Main   Jan 2021

PRAISE FOR
ALONE IN THE WOODS

"A masterful and realistic portrayal of the descent into survival mode, told with authentic voice and ominous details, yet still managing to read like a love letter to the Northwoods."

—Terry Lynn Johnson, author of *Ice Dogs* and *Dog Driven*

"Writing with a genuine love for the Wisconsin wilderness, author Rebecca Behrens remembers what it feels like to be a middle schooler. The deeper readers go into the woods with Joss and Alex, the more they'll be rooting for the girls' survival—and the salvaging of their friendship."

—Caroline Starr Rose, author of *May B.* and
Jasper and the Riddle of Riley's Mine

"Thrills—the kind you get from a wild tube ride through the rapids—and chills—the kind you get struggling to stay alive in the woods in wet swimsuits—are what we've come to expect from Rebecca Behrens's truly exceptional survival tales. Add this one to your must-read list!"

—Rodman Philbrick, author of *Freak the Mighty* and *Wildfire*

"Rebecca Behrens writes a universal story—two best friends growing up and growing apart—except the backdrop is a survival thriller set in the deep, dark, tick-infested Northwoods of Wisconsin where the stakes are life and death. A fast and frightening read that has me rethinking my summer river-tubing plans."

—Erin Teagan, author of *Survivor Girl*

PRAISE FOR
THE DISASTER DAYS

A Junior Library Guild Selection
A Bank Street Best Children's Book of the Year

"A realistic, engrossing survival story that's perfect for aspiring babysitters and fans of John Macfarlane's *Stormstruck!*, Sherry Shahan's *Ice Island*, or Wesley King's *A World Below*."

—*School Library Journal*

"The strength of this steadily paced novel that stretches over four days of a scary disaster scenario is that Hannah doesn't figure everything out; she stumbles, doubts, and struggles throughout it all."

—*Bulletin of the Center for Children's Books*

"Fans of survival thrillers in the vein of Gary Paulsen's *Hatchet* will enjoy this tense, honest tale of bravery...an excellent (and refreshingly not didactic) teaching tool on natural-disaster preparedness."

—*Booklist*

"Disaster-related action keeps pages flipping... A believable heroine finds her strength during a disaster."

—*Kirkus Reviews*

ALONE
IN THE
WOODS

ALSO BY REBECCA BEHRENS

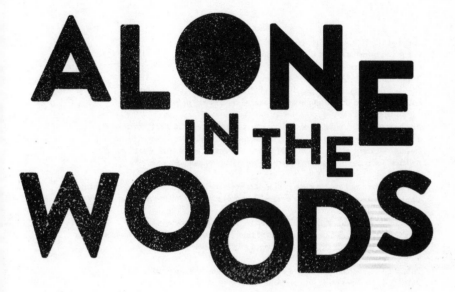

ALONE IN THE WOODS

REBECCA BEHRENS

sourcebooks
young readers

Copyright © 2020 by Rebecca Behrens
Cover and internal design © 2020 by Sourcebooks
Cover art © Levente Szabo
Internal design by Ashley Holstrom/Sourcebooks

Sourcebooks and the colophon are registered trademarks of Sourcebooks.

Published by Sourcebooks Young Readers, an imprint of Sourcebooks Kids
P.O. Box 4410, Naperville, Illinois 60567-4410
(630) 961-3900
sourcebookskids.com

Library of Congress Cataloging-in-Publication Data

Names: Behrens, Rebecca, author.
Title: Alone in the woods / Rebecca Behrens.
Description: Naperville, Illinois : Sourcebooks Young Readers, [2020] |
    Audience: Ages 8. | Audience: Grades 4-6. | Summary: Rising
    eighth-graders Jocelyn and Alex, former best friends forced together on
    a family vacation, must cooperate to survive when they get lost in the
    Wisconsin Northwoods. Told in two voices.
Identifiers: LCCN 2020018456 | (hardcover) | (trade paperback) | (epub)
Subjects: CYAC: Survival--Fiction. | Cooperativeness--Fiction. | Lost
    children--Fiction. | Forests and forestry--Fiction. |
    Friendship--Fiction.
Classification: LCC PZ7.B38823405 Alo 2020 | DDC [Fic]--dc23
LC record available at https://lccn.loc.gov/2020018456

Source of Production: Sheridan Books, Chelsea, Michigan, United States
Date of Production: August 2020
Run Number: 5019343

Printed and bound in the United States of America.
SB 10 9 8 7 6 5 4 3 2 1

For Megan

ONE

I SHOULD'VE KNOWN ALL HOPE was lost when Alex refused to eat a doughnut.

There were certain vacation moments that we looked forward to all year. The first being when the huge, slightly creepy, grinning lumberjack came into view at the end of the drive. Clutching an ax so big it shaded the cars in the parking lot, the lumberjack—Paul Bunyan—was there to welcome you to his Cook Shanty restaurant and, unofficially, the Wisconsin Northwoods.

It wasn't a real lumberjack, of course. Just a huge wooden cutout next to the yellow sign touting the restaurant's dinner special (usually walleye, which our parents love, but if you ask me just sounds too gross to eat) and, of course, the "logging camp breakfast" served from 7:00 a.m. till noon.

That breakfast was why we always left Madison so early—because the drive to Minocqua usually took between three and four hours, depending on how many times our little brothers had to pee and which parents were driving. The flapjacks, camp potatoes, and warm buttermilk doughnuts would disappear from the red-and-white-checked tables at twelve on the dot. One year, we got a late start because Nolan couldn't find his glasses, and then vacationer traffic was slow along Highway 51, and we didn't pull into the lot until 12:11 p.m. It was too late; they'd already moved on to lunch—and were out of doughnuts. Alex almost cried. We had to settle for doughnut holes from the Kwik Trip gas station, and that was not the proper way to start our week at the cabin.

Our families took this vacation together at the end of every summer. It was tradition. "Allard's Roost," our cabin on the edge of Buttercup Lake, used to belong to my grandparents. We've spent a week there every summer of my life, and after Alex and I became best friends in kindergarten, the Benavides family—Nick, Carmen, Lucy, Alex, and Mateo—started coming along. The A-frame cabin is pretty roomy, with lots of places to sleep, so all nine of us were a tight but manageable squeeze. It helped that Nolan, my little brother, and Mateo actually liked to crash on the musty pullout couch in the den.

My favorite thing about our week "Up North" was...everything. I loved jumping off the sizzling-hot pier into the ice-cold lake for a swim, stargazing from the Adirondack chairs at night, listening to the loons hoot, and hiking around the woods to collect leaves and pine cones. I even loved the notoriously big mosquitoes because their presence meant being surrounded by the glow of citronella candles every night while we gathered on the patio to grill our supper. Stopping at Paul Bunyan's Cook Shanty for doughnuts was just the first favorite thing in a week brimming with them.

This year, though, everything about the trip was slightly wrong. Like we'd begun singing half a note off-key, and as the song went on, it only got worse and our voices more out of tune.

Starting with the car arrangements. It took two jam-packed cars to get all of us (and all our stuff) up there, but we didn't always drive as separate families. Usually, Alex and I begged to be in the same car, so we could play the license-plate game and share chalky-but-sweet Necco wafers—a car-ride candy tradition dating back to when my dad was our age.

Except this year, Alex slid into the back seat of the Benavideses' brand-new car, buckled her belt, and announced, "I'm beyond tired so I'm just gonna sleep the whole way up." Then she put on her headphones and pulled her hoodie down so it almost covered her eyes. It felt weird to climb over Lucy to claim the middle seat, so I rode with my parents and the boys, sitting by myself in the wayback of our messy old SUV. Nolan and Mateo played games the whole ride, and the car was loud, and after a while kind of smelly, and I felt vaguely carsick. Possibly because I was trying to read in the back seat. Possibly because of what it meant that a big bag of groceries—and not Alex—was sitting next to me.

It's going to be okay when we get there, I told myself. *It'll be like hitting a reset button. We'll finally talk about what happened. Then everything will go back to normal.* I tried not to think of how far from normal we'd already veered.

I finally spotted Paul Bunyan (and his famously blue ox, Babe) at eleven thirty, which meant we had plenty of time. The boys cheered as we pulled into the parking lot. Even though my legs were stiff from the drive and I was still queasy, I bounded out of the car.

"Doughnuts! Doughnuts doughnuts doughnuts!" our brothers chanted as they raced inside.

"Coffee," Lucy said with a dramatic sigh as she chased after them.

Alex lingered in her seat, her fingers flying over the keypad on her phone. *So much for sleeping the whole way.* I lingered next to the open door, tracing shapes on the sticky-hot blacktop with my sneaker toe.

"Are you coming?" I finally asked. "They're going to stop serving breakfast soon." Everyone else had gone inside but us. My stomach growled.

"Sure, just a sec," Alex mumbled, still typing. Then she clicked her phone's screen off. Before she'd even shut the car door, it buzzed and lit up again with a rapid-fire stream of texts. "Ugh, I haven't had decent cell service for the last hour. I'm dying."

"I'm dying to eat something," I muttered, moving slowly

enough to keep pace with her as she walked-while-texting into the restaurant.

The lightning-quick servers had already brought platters of family-style food to our long picnic table, and everybody was loading up their plates. My dad stared at his biscuits and gravy with the same loving expression he has in the framed wedding photo of him and my mom on our mantel at home. "I'm in heaven," he said with a happy sigh.

The two empty seats at the table for Alex and me were next to each other, like always. I plopped down and grabbed a plate, still warm from the dishwasher. "Pass the doughnuts, please!" I made grabby hands in anticipation.

When Nolan handed them off to me, I dropped two onto my plate. The first one you gobble up because you're starving after that long drive. The second is to savor the flavor, because it'll be a year before you come back. Before the servers clear the platters, you snag a third doughnut and wrap it in a napkin for later, a midnight snack.

I plopped the first of her two doughnuts onto Alex's plate.

"No, thanks."

I had just grabbed her second when she said it again, a little louder and sounding slightly annoyed. "I said, *no*."

My hand hovered over her plate, waiting to drop the dough-nut like a bomb. "You're kidding, right—"

"I don't want a doughnut, Jocelyn!"

Everyone at the table quieted, except for Nolan, who is an extremely loud chewer. Lucy frowned. I could tell my mom was sneaking a glance at us.

"But we have them every year," I said in a very quiet voice. My face flushed, and I moved my hand—and the doughnut—away from Alex.

"Well, things change." Alex grabbed her fork and scratched at her almost-empty plate.

I didn't understand why she seemed so angry. *I'm the one who deserves to be mad.*

Her mom cleared her throat. "Alex, honey, are you feeling okay? Aren't you going to eat something?"

"This food is kind of gross," Alex grumbled, but she scooped up a bit of the scrambled eggs. "It's unhealthy."

I stared down at my plate, with its two greasy doughnuts staring back at me like wide-open eyes. Suddenly, I didn't want to eat them, either.

"I'll tell you what's gross: this coffee," Lucy said, wrinkling her nose. "It needs *all* the sugar." Her voice was a touch too loud and upbeat. But it worked—everybody else went back to talking and eating. Except Alex. She pushed her eggs around her plate for a while, eating maybe half of what was there.

While the rest of us went back for seconds, she mumbled something about looking for a signal and wandered off in the direction of the gift shop.

"Somebody woke up on the wrong side of the car, huh?" her dad said, shaking his head.

Nobody was looking at me, which made me think they were all embarrassed on my behalf.

I ate only one of the doughnuts, and I picked at the rest of my food. It didn't taste right. When it was time to leave, though, I wrapped up two doughnuts in a big paper napkin. Maybe we'd eat them later, sitting cross-legged on the pier underneath the stars, which twinkled so brightly in the Northwoods night sky. After the cabin worked its magic and turned my best friend back into herself.

I felt stranded in the wilderness, without her.

TWO

MY SECOND FAVORITE THING about our week up north
was the inaugural lake jump. By the time we reached
the cabin, after another forty-five minutes in the car from
Minocqua, we'd be itching for a chance to cool off. That's why
Alex and I always wore our swimsuits underneath our clothes
for the drive. As soon as the car crunched to a stop at the edge
of the gravel driveway, under the shade of my favorite tamarack
tree, we would hop out. We'd peel off our T-shirts and shorts,
pull off our sneakers, and then race across the yard, down the
footpath, and onto the pier. (My mom would chase behind us
with a can of tick repellant, but we never slowed down enough
for her to spray us.) We'd start counting to three on the raised
slat that's halfway down the pier, and then we would clasp hands.
At the end, we'd raise our linked arms and leap, landing with a
huge splash in the deliciously cool water. Blinking my eyes open
after surfacing, I'd get my first real view of the cabin, perched
above us on the gently sloping hill and surrounded by trees. My
heart would swell with happiness. Then Alex and I would climb

out and run back up for thick towels, and to actually help lug everything inside.

Perhaps after the doughnut awkwardness, I should have dialed down my expectations for this year's lake jump. Maybe, I thought, Alex's crankiness was just about the food, which, aside from the doughnuts, is not the finest. My dad's scrambled eggs are way better, and the sausage links can be a little rubbery. At least they used to be—I haven't had one since I became a vegetarian in fifth grade. But nobody expects haute cuisine up north, the land of "supper clubs." Old-school food is part of the charm.

Anyway, why wouldn't Alex still love the tradition of jumping off the pier?

Her car had led the way from breakfast, so they were parked and Lucy had already stepped out to stretch by the time ours came to a stop.

"Hurry, hurry, hurry!" I urged Nolan and Mateo, whose seats I had to fold down in order to escape the wayback.

I nudged past them and their mess of action figures and activity books, then hopped onto the gravel, squinting at the bright midday sun. The tamarack's branches seemed to wave hello. Scents of pine and cedar enveloped me. I felt better than I had in weeks, better since the morning Alex had left for her camp. We were at Buttercup Lake, finally. *Just us—no Laura in sight.* I pulled my T-shirt over my head and adjusted the straps of my swimsuit into place. It was from last year—because I wasn't doing swim team this summer, Mom hadn't wanted to spend money for a new suit. My old turquoise one fit mostly fine, anyway.

"Time for the lake jump?" Mom smiled at me, reaching her arms overhead and rolling her neck, easing away the kinks from the drive. "Should I ready the tick spray?"

"Oh yeah." The tie on my drawstring shorts was refusing to unknot. I glanced toward the Benavideses' car. "Come on, Alex!"

Thanks to her head start, she should've been down to bare feet already. Finally, the knot came loose, and my shorts dropped to the ground. I bent to unlace my sneakers.

I was shoeless before Alex even got out. I shifted from one foot to the other—the sunbaked gravel was sharp and hot. Normally, I didn't stand on it long enough to notice. "What are you waiting for?" Maybe it was the lumberjack breakfast making my stomach hurt a little. Maybe it was something else. A hearty serving of worry, garnished with a dollop of anger.

Alex clutched her phone in her hand. "Sorry, I wanna go in and hook up to the Wi-Fi first." She paused, then added in a half-hearted tone, "Maybe a swim later?" Alex shrugged, like even she thought that was doubtful, and then she turned to follow my dad up the walkway to the cabin.

A cloud passed over the sun at that exact moment, but even if it hadn't, I still would've felt the chill.

By the time we got to my third favorite thing, I'd begun to manage my expectations. For dinner the first night of the trip, our dads cooked everything. They grilled, usually fish for all the parents, hot dogs for Mateo, regular burgers for Nolan and Alex, and veggie burgers for me and Lucy (who joined me in vegetarianism once she got her part-time job at the zoo). After dinner, we built a fire in the firepit to roast marshmallows. Alex's mom always got out her guitar, and we all sang campfire songs and ate s'mores until we could burst. It's a scene as perfect as a car commercial on TV, but it's real.

Alex sat next to me on the wooden picnic bench, but there was so much space between us you almost could've squeezed Nolan in there. Or Tampoco, the Benavides family cat (who Lucy named the Spanish word for *neither* because he's so contrary). Alex picked at her burger but gobbled about seven pickle slices. Which was weird.

"You sure you got enough to eat, Alex?" her dad asked while gathering all the s'mores stuff.

"Yeah." Her head tucked toward her chin, so her voice was slightly muffled. It was because she had her phone on her lap, below the table. It was lighting up with notifications, as frequent as the fireflies drifting through the trees and yard.

"Sorry the burger was a little overcooked," my dad said. "Am I going to have to give up my title of grill master?" He was joking, but there was a hint of seriousness in his voice, like he really felt bad if she hadn't enjoyed her food.

"It was great, but I don't think the buns were organic—ow!" Alex interrupted herself with a loud slap on her forearm. She got the mosquito but too late: a smear of blood spread across her bare skin. This is why up north, you wear long sleeves after dusk. Layers are your friend. No matter how hot and sunny the day got, I always carried around my sweatshirt.

"These mosquitoes are so ridiculous. I can't take it anymore." She hopped up from the table, swatting around herself as she moved for the patio door. "I'm going inside."

"You don't want a s'more?" My voice had that strained, tinny quality to it again, like when I get called on to answer a question in class and everyone is suddenly listening and my public-speaking nerves kick in.

"I want to not be eaten alive." Alex paused. "I guess you could bring one in for me." Then she slipped inside. Through the sliding door, I could see her curled up on the couch in the darkness, her face illuminated by her phone. Whatever she was looking at on it made her smile. Perhaps for the first time all day.

"Okay," I said quietly, even though she was already gone and couldn't hear me. When I glanced back up at our families, every-one was acting totally normal, but I could sense that they were avoiding eye contact with me again.

It's fine. Every single time we've had a fight, we've gotten over it. This is just a particularly bad *fight. Like the time I accidentally spoiled the ending of* The Westing Game. *It took weeks for Alex to stop the silent treatment after that, even though I apologized a million and one times.* The thing was, though, we hadn't actually been fighting. Since registration, we'd had no contact, till this morning. And if anyone should be giving the silent treatment or waiting for an apology, it should've been me.

I made a truly perfect s'more for Alex. It could've won an award. I put the chocolate square on the graham cracker near the fire, where it would warm and soften the chocolate so it hovered between being a liquid and a solid—I think the science term is colloid. I roasted the marshmallow low and slow, so that it grew fatter and fatter but didn't crumple and blacken on any sides. When it was about to ooze off the stick from its own weight, I pulled it away and plopped it on the cracker, quickly pressing the top piece down. The gooey marshmallow and jellylike chocolate immediately melded. I placed the s'more on a napkin and crossed the patio while cradling it in my palms. Maybe, once she tasted it, I could lure Alex back outside. To where we were all sitting around the fire, laughing and singing, licking sticky traces of marshmallow off our fingers. Yes, I had probably six new mosquito bites despite the repellant, the citronella candles, and my long pants. But if they were the price, it was well worth paying.

"Hey," I said as I let myself into the living room, careful not to let out Tampoco (who strictly stays inside the cabin, to keep all the Northwoods songbirds safe). I stood awkwardly next to the couch. I wasn't really sure what to say. It felt like approaching a stranger. Which is an awful way to feel around your best friend.

If she was still truly that.

"Hey." She yawned and glanced warily at me. Alex seemed as uncomfortable being alone together as I was.

"I made you a s'more." I held it out for her.

"Thanks." She took it but just set it on the coffee table. I wanted to tell her she should eat it right away, while it was still warm from the fire, that it was better that way. But after the doughnuts...

"It's really nice out there," I said. "The stars are so pretty. I wonder if you can see Sirius." In sixth grade, I did my TAG—talented and gifted—project on constellations. I remember almost all of them. Sirius, the Dog Star, is part of the constellation Canis Major. It's also where we get the phrase "the dog days of summer," because ancient astronomers noticed its rising with the sun marked the hottest days of the year. Summer isn't the best time to see Sirius at night, but it is the brightest star, and the Northwoods sky is always so dark. "I could show you?"

"Maybe another time. I'm kind of tired."

I glanced out the window at the silhouettes of our families enjoying the glow of the firepit. I longed to be out there, but not without Alex. I'd stay inside the whole week if that's what it took for things with her to be right-side-up again. If I let myself actually think about how weird things had gotten between us, I felt sick. "I'm tired too. Should we go up to bed?"

We've always shared the "aerie," the nickname for the sleeping loft that is the very top triangle of the A of the cabin's frame. The aerie is a small space—at the edges, even a kid can't stand up straight—and there's only room for a full-size mattress on the floor. But it's cozy, and it's always been ours. Someday we'll outgrow it, and then Nolan and Mateo will inherit it. Until then, each summer we've scratched our names and the year into the wooden beams of the ceiling, along with a single word or phrase that encapsulates what that week was like. One year, it was *fox,* when we found an orphaned baby fox underneath the patio and fed it with an eyedropper. Another year, *endless rain,* when five of the six days we had to spend inside playing cards and looking up random dictionary and encyclopedia entries because the weather was so bad.

I wondered what this summer's word would be. So far, I could suggest: *awkward.*

Alex looked up at me. Her expression was hard to read. "Actually, I'm going to bunk with Lucy, I think." Her eyes darted away from mine. "The aerie is kinda claustrophobic. Like being in a tomb or something."

"Oh." Tears pricked at the corners of my eyes, and I willed

myself not to let them slide out and roll down my cheeks. I didn't want her to see. "Well, good night, I guess." There was a telltale throatiness to my voice, so Alex must've known I was upset, but she only said a distracted "g'night" as I hurried to the stairs, snatching my bag from the luggage pile still untouched by the landing.

Up in the aerie, I dove onto the mattress. My mom had put on clean sheets, which I knew because I buried my face in them, and as I cried—silently, because the cabin's walls are thin—I could smell fabric softener instead of musty cabin dust. A window facing the lake takes up one whole wall, and eventually I raised my head to look out at the first-night festivities below, still going strong. Mateo and Nolan were running around the yard catching fireflies. The fire's embers glowed. Everyone was smiling. Watching all that golden-lit happiness below me only made me feel worse.

I unzipped my bag to pull out my favorite sweatshirt. Not just because it gets cold up in the aerie at night but because my sweatshirt is super comforting. I wear it whenever I'm nervous, or sad. I fell asleep before putting it on, hugging it to my chest like a security blanket. Babyish, maybe. That's probably what Alex would think. But, after all, I was alone. There was no one else to see.

ALEX

THE BEGINNING OF THE END

IT WASN'T MY FAULT. It was the sweatshirt's. If your best friend had been walking down the hallway wearing it, you would've reacted the exact same way as I did. Especially on registration day. And it's not like I hadn't tried to tell her before. But Jocelyn, for someone so smart, can be kinda dense about certain things. Like that stupid wolf sweatshirt.

So maybe it was actually *Joss's* fault that I dumped her. Friend-dumped her. (I feel like that should have its own term. "Fumped her"? Or, "We froke up"?)

Anyway, it's not like I planned for any of this to happen. I want to make that clear. And when I try to pinpoint when it all started, it wasn't registration day. It's like when you drop a tube of lip gloss and the clear plastic cover gets one long crack, but it still snaps on the base so everything's fine. But then you drop the tube a few more times, and the cracks get worse—there's not one but a bunch—and eventually one day the cover breaks apart, and unless it's, like, a really special color, you have to throw away the tube, because without the cover, the gloss will get all over everything, and lint from your pocket or whatever junk is in the bottom of your bag will stick to it, which is disgusting. My point is, the first crack in our friendship formed way earlier. Maybe at the end-of-the-year dance.

Joss and I had never actually gone to a dance at Walden Middle School, despite the fact that there's one each semester. The main reason was that we both were intimidated, me slightly and her super: of popular girls like Laura Longbottom showing off their shiny new dresses, of boys attempting to break-dance with no regard for soda-spilling consequences. Of the potential for seeing our gym teacher "bust a move" (her words, not mine). But at some point, I decided that before we started eighth grade, Joss and I *had* to go to a dance. Because...I wanted to. I mean, what if dances were actually not scary and awkward, but fun? I didn't admit this to Jocelyn, but I honestly hoped to dance with a boy. No one in particular, although Josh Haberman is kind of cute.

I couldn't convince Jocelyn, so eventually I half-tricked her into a pinkie-swear that she'd go. She still resisted until the very last minute, trying to lure me into staying home with the promise of an evening full of rom-coms and the kind of ice-cream sandwiches that are made with big chocolate-chip cookies. Tempting. But as we walked into the gym that night, lights pulsing and music blaring, my heart swelled. I felt, like, part of something. I wasn't watching a party scene in a movie but actually at one myself. I wanted to run right onto the dance floor. Except Jocelyn was frozen with one foot in the gym and one foot out.

"Whoa, Alex, there are so many people here." Her eyes were wide like a Disney princess's, out of fear. "It's too hot. And way too loud."

"It is kinda loud." We had to shout to hear each other. My grin faded as I searched the dark, crowded corners of the gym for familiar faces. The shiny people pushed past us as they hurried through the door, almost knocking us over. I tugged at my skirt, which suddenly looked and felt all kinds of wrong. "C'mon," I said after a deep breath. "We can't just stand here. Let's do this."

Jocelyn still didn't budge. "I don't *want* to do this," she said, shaking her head, right as a girl, teetering in heels, stumbled next to us and sloshed punch onto Jocelyn's top. Well, actually it was my top—I'd picked an outfit for Jocelyn because clothes are not her thing. Joss's face scrunched up, and I knew she was dangerously close to tears. So I steered her to the edge of the gym floor, pulled a wad of napkins out of my purse, and then started blotting while doing emotional damage control.

"You totally can do this. Come on—we're in it together. Just give it an hour." I kept dabbing at her/my shirt, dipping the napkin wad into her reusable water bottle, which was covered in stickers with environmental slogans. "Plus, I'm leaving tomorrow morning. This is our last night until after camp. I need to bank good memories—I'm gonna be stuck in the middle of nowhere for two weeks, remember? They don't even let you bring real shampoo there. Because you have to wash your hair in a *lake*." I shuddered, thinking of stinky weeds.

She cracked a smile. "That actually sounds awesome."

I wasn't surprised. Jocelyn really loves all that outdoorsy stuff.

I stepped back and studied the stain. You could hardly see the pink blob of punch. "All good now." The music had switched to one of my favorite songs. I stared at the dance floor with something like longing. I glanced back at Joss. She didn't look like she'd cry anymore, but she was hunched over with her arms crossed over her chest. "Can we try dancing?" I asked. "Please?" It just looked like so much fun.

She shook her head forcefully.

For a second I thought of grabbing her hand and yanking her to the floor. But I figured she would fight it like Tampoco did the time we had to give him a bath. And I didn't want to make her uncomfortable. I let out a sigh, which I don't think she heard over the blaring music. "Okay. Then let's get food." I linked elbows with Joss and led us both over to the snack table.

We stood there awkwardly for a few minutes, assessing the cookie situation. That good song was still playing, so the only other person hanging around the table was this kid from our neighborhood whose all-encompassing obsession with sharks—seriously, I don't think he owns a single item of clothing that doesn't at least have a picture of a dorsal fin on it—had earned him the nickname Shark Boy. That night he had on a button-down covered in tiny chomping great whites.

"Cool shirt," Joss said to him, and he grinned.

I scooted farther away and motioned for Joss to do the same. I didn't want anyone to think we were there *with* him.

"Hey! I know. Let's do a blind taste test of all the sodas." Joss grabbed a few cups and started pouring. "Don't look!" That is classic Jocelyn, Miss Talented and Gifted—turning a school dance into an impromptu science experiment.

But tasting drinks was better than just standing around, watching everyone else. Joss handed me a cup, and I took a sip. "Tastes like bubbles. Clear bubbles." Another sip. "Licorice-y? And not in a good way." I'm not the hugest soda fan.

Shark Boy, circling us, piped up, "I like licorice. That flavor's called *anise*."

I almost choked on my cookie while stifling a laugh. Next to me, I could feel Jocelyn shaking with held-back giggles. I knew if we made eye contact, we'd get hysterical, and I didn't want to be mean.

Eventually, our friends Houa and Kate found us, and then we all danced in a tight circle on the farthest edge of the floor, even Jocelyn, although she mostly just swayed in a sorta self-conscious way and watched the second hand travel around the big clock on the wall. At one point, our gym teacher did bop by "busting a move" with her arms in the air, but I did not suffer death by cringe. Across the floor, in the middle of the gym, Josh Haberman danced next to Laura Longbottom, who was acting all cool and casual about it (but grinning at her friends like maybe she agreed with me about his cuteness).

At eight thirty, my mom picked Joss and me up and took us back to my house for one last pre-camp sleepover. As soon as we were in the car, Joss perked up like a flower after being watered. I felt kind of...I don't know. Gloomy? Joss would know the right word. Disappointed, I guess, because the night hadn't gone like I'd planned or hoped, even though it hadn't been bad. As long as we were together, Joss and I could have fun. It's just, we were going to be eighth-graders. Even if Joss wasn't ready for fun in the form of dances and guys and stuff—maybe I was?

We clambered up to my room, our clicking heels on the stairs reminding me of the dance floor I hadn't fully gotten to enjoy.

"Wanna watch a movie?" Joss chirped, scrolling through the choices on my computer.

"Sure, but something we can have on in the background. I haven't packed."

She shook her head at me. "Procrastinate much? Aren't you leaving first thing in the morning?"

Jocelyn would've packed, like, a week ago. She's so on top of things.

I flopped onto my bed. "Yup. I'm pretending that camp isn't happening." Then I rolled over and finally tugged my suitcase out from underneath my bed. "Time's up, though. You know camping stuff better than I do. What do I need?"

"Same stuff you bring up north." She hopped over to my closet and started pulling out my most boring T-shirts and shorts. "Where's your swimsuit?"

"In there." I pointed to my dresser. She pulled open the top drawer first, forgetting that it's my junk drawer, full of Happy Meal toys and old birthday cards and intricately folded notes Joss had slipped me in the hallway at school. In the middle drawer was my turquoise racing swimsuit. Joss wadded it up and shoved it into the inside pouch of my suitcase, where I added my underwear and pajama shorts. When she wasn't looking, I replaced some of her choices with cuter tops. I mean, it's not like I was going to be alone in the woods.

"I'm so jealous," I said, throwing a pack of stationery on the top of my now-overflowing suitcase. "You get to wake up tomorrow and start summer. I get a daylong bus ride to nowhere. All because my grades in Spanish were so bad." I was sentenced to Tierra de los Lagos, a Spanish language-immersion camp, on the strong recommendation of my Spanish teacher. Unlike Jocelyn's, my grades last year had not been fantástico. "I wish you were coming along. I'm not going to know anyone there."

Her mouth twisted downward. "Yeah, well, this year it was

either camps or the cabin for us. According to the budget. And I wouldn't miss the cabin for the world." She let out a small sigh. "Maybe camp will be fun. Remember Echo Valley?"

Years ago, we'd done a weekend camping trip at this place called Echo Valley with our moms. The whole valley part of it became a problem during a huge rainstorm, when our tent flooded in the middle of the night. There was nothing we could do about it until morning, since we were a mile from the main building, so we loaded our stuff into garbage bags and pretended the tent was a Slip 'N Slide for the rest of the night, while our moms sleepily watched.

"Okay, now I'm having flashbacks to those sopping wet sleeping bags."

"Won't your cabin have beds?"

"Yeah, good point. I just hope the sheets aren't scratchy." I pushed down on the fabric top of my suitcase, trying to ease the zipper around the side. It was too full.

"Here." Joss hopped through the obstacle course of stuff all over my floor. "Watch out." She plopped her butt down on the suitcase, balancing with her knees pulled up to her chest. "Quick! Zip it!"

I wasn't quick enough, though, because she toppled off the suitcase and onto my rug with a huge thump before I could get the zipper even a quarter of the way around. I dropped to the floor next to her, laughing hysterically. We stayed like that, giggling and talking, until we got too tired and abandoned the unzipped suitcase to get ready for bed.

"Don't worry. It'll go fast," Jocelyn said, yawning as she lay back on her half of my bed.

"I know." I switched off the light. "Then our real summer can start."

It makes me weirdly sad to think about that moment now. I bet my math teacher could draw up some kind of equation to show how the two sides of any friendship breakup are related— like how if the Before friendship is particularly great, the After feels particularly terrible. And in terms of me and Joss, our Before was, well, the best.

Then I went to camp.

THREE

THERE IS NO SUCH thing as "sleeping in" at the cabin. For starters, half the windows don't have any coverings, and the ones that do only have faded, gauzy curtains that my grandma stitched together way back in the day. So when the sun wakes up at sixish, we do too.

But we had a good reason to be up early the next morning. My dad had this idea that we should all go on a trip down the Wolf River, like he and his brothers used to do when they were kids. My mom vetoed the idea of whitewater rafting because the boys aren't big enough. But she found a place that does easy three-hour tubing trips along a pretty gentle section of the river. The coolest part is that it's a stretch where the Wolf flows through the Chequamegon-Nicolet National Forest. Well, technically there are two separate forests, the Chequamegon and the Nicolet, and they're actually miles and miles apart. But at some point the US Forest Service merged their management, so now they share the official name. Last year, I did my TAG project on the national forest, so I kind of nerd out about it.

The Nicolet is home to all kinds of cool plants and wildlife—deer, moose, bobcats, bears, river otters, elk, and even wolves. (I mean, it was named the *Wolf* River for a reason.) I've never seen a wolf in the wild, and that's one of my life goals. Someday, when I'm a naturalist or biologist, I'd love to study wolves. They're really misunderstood—people think of them as these awful, dangerous predators thanks to them being portrayed as the villains in tons of fairy and folktales, but in real life, they're not like that. Wolves are generally afraid of people and rarely attack or hurt them, and they only hunt what they need for food. To put it in perspective, dogs that people keep as pets cause far more injuries each year. But nobody uses that as an excuse to hunt them till they're endangered.

The website for the tubing trip said that while we leisurely float along the river in our flotilla of inner tubes, we can expect to spot some of the forest's wildlife along the banks. Which was super exciting. And after the first day of vacation being such a letdown, I really needed something to look forward to.

I shuffled into the tiny galley kitchen, where the coffeemaker was already gurgling and a bunch of bagels were laid out on the counter next to all the fruit we'd picked up at a farm stand. Lucy was perched on a stool, reading. I could hear Mateo and Nolan thudding around on the patio. Our parents were spread out in the living room, slurping from chipped mugs and enjoying the view to the lake. Even Tampoco was up, stretching out in a morning sunbeam on the worn wooden floor. Alex was nowhere to be found.

Lucy put down her book and smiled at me. She patted the worn wooden stool next to her. "Get something to eat, then come sit with me."

I grabbed a knife to spread a thick layer of peanut butter on a blueberry bagel. I smushed a bunch of strawberry slices on top: DIY jelly for a PB&J. Lucy was watching me the whole time. Her sympathetic smile never wavered.

Please don't say anything about Alex sleeping in your room and not up in the aerie last night.

"I wanted to tell you," Lucy started, her voice sounding awfully similar to a guidance counselor's in its careful, empathetic tone. "That whatever's going on with you and Alex, it's probably a blip. She's just, you know, a little enraptured with Laura Longbottom right now." She wrinkled her nose, to remind me that she didn't see the appeal, either. Sometimes I felt that Lucy and I were more alike than Alex and I were, and if Lucy were four years younger, we'd be best friends instead.

I didn't really want to talk about what was going on, though, and especially not about Laura, so I just nodded and took a huge bite of my peanut butter bagelwich.

Carmen saved me by calling from the living room, "Is Alex

out of bed yet?" Then she glanced over to the kitchen, saw me at the breakfast nook with Lucy, and smiled. "Oh! I see Joss, so there's my answer."

I felt my cheeks start to burn. Alex and I had been inseparable since we were five. "A package deal," as my dad liked to say. We basically shared a circadian rhythm. It was normal to assume that if one of us was up, so was the other.

"Um, I'm not sure what Alex's deal is…" I eventually said. This was uncharted water, for everyone.

Lucy stepped in to save me. "Alex bunked with me last night because I demanded sister time."

"Oh!" Carmen let out a small, embarrassed laugh. "Okay, I'll go wake her. We should get a move on."

"Want me to play 'Taps'?" Nolan asked.

Mateo held up a bugle, which they must've found in the den. There's all kinds of random stuff squirreled away in the cabin.

"That's typically a song for dusk, but maybe also an appropriate punishment for being the last one up," Alex's dad said with a grin.

The boys scrambled up the staircase, and seconds later, I heard the bugle make a great and terrible honk, followed by Alex shrieking. I'm a little ashamed to admit that for the first time that morning, I smiled.

We drove about an hour southeast to get to the starting point of the tubing trip. The winding roads were hemmed in by tall stands of conifers, and yellow wildflowers blanketed the ground, making everything green and gold. It always felt so different from driving around Madison, which is a small city with traffic and billboards and museums and shopping centers galore. Up north, you can go miles and miles and see not much but signs for Pine Tree Road (every little community seems to have one). Places whose names are in bold print on the state highway map—which normally means they're bigger, like a real town—turn out to have only a gas station, a tavern, and maybe a church or a VFW post. All of which probably sell fishing tackle. It's a whole other world in the Northwoods. I kind of like the wildness of it all. Especially with the spotty cell reception, it feels like time travel.

Even though we'd unloaded all our stuff yesterday, the cars somehow still felt crammed. Maybe it's because I was riding with the Benavideses this time, wedged in the back seat between Alex and Lucy. Some roads were bumpy, and my stomach churned with the early stages of carsickness. Alex's new body spray wasn't helping. It smelled like she'd bathed in vat of sugary mango smoothie.

Just wait until the mosquitoes and flies along the river got a whiff of that.

After spending the night alone up in the aerie, my feelings

toward Alex had begun to curdle, like old milk poured unsuspectingly into hot tea. Till now, the only person I'd been truly angry with was Laura, who I viewed sort of like a kidnapper. She'd taken Alex hostage at their camp, maybe even against her will, and Alex couldn't be blamed if now she was suffering from Stockholm syndrome.

But up north, Laura was nowhere to be seen—except in endless texts on Alex's phone—and yet my best friend was still acting like a stranger.

I kept shifting in my seat, tugging to adjust the straps of my suit. I was wearing it plus a pair of thin athletic shorts. I was also wearing water shoes. As much as I love splashing around in rivers and lakes, I do not love how underwater plants and weeds feel on bare feet. They're slimy, and at first brush, I always think I've encountered an eel. Like my suit, the water shoes were slightly too tight. That was sort of my trend of the summer: wearing things I'd outgrown. Partly because I'd had a growth spurt and partly because money was still too tight for Mom to take me shopping for a bunch of new clothes. I didn't really care, except for how I noticed Alex side-eyeing my outfits sometimes. I tried to remember if she'd done that at all last year at Walden, or if it had just started after she came home from camp. Her obsession with fashion had definitely gone to the next level since then. It made me second-guess what I was wearing. Or, more accurately, whether I should care more about what I was wearing.

For the tubing trip, Alex had on the same teeny bikini that she'd worn to the pool party. I was curious to see the reaction from her mom when Alex took off her fancy cover-up. And instead of water shoes, Alex wore a thin pair of fuchsia flip-flops that loudly slapped with each step. It was the kind of outfit that maybe made sense for a pool day but not one spent being active in nature.

We got to the tubing outfitter late because the GPS in the Benavideses' car took us down the wrong Pine Tree Road— twice. It had been a busy morning, apparently, because two groups had already gone out ahead of us on the river. So the tubing people were down to their last seven tubes.

"That's totally fine, some of us can double up," my mom said, turning to assess our group. "It'll certainly be easier to keep track of Nolan and Mateo if they're in one tube instead of two. And also—"

Before she could finish, I burst out, "Alex and I can share."

"Great!" Mom turned back to the guide, who began pulling the tubes down from a big rack, bouncing them against the ground to make sure they were properly inflated.

I sneaked a glance at Alex, to see if she seemed happy that we were going to be together all day. She was busy riffling through her bag. Then she pulled out a tiny jar and swiped more greasy lip stuff across her mouth, which was already glistening and pink, like she'd just eaten a full box of strawberry Popsicles.

"This one should fit the two of you," the guide said, rolling a big green tube toward me. It looked older than the rest, with a few marks and faded spots dotting its sides. I scooted forward to catch it. Because it was shaped like a humongous doughnut, I thought it would have a hole, but there was actually plastic in the middle. Good for keeping our legs out of the rocky river, I guessed.

"How rough does the water get?" I asked, pushing my hair off my face.

"The part you're on, not real bad. Only a couple of baby falls, and the water is pretty low right now. Think more of a lazy river experience." He motioned to my backpack at my feet. "That still might get splashed, though."

For a moment, I considered taking my bag back to the car, because would I really need all this stuff for a day drifting along the river? Maybe I had overpacked: two bug-spray wipes, an almost-used-up tube of sunscreen, one of the cabin's thinner beach towels, my sweatshirt, a mini first aid kit, my grandma's binoculars, and my camera. I still used an old-school digital camera because I wouldn't get a real phone with a functioning camera until next year. Until then, if I needed a cell phone, Mom gave me a clunky old flip phone to carry around. It had been kind of an issue ever since Alex got really into her phone this year. Sometimes I think if she could've been sending me elaborate emoji sentences and gifs all summer long, she wouldn't have needed constant contact with Laura. I did see why my parents were hesitant, though, because Alex had already broken her screen twice. The first time her parents paid to get a new phone, but after the second, she just had to live with one long crack zagging across the display.

I knew Alex's phone was full of pictures of her and Laura hanging out—at their camp, and later all around Madison, posing at sunset in the iconic chairs at the Union Terrace, celebrating a hole-in-one at Vitense mini golf, even sunbathing out in a paddleboat on Lake Wingra. I wanted to take some photos of her and me on this trip. So that meant bringing along my backpack.

Also, I was willing to bet those bug-spray wipes would come in handy. The mean blackflies that hang out around water can be merciless.

I shrugged to the guide. "Except for my camera, everything in my pack can dry."

"Hope the same is true for your friend," he said, nodding toward Alex.

A fashion magazine was sticking out of the top of her bag, which bulged with beauty products. She'd probably freak if all her lotions and potions got a drop of water on them.

"We'll find out." I sighed.

"Here," he said, reaching for something on a shelf. "Take a dry bag, just in case." He handed me an enormous ziplock bag that could fit both my backpack and Alex's tote inside.

Dragging or rolling our tubes, we followed the guide like

ducklings to the water's edge. He gave my parents instructions, some of which I overheard. There was a bridge about three hours downstream, which is where we would get out to be picked up. He gave my mom his cell number, in case there were any issues along the way. "Coverage isn't great, though, as I'm sure you've noticed. But really, the only problem you might encounter is too much fun!" he said, grinning. I caught Alex cringing at his joke.

Then the guide opened up a big plastic chest and pulled out life vests. They were the basic kind—three pieces of foam, or some floatie material, covered in yellow fabric and tethered to one another with thin straps that snapped around the wearer's waist. "Everybody here can swim, right?" the guide asked.

"Yes," we chimed.

"That's great. But you're still taking these out with you."

"Do we have to wear them?" Alex looked skeptical.

Nick was wrestling Mateo into his vest. "Absolutely you do. Currents can be unpredictable."

The guide tossed Alex a dingy one. "We require that everyone under the age of eighteen wears a vest the whole time they're on the water. Grown-ups, you can do what you want—but remember, you *are* role models."

Our parents nodded seriously. It's funny and slightly disconcerting to see another grown-up telling them what to do.

"This is ridiculous," Alex mumbled. "It's going to look so dorky in pictures."

I ignored her, tightening my straps.

With the guide's help, we waded into the water. Alex went ahead of me, shrieking when she made contact with the cold. She was still wearing her cover-up—it was going to come off once we were on the river, when our parents weren't paying attention. The gauzy fabric swirled around her legs. She clambered onto the inner tube, huddling on top of the plastic ring.

I stopped judging her shriek when I plunged into the river myself—it was way colder than the already-pretty-cold Buttercup Lake. "Yowza!"

"Don't worry! The sun will warm you right up," the guide said cheerfully.

I hoped he was right. I struggled to get into the slippery tube. It took me three tries to swing both of my legs up and inside the hole. The bottom of my backpack already had dipped into the water. Maybe using the dry bag was a good idea after all. Alex huddled on the opposite side of the tube, shivering.

Everyone else had settled into their tubes and were hanging on to one another's cords. The guide held on to Alex's and mine. Looking at all of us bobbing in the gentle current, we were like a pod of sea otters. Our moms were in the lead, followed by Nolan and Mateo, and the dads completed the parental sandwich, which seemed like very smart thinking—penning in the boys. Lucy followed, her tube twirling aimlessly—she already had her book open on her lap. Alex and I were last.

"And you're off." The guide let go of our tube, gave a gentle push, and slowly the current pulled our pod downstream and toward the middle of the river, where the water flowed faster. The guide and the tubing shack began fading into endless trees behind us. "Have a great time!" he hollered, with a wave.

As the last of our group, I felt kind of like its envoy, so I waved goodbye to him. Alex didn't join me. She was busy getting settled in the tube, wiggling around and trying to figure out where to position her tote bag so it didn't get wet. "Am I going to have to balance this on my lap the whole time?" she grumbled.

I shook my head. "The guide gave us this," I said, holding out the big Ziploc. "A dry bag to seal our stuff inside."

She rolled her eyes, which was confusing because I was offering her a solution. "Remind me why is this better than just hanging at the lake?" She slid down the inner tube, and it made a farting noise. I laughed, and she rolled her eyes again.

From ahead, her mom yelled back, "Lucy, keep an eye on the girls, please?"

Lucy raised her arm and made a thumbs-up. "Okey-doke." But she didn't look up from her book.

Alex continued to wriggle around and huff, but I leaned back against the warm plastic of the tube. My life vest functioned great as a neck pillow. I stared up at the cloudless blue sky, letting the sun kiss my face. The guide had been right: it was warming up already. I took a deep inhale, savoring the smell of the pine trees and fresh water. I wanted to soak in this moment, the start of our ride. Who knew where this little adventure was going to take Alex and me. Hopefully, back together.

FOUR

WHEN AN ACCIDENT HAPPENS—SOMETHING serious like a plane crash—experts like to talk about the "Swiss cheese model" to explain how it came to pass. Pretend the accident is failing a test. You do a lot to prevent that from happening: studying in the days leading up to it; getting a good night's sleep beforehand; eating a brain-boosting breakfast the morning of; and making sure your pencils are pre-sharpened and you have an eraser that actually works, instead of one that just leaves messy smear marks on the paper. Those defenses are like layers of cheese, and when they stack up one on top of the other, no hazards can pass through their protective barrier. (The thing about this analogy that has never made sense to me is why random hazards are trying to fly through cheese. Oh well.) If you have a whole bunch of layers defending against something going wrong, it's almost impossible it will, right? If you study, sleep, eat breakfast, and sharpen your pencils and check your eraser, you're set up for testing success!

Except: What if the layers of cheese are *Swiss* cheese, which everybody knows has holes. Little gaps and big ones: You studied the wrong section; maybe you had insomnia the night before; you overslept the day of and didn't have time for a real breakfast; then your only pencil snapped midway through the test, and its eraser was too dry. One "hole" in a slice—a crummy, rushed breakfast—isn't going to cause trouble because you still have the other layers of cheese stacked on that piece. But what if holes in *all* those layers of Swiss cheese perfectly line up—even for only one moment? No protective barrier. The accident happens. Unprepared, sleepy, hangry, and without a decent writing/erasing utensil, you flunk the test.

Several layers of Swiss cheese prevented something from going wrong on our families' low-key, scenic float down the Wolf River:

- We were on a calm section of the river with barely any rapids.
- The tubes were all intact and fully inflated.
- We were all wearing life vests.
- Our inner tubes were tied together so nobody could drift away.
- If we did get separated somehow, our parents, Lucy, and Alex all had phones.
- Lucy was keeping an eye on Alex and me.

Pretty quickly, though, our slices of Swiss cheese showed their holes. As soon as we were away from the guide, Alex unsnapped her life vest and flung it into the bottom of the tube.

"You're supposed to keep that on," I said, toying with the strap dangling from my waist. I didn't exactly blame Alex— the vests were scratchy and smelled vaguely of fish. Which made sense, considering how often they were dunked in river water.

"No way. It stinks and looks super dorky."

"Alex, there is literally nobody around to see or smell," I said, exasperated. "Except our families, and they've all seen you in footie pajamas."

"There's nobody to witness my dorkvest—until I post photos." Alex shook her head at me in a way that said *duh*. "Not like there's *any re*ception. How do people even live up here? Must be so boring."

I glanced around us. The Wolf River flowed smoothly through a deep, dense old-growth forest, with tall trees lining its banks like watchers at a parade. The leaves and needles formed a patchwork of green, every shade imaginable. The water was more silver-brown than blue—and with the bubbly froth from the current, it reminded me of soda. Birds flitted across the canyon of treetops. It was a truly brilliant blue-sky day, and the forest was one of the prettiest environments I'd ever been in—it felt like we were sitting inside of a screensaver image. Who wouldn't want to live up here and get to experience natural beauty like this all the time? I didn't tell that to Alex, though.

After sneaking a glance at the front of our tube flotilla to make sure that her mother wasn't paying attention to us, Alex whipped her cover-up over her head and balled it up in her tote bag. She didn't seal the Ziploc over it, which made the dry bag sort of purposeless, but I kept my mouth shut. In her teeny bikini, she held up her phone and started checking her angles. "Could you move a little that way?" She pointed, and I scooted left. "More," she said.

I guess she wanted to make sure I wasn't in the frame.

I dipped my hand in the river, the chilly current massaging my palm. I tried to let the water wash away how annoyed I was feeling. I glanced down at my swimsuit, faded and kind of stretched out in the butt. But I was still comfortable in it. I couldn't imagine wearing something as skimpy as what Alex had on. It seemed impossible to actually swim in that without a bikini fail. I'd be nervous the whole time. I let out a little sigh and tried to focus on the nature around us. But it was hard, especially with Alex jostling the tube to take her selfies. We kept bumping into Lucy's tube because of it.

"Hey! Can you guys stop it? Some of us are trying to read," Lucy grumbled, dropping her book to her lap and scowling at Alex. "Oh my God, are you really wearing that? Does Mom know?" Lucy turned toward the rest of the group and raised her hand to wave.

"Shh! Don't get her attention. Once I take some pictures, I'm putting the cover-up and vest back on."

Lucy paused. "I won't tell Mom if you stop bumping into me."

"I'm not doing that on purpose—it's because we're tied together." Alex grabbed the piece of thick, waxy rope that connected us with one loose knot. She easily untwisted it, and with one last push away from Lucy's tube, she set us free. "Happy?"

Lucy picked up her book again. "Yes." She readjusted her sunglasses and settled back into her reading position.

"I'm not sure we're supposed to be untethered," I said quietly, marveling at how quickly Lucy's tube had drifted from ours. Even if I stretched out my arm and hung halfway off the tube, I couldn't have reconnected us.

"Relax, Jocelyn. Where exactly could we get lost? This isn't, like, the Amazon."

I supposed Alex was right.

By then, the sun was blazing. I unzipped my backpack and took out my sunscreen to reapply. When I offered it to Alex, she looked like I'd just offered her a lutefisk-flavored fluoride treatment at the dentist. "I don't want to mess up my makeup." After I'd recoated my arms and legs and made a thick triangle of chalky goop covering my nose, I pulled out the binocs. Then I sealed my backpack in the dry bag.

I fiddled with the dials on the binoculars, setting them so

what I could see wasn't wobbly and blurry and I could check out the deciduous trees growing along the other side of the river. When I was doing my Nicolet Forest project, I learned about a kind of special apple tree that first grew along the banks. "Did you know the Wolf River apple tree grows fruit that is abnormally big? Like, each individual apple can weigh a whole pound."

Alex wasn't listening but held out her phone, waving her arm through the air as she shifted and stretched, searching for a signal. *Really? You can't just put the phone away for three hours and pay attention to your surroundings...or me?*

"Yes!" she squealed, pumping her free fist in the air. "Two texts just came through! Finally." She hunched over her phone and started typing madly. One of her swimsuit straps was already twisted, proving my point about bikini fails. We were sharing an inner tube—so close to each other our knees occasionally bumped—but it felt like we weren't even on the same plane of existence. I made a silent wish that we'd drift into a "No Service" zone again, or that she'd at least run out of battery.

I went back to scanning the rocky outcroppings and treetops, looking for signs of forest life. Like...a nest! "Alex! I think there's great blue heron's nest!" I pulled the binoculars from my face and held them out for her. "Take a look!"

"Yeah, I'm good," she said, waving me away with her left hand while furiously texting with the right.

"Stuff like this is the whole reason why we're here." I couldn't keep the frustration out of my voice. She might as well have stayed in the cabin all day, huddled around the Wi-Fi router like it was a campfire.

"Is it, though?" Alex said distractedly. "The reason I'm here is because my mom said I *had to* be."

I curled into my side of the tube. I swallowed hard, feeling a tightening and rawness in my throat that I knew meant I might start crying. But I hadn't cried in front of her at registration day, and I certainly wasn't going to now.

Maybe Alex didn't mean to hurt my feelings when she said stuff like that—implying that she was only hanging out with me by force. But it did hurt. A lot. This trip up north was supposed to fix things. We'd have fun together, like we'd had at the Walden end-of-the-year dance, and then she'd remember why we were— *had been?*—best friends in the first place. I knew I'd fallen a little behind Alex, in terms of all that social stuff. I just needed to convince her to give me time now to catch up. But I couldn't do that if she never gave me a chance.

Over on her side of the tube, Alex was giggling to herself. The constant upbeat chime of those text notifications pierced the peaceful nature soundtrack. I glanced ahead to see if Alex's phone was bugging the rest of our group. They were alarmingly far downstream—probably because Nolan and Mateo were paddling to go faster.

"Hey, we should try to catch up with everyone." A bend in the river lay ahead, and for the first time we wouldn't be able to see the rest of our tubing pod once they made that turn. Nobody had noticed that we weren't linked up anymore because Lucy's eyes weren't on us but still fixed on her book and the boys were so rambunctious, all the parents were busy watching.

Alex grunted in response.

"Seriously, help me paddle." I set the binoculars on top of the dry bag so I could use both arms.

Alex leaned over her side of the inner tube but not to help me. She'd flipped herself so the sun was on her back, bare except for those thin, twisted straps of magenta fabric. I could still see faint tan lines from her old racerback suit, identical to the one I was wearing. But they were so faded. A few more days in the sunshine with that bikini on, and they'd be erased. Which seemed significant, somehow.

Meanwhile, our families approached the bend. The water was frothier there, like maybe a small set of rapids was churning it up. The river definitely moved faster after the turn—I could see the current's forceful pull. The thick trees lining the banks had given way to granite-colored rock ledges.

"Alex! Come on. Could you put down your phone for one minute?" I didn't bother trying to hide the concern and frustration in my voice.

"Chill, Jocelyn." Her eyes stayed glued to her phone, its bottom resting against the rounded top of the tube. She muttered something to the screen. *Wait, is she talking with someone? Laura?*

I was churning up inside, just like the rapids ahead. I glared at Alex, willing her to face me and see that I was upset. Willing her to care. She kept staring at her phone, fingers dancing across the keypad. *Chime, chime, chime.* If I heard one more notification, I would implode.

Chime.

I didn't implode, but the pressure building inside me had to go somewhere. So I slammed down my fist and bounced the tube. On purpose.

ALEX

SPANISH CAMP

I WAS WRONG. I DID know someone at camp: Laura Longbottom. Although I didn't *know her* know her. We'd gone to school together since third grade, I think, or whenever her family had moved to Madison. But we'd never been friends. Or even very friendly. In fifth grade, a substitute had butchered my full name—Alejandra Benavides—reading the attendance sheet, and even though I quickly corrected her to call me Alex, Laura had giggled and started calling me *Alej*, like "A ledge," after that. For a few days, everybody else in our class did too. You'd think someone with the last name *Longbottom* would have, like, an awareness of making fun of people's names, but apparently back then Laura hadn't been coded for empathy.

I saw her right when I got off the bus, and I didn't know whether to be relieved to have one familiar face in the sea of campers or to be afraid that she'd get all these kids to call me "A ledge" too. So I avoided her, making sure to get in the farthest-away check-in line. I kept glancing around, trying to spot her signature high ponytail, so I could steer clear.

When I finally dragged my bags to Cabin Ronda (all the cabins were named for Spanish towns), I stumbled through the doorway and saw it. That high pony. Laura was sitting cross-legged on a bed, and the only empty one left was right next to hers. I sucked in a deep breath, for strength.

But Laura's eyes brightened as she looked up to see me, nervous and tired, standing in front of her. "Alex!" She jumped off the squeaky bed and tackle-hugged me. "You have no idea how happy I am to see you. And, oh my God, we're in the same cabin!" It took me a second to free an arm to tentatively hug her back. She squeezed me tight, and all I could think about was how gross-sweaty I must be, and that my breath probably still smelled like the cheese curls I'd been munching on during the bus ride.

"But what are you doing here? Don't you, like, know Spanish?"

I couldn't help but roll my eyes, as I untangled myself from her hug and started dumping all my stuff next to my bed. "Why, because my name is Spanish? I was born at Meriter Hospital, Laura. In Madison. My parents were born in Wisconsin too." *Wait until I tell Joss about this.* Imagining her shaking her head was comforting.

Laura's face flushed. Which almost made me feel bad, except for the fact that she'd been the one to make an insensitive comment. I simply hadn't let it slide. "Sorry—I didn't mean it that way, Alex. I just, you know... I thought you were good at Spanish...definitely better than me." She trailed off into an awkward silence. I softened. Learning languages is hard, at least for me. That's why I was at this camp. It was kind of nice if she actually thought I was good at it. "Anyway. Do you need help unpacking?"

I shrugged. "Sure." Laura seemed sincere. And now we were going to be in close quarters—literally—for the next two weeks. Ronda was the smallest cabin at Tierra de los Lagos, with only six girls assigned to it. I paused next to her for a second, scratching at what I knew would not be my only mosquito bite. I remembered watching Laura shine on the dance floor at Walden. For the most part, I'd always felt invisible to popular girls like her. Now here Laura was, helping me pull the stiff sheets across my camp bed and rooting through a bag that had two weeks' worth of my underwear in it. Life is weird.

———————

If you'd asked me, when I first got there, how I expected to feel on the last day of camp, I would've said super happy. Thrilled. Over-the-moon. Instead, I was sitting on my bed, clinging to Laura and the four other Cabin Ronda chicas. We were all ugly-crying.

"¡No quiero salir!" My Spanish had improved a bit over the two weeks, even though I had spent very little time actually working on it. That was mostly because of Laura.

"Text me as soon as you get home, okay, Lexie?"

That was Laura's new nickname for me. Much better than "A ledge," which she'd actually apologized for, the night we totally bonded at the campfire.

"I promise!" Our goodbye was kinda overdramatic, considering we were heading to the same place. We were separating for the drive only because Laura's mom was picking her up, and I was on the list to take the bus back, and camp doesn't allow you to change your travel plans without a parental signature. Still, I wondered if, once we were home in Madison, everything would be different.

With our hands clasped, you couldn't tell Laura's fingers from mine—we'd painted our nails the same shade of shell pink, with contraband polish she'd sneaked into camp. (It hadn't been on the approved toiletries list.) At first, I'd been worried about using the polish because it was against the rules. Same with using the real shampoo that Laura had also smuggled in—only lake-safe shampoo was allowed, this peppermint-y kind that barely sudses that they sell at the health food co-op on Willy Street in Madison. But I got over the worry because Laura didn't seem concerned at all, and her attitude was sort of contagious. Or, not really contagious—it was like she walked around in this spotlight of good luck and good vibes only, and if you were walking next to her, then it was yours to bask in too.

Laura had been just as popular at Tierra de los Lagos as she was back at Walden. And from the moment I walked into our cabin, I became her closest camp friend. So that meant that I, too, had been super popular. Can I be honest? Popularity felt great. It was as warm and bright and energizing as sunshine.

When Joss and I would walk into the cafeteria at Walden, if we couldn't make a beeline to a table with our friends Houa and Kate, we would find whichever looked the emptiest. We'd slide in with our trays, nodding hello to the quiet kids sitting at the other end. We'd never, ever plop down at the table in the center of the lunchroom where Laura and her friends sat, always laughing at whatever thing the boys across from them were doing to get their attention. If we were near their table, Jocelyn would watch them with disgust. "Don't they know that plastic straws are terrible for the environment? And they're just wasting them! Ugh, they're so immature." Were they, though? To me, they looked like they were just having fun. The straws already existed; it's not like it mattered at this point whether they were used for their intended drinking purpose or to turn the paper wrappers into missiles. (Although Joss had a point about whether our school should switch to eco-friendly straws.) And hanging out with guys didn't seem immature but the opposite. Grown-up. Cool. Why did Joss have to make me feel bad for wanting to be a part of that?

At camp, *I'd* sat at the cool table, giggling with Laura and ducking soggy french fries that Sanjay and Kelvin were flicking at us, while Laura whispered in my ear, *"Oh my God, Kelvin totally has a crush on you!"* A fry hit my cheek right then, but I didn't care. In fact, after I looked up and caught Kelvin's big brown eyes, I kind of wanted to save that fry forever. Someday I'll be going through my memory box with my granddaughter, and I'll pull out a petrified fry and be like, "This was the first fry your grand-father ever lobbed at my face, way back at Spanish camp."

That's not a totally unrealistic flash-forward. At the end-of-camp party, Kelvin and I danced together three times, and one was a slow dance. He held my hand even after the song stopped. We'd exchanged email addresses and were going to friend and follow each other on everything, once we got our phones back from camp's quarantine. He lived in Minneapolis, which is pretty far from Madison, but Laura kept saying how romantic long distance could be...

Afterward, Laura and I had stayed up all night. First we packed up her stuff, then mine. She sprawled on my bed, handing me clothes from my drawer. She tossed a wad of turquoise at my head. "Okay, first order of business when we get back to Madison: Shopping. You need a bikini. No more one-pieces, okay?"

I caught the swimsuit and ashamedly shoved it in my suitcase. My mom might be okay with a two-piece—I wasn't doing swim team this summer, so I didn't need a racing suit anymore. But she would definitely veto a skimpy one like Laura's. "Absolutely," I said. The thought of a shopping trip with Laura was super exciting.

"But you can always borrow one of mine. Mi closet es tu closet!" Neither of us had learned the Spanish word for *closet*, which really seemed like an oversight considering how much we both loved clothes.

My drawer was empty, so Laura moved on to all the junk I'd put on my bunk's shelf. Most of it, I hadn't touched since the first day. Like the pack of stationery, unopened, which she handed to me next.

"Were you actually, like, planning to write letters home? Oh my God, the envelopes are even stamped."

I had been. I hid my blush with a laugh. "To be fair, I thought I might get pretty bored."

"But you got letters from someone!" She waved three envelopes in the air above her head. "Dude, are they from Kelvin?!"

I shook my head. "Laura—think about it. He's *here*. Why would he mail me a letter?"

"Whatever, maybe he's a hopeless romantic or something." Had she seen him flick the fries? Laura studied the return address. "Two are from 'Jallard.' And the other is from 'Special Agent Lupine'? Huh?"

I blushed again. "They're all from Jocelyn." *Jallard* is one of my nicknames for her: J (Jocelyn) Allard. And Joss and I used to play this elaborate game we made up that involved both spies and mythological creatures and scientists—she called them cryptozoo-somethings—and her character's name was Special Agent Lupine. I had never realized how dorky that sounded till Laura read it aloud. "That's, um, an inside joke."

"Are you still, like, really close with her?"

I shifted my position on the floor. "Yeah, I mean, she's been my best friend since, well...forever." The kind of friend who mails a letter to you at camp three days before you even leave so that on the second day, when you're peak homesickness and unsure about everything, you have an envelope to slit open and comforting words from home, along with a handy "Days Left" countdown filled out on an index card.

"That's cool," Laura said, with a tone that kind of suggested it was the opposite. "It's just that, you're really fun and supercute. Kelvin agrees." She giggled. "It seems like maybe you wouldn't have a ton in common anymore with someone like Jocelyn Allard. You know?"

What was unsaid was that she thought Jocelyn—my best friend—was neither of those adjectives. Not really fun, not supercute. It made me cringe to think she felt that way. If Laura knew her like I did, she'd know that Joss can sometimes be dorky, like anyone, and it's true she's not into clothes, but she's also hilarious, and loyal, and fun. Just in a very different way.

I nodded in agreement. Guilt formed a pit in my stomach, or maybe it was the loaded baked potatoes and grilled hot dogs they'd served us for dinner. But I still said, "Yeah, I see what you mean."

"Anyway, I'm glad I got to know the real Alex. Lexie." Laura grinned at me, and it felt like winning a prize. *The real Alex. Lexie.* Maybe she was right. This cool version of me had been trapped inside for a long time, and camp had finally given her—Lexie—a chance to shine. "What should I do with these?" The letters from Joss were pinched between Laura's shell-pink nails. "Pack or trash?"

"Trash," I said without a second thought.

FIVE

I T WAS LIKE I was watching one of Alex's cell phone videos with the slow-motion effect turned on. After I heard that final chime, the expanding bubble of rage inside me popped, and the force of it sent my arm flinging down, hard, onto the side of the inner tube. Kind of like a karate chop. Alex was still draped facedown across the tube, so she didn't see the chop coming.

I wasn't thinking when I whacked my side of the tube—I was *feeling*. So I'm not sure it would be 100 percent fair to say I did it on purpose. Honestly, my action surprised me, too.

As my side sank slightly, Alex's bounced upward, separating her stomach from the plastic momentarily as she hovered a tiny distance above it. Her limbs all flung out instinctively, kind of like when you squeeze one of those rubber pet toys to make their eyes pop out. Startled, her fingers loosened her grip on her phone, and it went flying free.

It dropped onto the very top of the tube's curve, where it bounced up again. The phone hung in the air, debating which way physics was going to take it: left, and it would fall into the middle part of the tube, or maybe even into the partially unsealed dry bag. But if her phone veered to the right, it was going to plop into the cold, murky Wolf River.

It fell to the right.

I gasped as soon as I heard the splash. Alex was too stunned to make a sound. She gripped the sides of the tube, which had resettled on top of the water. She slowly turned to me, blinking and gaping, and then back toward the spot where it had entered the water. "My phone!" she finally screamed.

Then Alex flung her legs over the side of the inner tube, like a runner going over a hurdle, and splashed into the water herself.

"Alex!" I shrieked. She wasn't wearing her life vest anymore. I had no idea how strong the current was or how deep the water.

We'd drifted close to the shore before the bounce had happened, so the river was shallow, coming up to Alex's thighs once she found her balance and stood tall. I wondered if her flip-flops had managed to stay on. Then she hunched over, arms sifting through the silver-brown water, hunting for her phone. I needed to stop the tube from floating farther away. *This is my fault.* I had to help her, even if I hated that phone with a fiery passion.

I tried to paddle the tube toward her, but no matter how furiously my arms cut through the water, the current kept pulling me downstream. Up ahead, our families had hit the river bend. I could hear Nolan's and Mateo's squeals as their tubes bounced along the patch of rapids. In seconds, they'd float out of view. "Hey! Help!" I screamed at them. I wasn't sure if they heard me over their own noise and the churn of the water, so I kept yelling as I turned back to Alex. The only way to not leave her behind entirely would be to also jump out of the tube and then wade over to her, near the river's edge.

When I whipped back around to check on our tubing pod, I thought I saw Lucy turn to stare in our direction, her hand shading her eyes. But it was hard to tell if she was looking at us or her open book.

When we'd gotten into the tube, the guide had been standing in calm, knee-high water next to us. He'd held the tube steady while first Alex clambered in, and then while I did. But now there was nobody to help me keep things balanced, and the tube was in the middle of the fast-flowing river. I swung one leg out and into the cold water. Alex's now-empty side rose in the air like a teeter-totter. As I swung my other leg over, the imbalance became too much. The tube flipped, sending me tumbling face-first into the Wolf River.

"Gah!" My mouth had been open in surprise, so I swallowed a huge mouthful of river as soon as I plunged in. My life vest pulled me back up above the surface, where I sputtered the water. The tube landed on top of my head, and all its contents bobbed around me. I grabbed the dry bag containing my backpack and Alex's tote bag, then clamped my palm around the handle of the inner tube. With my free hand, I pushed upward to flip it right side up. The tube was much heavier than I expected, or maybe it's because my feet were still kicking around the bottom, and without having my footing, I couldn't use a lot of force to push it. After three tries, I got it to flip over. Before it could float away, I snatched the dangling piece of waxed rope that had connected us to Lucy's tube. My feet finally planted onto the slippery bottom of the river. I blinked water out of my eyes. Alex stood only a few feet away, near the rocky bank, still frantically searching for her phone. I pushed myself through the water toward her. I glanced back once, seeing two things: One, that Alex's life vest was now floating downstream, along with anything that hadn't been inside the dry bag. Such as my grandma's binoculars. And two, that our families had made it around the bend and were no longer in view.

Surely they must've heard all the commotion, right? Lucy had noticed that we'd drifted, right? And they'd come back for us, or at least stop around the bend and wait for us to catch up...right?

I tossed the dry bag—which unfortunately hadn't been totally sealed when I'd capsized—into the wet bottom of the tube. "I'm coming back, Alex!" I waded as fast as I could, but it was hard to navigate the riverbed, full of sharp and slippery stones and sticks. *Thank goodness I'm wearing water shoes.* Some rocks jutted out near the surface, almost like icebergs. I could hear them noisily scrape the plastic as the tube dragged along behind me.

Panting, I stopped next to Alex. She whimpered as she turned in circles, her arms still plunged in the cold water, desperately groping the riverbed below. "I can't believe this happened." Her tone was distraught. I could empathize. I felt really bad about Grandma's binocs.

"My fingers are numb. I can't even *feel* what I'm feeling around for anymore." Alex sniffed and raised a hand to rub her nose. Goose bumps covered her arms and legs. Even with the sun out, once you were wet in the river, it was freezing. Especially if you happened to be wearing a super-skimpy two-piece.

"Hold the tube and take a break. I'll search." I passed her the tube's rope, then hunched over to feel my way along the riverbed with my hands. It would be a miracle to find the phone, which could've settled in the rocks or silt or weeds or, with the swift current at work, might already be far downstream. Not to mention, after several minutes in the river, it was sure to be waterlogged and ruined. Especially because Alex's screen already had that one long crack zagging across it—definitely not watertight.

But Alex was really upset, and I felt at least partly responsible, so I fished around for it anyway.

Although Alex was supposed to be holding the tube, after a few minutes, she angrily shoved it onto the rocks, leaving it wedged in a spot crowded with fallen logs and branches, out of the water enough that it wouldn't float away. Then, shivering, she waded back to where I was still searching. Her teeth chattered.

"You should stay out of the river for longer," I said. "Dry off. You're too cold." Soon, I would need to do the same. It's not like my one-piece and shorts were keeping me much warmer. I could hardly feel my toes, even when I scrunched and wiggled them in my water shoes.

Without a word, Alex slumped, splashed her way over to the tube, and dropped herself into it. The tube made a weird exhalation sound as she did, like a person having the wind knocked out of them.

Why haven't our parents circled back to us yet? Maybe, if they hadn't seen that we were lagging behind—and having trouble— until they'd hit the bend, it had been too late to stop before the turn. If you're going through rapids, even little baby ones, you have to ride them out. Plus, it had been hard enough to get our inner tube to stay in one place after Alex had dived out of it. It would be even harder to maneuver a whole pod of connected inner tubes upstream, against the current.

I stepped a few feet closer to shore and bent to touch my hands to the bottom. Sliding my palms across the scuzzy rocks was creepy. It reminded me of that Halloween party game where you blindfold someone and then have them feel a bowl of peeled grapes, telling them they're touching eyeballs. I shuddered. I totally respect nature, and I think even the sort-of gross things— like earthworms and egg sacs and cocoons—are at least theoretically cool, but it's a whole other thing to be touching unknown stuff at the bottom of a river. Or unknown creatures. There *are* water snakes in the Northwoods. And then my palm brushed against something smooth that definitely didn't feel like a rock or slimy stick. I shrieked and yanked my hand away in surprise.

The thing I'd felt wasn't snakelike but hard, rectangular, and thin, with a shape so deliberate I knew it hadn't been made in the forest. The object loosely balanced between stones, like it hadn't been there a very long time. I blinked, took a deep breath, then plunged my hand down till my fingers closed around it. I pulled my arm out of the water, triumphantly, clutching Alex's phone.

"I found it! I actually found it!"

She sprung off the inner tube, causing it to make another loud exhalation. "What? Are you serious?" I nodded. "Oh my God! You're my freaking hero!" A smile overtook my face. *Maybe this is the start of our turnaround. I mean, what says love more than fishing around in a freezing-cold river to rescue your friend's presumed-dead phone?*

On numb feet, I stumbled over to her, holding out the phone like a prize. Alex reached to grab it. She looked happier than she had all summer; as happy as she normally did when we pulled into the parking lot at Paul Bunyan's. So happy that I grinned right back at her.

Her smile faded, though, once she started tapping the screen.

"Yeah, I don't think it's going to work. It was in the water a long time." Alex kept pressing the home button, like a cell phone version of CPR chest compressions. "I mean, I've heard if you stick a wet phone in a bag of uncooked rice, it will absorb all the moisture, and then in a couple of days, the phone will work again."

"Seriously? Where can we get a bag of rice?" Her head whipped around, like she almost expected a rice emporium to pop up out of nowhere, in the middle of a national forest.

"Um, Minocqua? There might be rice in the cabin..." Probably faded boxes of Uncle Ben's wild-rice mix from the 1990s.

"We need to get home fast."

"Alex, I hate to break this to you, but it's probably a lost cause." I paused, trying to find the right tone. "Now might be the time to say your goodbyes." I was being sarcastic but also not. "I'm going to prepare a eulogy for those binoculars." I thought of all the times I'd used them to get up close and personal with loons gliding along Buttercup Lake.

"This isn't funny, Jocelyn." She pressed the home button again and made an anguished moan. "Not at all."

I turned away, staring in the direction of the river bend. I couldn't see anything beyond it, and there was no sign yet of our families coming back for us. Alex's life vest had floated away downstream, out of view. I swallowed hard, thinking of how much it would freak everyone out to see that drifting alone, before they knew we were perfectly fine.

"Ow!" Alex frowned, slapping at a fly that had landed on

her leg. They love wet skin, for some reason. I could see—and hear—a few others circling us.

"Maybe we should cover up, so we don't get eaten alive waiting here." I moved past Alex, still clutching her dead phone, and toward the tube. The sun beat down on us, and I felt really exposed, standing in calf-high water. "On second thought, we should probably get back in our tube and head downstream. They're going to worry about us."

"My parents will be so mad I ruined my phone again," Alex grumbled, moving to follow me.

When I got close to the tube, I heard hissing. I turned back around because I thought it was Alex. But her mouth was closed in an angry pout. *Where's that coming from?* It sounded like the noise when you screw off the cap on your bike tires to fill them up at the gas station. *Wait a minute...tires.* Full of air, just like inner tubes.

I took off running, splashing wildly.

"Hey!" Alex called after me. "What's your deal?"

When I reached the tube, my stomach dropped. It was still safely wedged where she'd left it, but no longer puffed up and bouncy. The plastic ring drooped into the water and over the rocks, defeated. Deflated. It wasn't floating anywhere.

Which meant we wouldn't be, either.

SIX

"WELL, THIS IS A problem," I said, scratching at a mosquito bite on my thigh. I heard the buzz of a fly and swatted it away, then once again after it circled back. Blackflies are deceptively small but incredibly determined.

"How did that happen? They gave us a defective tube?" Alex kicked a flip-flop at it.

Aside from dull scratches and discolored spots, the tube had been perfectly fine when we got in. I remembered the guide carefully inspecting it. "This isn't the tour company's fault. Something probably poked it while we were getting out of the water." Or when Alex flopped onto the tube while it rested on top of a bunch of sharp objects like sticks and rocks. "Here, hold this?" I tossed Alex the dry bag, which had about a quarter inch of water at the bottom. Then I picked up the partially inflated inner tube and began inspecting it, searching for a hole. Maybe, if the air was leaking from the valve, we just needed to reseal it.

That wasn't it, though. "I found the culprit," I said, pointing.

A branch like a spear had impaled the side of the tube. When I held my fingertip next to the spot where it pierced the plastic, I could feel the air hissing out. I yanked the tube off the branch, which only made the hissing noise louder and the airflow faster. I plugged the tear with my pinkie to stop it.

"What are we going to do about that?" Alex asked, readjusting the dry bag in her arms.

"I don't know—maybe with the life vest, we'll still be able to travel downstream? Because that's a flotation device." *If* the tube could still support both of us. "I could keep the hole covered. We probably won't have to float far. Everybody must be waiting for us right after the rapids."

"Okay," Alex said, tossing the dry bag back in the bottom of the tube. "Let's push it out, and I'll hop in."

Shivering, we guided the tube a few feet into the river, and then Alex carefully grabbed the side. The tube sank from her weight. She slowly slithered herself onto it; the more she advanced, the more the tube smushed. I kept my palm pressed against the part with the tear so more air wouldn't escape, but I could still hear the hissing.

About three quarters of Alex was on the tube when it began taking on water. A few splashes at first, and I imagined crossing my fingers (because my actual fingers were stopping the leak) so it wouldn't take on much more. But once Alex tucked her flip-flop-clad feet inside, water poured into the middle. The tube, and Alex, began slowly sinking like the *Titanic*. My puny, stinky life vest was not going to overcome that.

"I don't think this is going to work," I said. "Maybe you should get out."

She nodded and slid off the sinking tube, holding the dry bag above the water.

"Ow! Jeez, these things are terrible," she said, slapping after another blackfly. "I'm covering up." She dumped the dry bag onto the rocky shore, then yanked it open, hunting for her cover-up. Still wet and wrinkled, it clung to her arms and legs awkwardly once she put it on.

"I guess we'll have to wait here for them to come back," I said, sitting on top of a large, smooth rock. The sun felt good on my river-chilled skin. I stretched my legs out in front of me. They were already dotted with bruises from working in Mom's garden and biking and stuff, although I'd gotten a fresh scrape while splashing around with the tube.

"I can't believe they're not back already," Alex grumbled, draping herself on a fallen log a few feet away from me. "Like, don't they even care?"

That was kind of odd. At the least, we should hear them calling for us, from around the bend, while they waited for us to catch up. I strained my ears to listen. The only sounds were the gurgle of the river, the rustle of the trees in the breeze, and the chirp of birds. No human sounds, except for—

"Ahh!" I heard a loud slap as Alex tried to nail another black-fly. "Why are they tormenting me?" she moaned.

"It's your perfume," I said. Because the flies were picking on her more than on me.

"I'm not wearing any perfume!" she hollered.

"Body spray, whatever it's called. They probably like the scent. Mango. Maybe they think you're a big piece of juicy fruit."

"Well, they need to *stop*." Alex tucked her knees up to her chest, straining the fabric of her cover-up. "This sucks."

I didn't disagree.

My legs were finally dry, so I stood and walked over to the bag, where I fished out my tube of sunscreen. The first squeeze only sprayed small blobs of the gel into my hands, and I had to shake it and squeeze superhard to get a decent glob out. "I'm almost out of sunscreen," I said. "Did you bring any?"

Alex snorted. "Nope. But you've gone through a tube *already*?"

I shook my head. "I was trying to finish this up before starting the new one. Anyway, you're supposed to use two ounces every time you apply, and reapply after eighty minutes." She acted like I had some kind of sunscreen obsession, like I was on one of those weird cable shows that Mom and I always watch in hotel rooms, about people with strange addictions to eating nonfood items, like paper and cotton balls. For the record, I do *not* eat sunscreen.

I checked on the inner tube again, which was slightly less

than half full of air. When our families came back for us, unless they had a patch on hand, we'd have to somehow double up with our parents or Lucy, and then Alex and I would be split up. Maybe I could still finagle things so we'd be together. Even if she'd probably just keep whining about the flies and her ruined phone, and possibly me.

"How long have we been here?" Alex asked. "At least a half hour, right?"

I nodded. "I think so." The sun had shifted, no longer directly overhead. We'd been out of the water long enough to dry off and for the tube to deflate, and there was also the time we'd spent in the river before the rest of the group floated out of view. They really should've come back to help us already. A nervous chill ran down my spine as I considered the fact that they hadn't.

"Maybe we should just go," Alex said. "If they're waiting for us."

"But we don't know where they are," I said.

"Downstream," Alex said, rolling her eyes. "*Duh.*"

"*Except we can't float there,*" I replied, rolling mine.

"Good thing there's a path." She uncrossed her arms to point toward the trees.

Wait, what? I hopped up and walked to the spot where the reeds and moss-covered rock piles of the shoreline began blending with spongy dirt and pine needles and green grasses of the forest floor. Sure enough, what looked like a trail led from the woods to the covelike area where we were waiting. The path was faint, like it wasn't used regularly. But it cut clearly, confidently through the space between the forest and the river, hugging the bank. We *could* follow it downstream.

Usually, if you get lost somewhere, it's a good idea to stay put. Whenever we take a trip down to Chicago to see all the museums, my mom drills this instruction into Nolan and me beforehand: Don't wander away from the rest of the family, but if we get separated, stop where you are and wait. It's easier to find someone if they're not moving. In this situation, though, our families might not be able to come back for us. If they hadn't realized a path ran along the bank, they probably thought the river was their only option. Except they couldn't float backward. They were probably frantically calling the tube people for a ride upstream or to send the guide down to fetch us.

Still, I wasn't sure. "I don't know, Alex. Maybe we should wait a little longer. If we take off, we might miss them."

"Gah!" Alex slapped furiously at another fly. "I can't wait one more second. I'm being eaten alive. Our tube is busted, anyway. You can stay here if you want, but I'm leaving." She yanked her tote out of the dry bag. Then she slung it over her shoulder and stomped toward the footpath, the soft ground muffling the angry slap of her flip-flops.

I didn't think we should go. But I certainly wasn't going to stay there alone, sitting on a deflated tube, while my best friend tramped downstream by herself. This was sort of what I wanted, right? A chance to be alone, really alone, with Alex. Some kind of experience, or adventure, to help us re-bond. Well, this was my chance.

I took one last glance at the Wolf River, and then I followed her.

ALEX

FIRST DAY BACK FROM CAMP

T HE YELLOW SCHOOL BUS left camp super early, so I got back to Madison around two. Only an hour after adult swim ended at the pool—meaning I had plenty of time to call Joss so we could hop on our bikes and head over for a swim. Historically, the first day of summer vacation is also an official Alex-and-Jocelyn holiday: the First Day at the Pool. Not once in the past seven years had we missed a chance to park our butts on the familiar striped lounge chairs and soak up the sunlight and chlorine smell. Even in bad weather, we'd still go and huddle under an umbrella, swaddled in towels. It was only because of camp that we'd missed it, so the day I got back was supposed to be this year's belated First Day at the Pool. Joss wasn't going to swim until I got back, out of solidarity.

Based on the letters Joss had sent me, and her index-card countdown in particular, I knew she couldn't wait for my homecoming. When my mom picked me up from the camp bus, she told me that Jocelyn had already called the house three times that morning. Now that I had my cell phone back from camp quarantine, I could see she'd also been texting me constantly from her emergency flip phone.

"Should I take you straight to Joss's house?" Mom asked. "You must be dying to see her." My phone buzzed with yet another message. "And she you, obviously," Mom added with a laugh.

That text wasn't from Joss, though. **LEXIE! Are you back? It's time for retail therapy ☻ Come over my brother will drive us**

I sort of couldn't believe we were back in Madison and Laura still wanted to hang out with me. "Actually, after we drop off my stuff, can you take me to my friend Laura's house?" Mom's right eyebrow raised, but she didn't say anything.

Another text from Joss popped up: **Are you home yet? I'm dying to swim! My mom is making me do yard work till you get back**. I swiped the notification away. I'd reply later and just tell Joss that the bus left after lunch, that I got home at dinnertime. Maybe we could do a night swim or something. Or, I mean, nothing was magic about going swimming *today*, aside from the fact that it was perfect pool weather: sunny and warm with no breeze. It was only a substitute First Day at the Pool.

When my mom pulled up at the Longbottoms' huge house, she turned to me. "Do I need to pick you up?" She pressed her lips together like she wasn't sure about what to say. "Maybe in time for a swim before dinner?"

I shook my head. "Laura's brother can drop me off when we're done."

"Okay," my mom said, tapping the steering wheel. The questioning tone of her voice said she didn't totally approve of my plans, and as my phone lit up again with a new text, she sneakily tried to read it. I pulled my phone away. Mom opened her mouth to say something, taking time to choose her words carefully.

"Loveyoubye!" I said, shoving my phone into my pocket and hopping out of the passenger seat. I had a feeling I didn't want to hear whatever she was hesitating to say.

The way Laura squealed when I got out of the car, you'd think I hadn't seen her in years, not hours. It made me feel really happy and also relieved—convinced that the friendship we'd formed wasn't just a camp thing. Laura and I were real friends now. *Friend*-friends. I wondered if at the next Walden dance, I'd be in the middle of the floor with Laura, one of the shiny happy people, instead of hugging the snack table with Joss. And Shark Boy.

Laura whined until her older brother, Zack, who apparently hadn't been informed of his role in our plans, agreed to drive us to the shops at Hilldale, even though the Longbottoms lived close enough that we could have biked. Before Zack agreed, I suggested that as an option.

"We'd get all sweaty biking, Lexie," Laura said. "And my hair looks really good today, so I don't want a helmet to mess it up." Her ponytail looked the same as any day. It was perpetually good, but whatever.

The stores were filled with back-to-school displays despite it not even being midsummer, but we managed to find a full rack of swimsuits at one boutique. You'd think that because a two-piece uses less fabric, it would be cheaper. But, no. I flipped the tag on a cool bikini and saw it would cost more than all the allowance and birthday money I had left. Nope.

"Too expensive," I said, starting to return the flimsy hanger to the rack.

"No offense, Lexie, but we're talking a need, not a want, here. This is not, like, 'discretionary spending.'" Laura beamed. "That's what my mom always says." I hesitated, staring at the cute print. "Just try it on, okay?"

I took the bikini back off the rack and headed into the changing room. The straps were confusing to tie—I couldn't tell at first which were just for show and which were there to, like, keep you covered. Once I finally had it on, I took a deep breath and stepped out.

"Oh my gosh, you look amazing!" Laura clapped her hands giddily. "So, so cute. Buy it!"

I did a twirl in front of the mirror. I felt kind of amazing, actually. Cool. Mature. "I don't have quite enough. Maybe I can come back with my mom to get it..." Who was I kidding? She'd never buy it for me.

Laura looked really sad for a moment, and then her face brightened. "Wait. When was your birthday?"

"April."

She pulled her wallet out of her purse and whipped out a bill. "Is this enough to cover what you're short?" When I nodded, she grinned. "Happy belated birthday! That's your present from me."

"Are you sure?" I asked, a little flustered by her generosity. Laura nodded happily. "Wow, thanks."

She reached over to give me a hug. "Eee, I'm so excited! You're gonna rock that at the pool."

Afterward, we sauntered back to the car, where Zack was still sitting, scrolling through his phone. "I'm hungry. Zack, drive us to Michael's," Laura ordered. He grunted in a way that I guess meant he'd agreed.

"Maybe we should get fro-yo instead," I suggested, because Michael's frozen-custard stand is really close to Jocelyn's house, and I felt guilty going near it when she didn't even know I was back. My phone buzzed nonstop in my pocket. If she called the house again, I hoped my mom didn't spill the beans that I was out shopping. So I sent Joss a quick message saying: **bus ride took forever, sooo tired not sure if I'm up for a swim. gonna take a quick siesta i'll call later.**

"Nope, I want custard. It's, like, my last hurrah of junk food after two weeks of camp slop." Laura was super into eating "clean" and organic. Her mom had mailed her a care package full of kale snacks to get her through camp. I thought they were awful at first, but the taste grew on me.

It's not like Joss will ever know we're there, I thought. She was still weeding in the backyard, according to her last text.

Zack parked and grunted again and then went back to scrolling on his phone while gnawing on a protein bar the size and color of a hockey puck. Laura and I headed for the superlong line. Her perfect ponytail bounced as she scanned the crowd, looking to see if anyone we knew from Walden was around. I slid my sunglasses down from atop my head, shading my eyes from the late-afternoon sun. Then I froze.

My heart thumped so hard and loud that whatever Laura was babbling about, I couldn't hear it. My head pulsed. I felt dizzy.

There was Jocelyn's frizzy topknot, three people ahead in line.

I closed my eyes briefly behind the shades, then finally peeked them open. She was alone. She was facing away from us. I don't think she'd seen me yet. There was still time to escape.

Why did I want to escape? Guilt, mostly, for all the messages I'd ignored and then my one reply that was more of a medium than a little white lie. For bailing on the promise to let Joss know the second I got home from camp. For skipping out on the rescheduled First Day at the Pool. I mean, it had been an *unspoken* agreement that I'd call her right away but...still an agreement.

Also guilt for side-eyeing the clothes she was wearing: a pair of scraggly jean cutoffs, the butt muddy from doing yard work, over her dry turquoise racing suit that matched mine. I was still clutching my bag from the boutique, with a replacement bikini inside that Jocelyn would never ever dream of wearing.

And, if I were being really, *really* honest, guilt for feeling like when I was around Laura, I didn't want to be around Jocelyn. I was the teeniest bit...embarrassed by her.

"Lexie!" Laura only called me that now. "Hello?" She waved a hand in front of my face. "Of course we'll share a dish because it's so much added sugar. I'm feeling like chocolate. Cocoa is an antioxidant, you know."

I nodded blankly. Jocelyn was up at the window, ordering. As soon as she was handed her custard, she'd turn around and see me. *Maybe I should hide in the bathroom, I could still fake a pee-mergency, dash inside right now...*

Too late. Joss turned, smiling lovingly at her turtle sundae, sticking out her tongue to lick the oozing hot caramel and fudge sauce that dripped down the side toward her hand. Then she must have sensed me staring at her, because her eyes flicked upward, and she recognized me.

The worst part is that, at first, Joss's face brightened, like when a cloud breezes away from blocking the sun. She must've thought I'd come there to find her, to surprise her. Her mouth spread into a grin, and she began to rush toward me, so eager that the maraschino cherry slid off the top of her sundae and fell to the pavement. She loves those gross cherries.

Laura chose that moment to throw her arm around my shoulder and pull me next to her. "This line is too looooooooooong, Lexie. And I'm staaaaarving." It was unmistakable that we were there together. Jocelyn stopped short a few feet in front of us.

My mouth opened and closed, then settled into a grimace to match Jocelyn's.

"H-hey, Alex," she finally sputtered. "Hi, Laura." Her voice turned up with confusion.

"Oh, hi. I think you got a little something on your shorts?" Laura gestured at Joss's crusty cutoffs. I couldn't see Laura's eyes, because of her mirrored shades, but I'm sure she was smirking at me. I elbowed her sharply while mouthing *Sorry* to Joss.

"Lexie! We're up!" Laura tugged me toward the counter.

"Um, hang on, I gotta get my custard," I mumbled, letting myself be pulled away.

Laura asked for a junior-size chocolate in a dish with no sprinkles and two spoons. The only good thing about that boring order is that it took about two seconds to scoop. I looked back to the round picnic tables, expecting to see Jocelyn sitting at one. We would head over, and I could explain that Laura had been at camp with me... I hadn't written Jocelyn a single letter, or even an email, so how would she know that Laura and I were friends now? But by then, three hyper toddlers were crawling all over the tables and Joss wasn't sitting down. I scanned the parking lot and adjacent playground. No sign of her.

"I guess Jocelyn left?" I asked, feeling my stomach twist.

Laura shrugged. "Whatever. Don't let me eat all this myself." She pushed the still-full custard dish into my hands, and I took a bite. The custard, too cold, gave me an ice headache immediately. I squeezed my eyes shut, willing it to go away. Even after it faded, I felt awful. "Actually, I don't think I'm hungry anymore." Abandoned and melting on the table next to ours was an untouched turtle sundae, missing the cherry. As I stared in the direction of Jocelyn's block, I imagined her hurrying up the sidewalk to her house, shoulders hunched, then slipping inside, the screen door slamming behind her. I didn't let myself imagine how sad and confused her face must've looked.

SEVEN

EVEN THOUGH THE INNER tube was pretty worthless with a hole, I dragged it along. Actually, *dragged* isn't the right word. I put my backpack on so my hands were free, and then I held the mostly deflated tube over my head, like it was a sun umbrella. Even though we were in a national forest, the path was dappled with sunlight. You can get burned even in the shady areas, I think, and I burn easily.

Alex turned back, probably to see why I was moving so slowly. "Why are you even bothering to bring that along?"

"For starters, we do have to return this to the tubing people. Also, it's a good source of sun protection."

She shook her head. "Literally the only good thing right now is that the sun is out. But you do you." She turned to face forward and kept stomping along the path. Her flip-flops kicked up little clouds of dirt and pulverized leaves with each step.

Truth was, we were both moving pretty slowly. The trail wasn't well defined, and clusters of rocks littered it—some of which were partially obscured by brush and a carpet of fallen pine needles, so you don't see them till you almost trip. Hidden tree roots were another hazard. I stubbed my toe really hard within a minute. Water shoes do not offer a ton of toe protection, unfortunately. At least not while you're on land. They were kinda slippery too. I wouldn't want to climb anything while wearing them.

For the first five minutes or so that we walked, the footpath hugged the curve of the river. I started to admit to myself that Alex had been right—following it downstream was the smartest course of action. But then, the path began to pull away.

It happened so gradually that I didn't notice until we were about ten feet from the too-rocky-to-walk-along shoreline. Looking ahead, the path—at least what I think was the path, because the longer we trudged along it, the harder it got to tell what exactly was a trail and what was a random bare patch of mud—veered into the forest. A thick line of trees would separate us from the river going forward.

"Hey, Alex? Hold on a sec."

She stopped and turned to me, wiping at her forehead. Her brow was sweaty, and her face was flushed.

"What is it?" She sounded winded too.

I dropped the inner tube to the ground to give my arms a rest. My muscles burned from holding it overhead. "Looks like we're walking into the woods," I said, pointing. "That doesn't seem right, if we're trying to follow the water."

She stared at where I was pointing to, scratching at a bite on her leg. "Huh," she said. "I guess so."

"Maybe this isn't going to lead us downstream. Should we head back?" That made the most sense to me.

She bit her lip. Alex doesn't like to be wrong. She's paranoid about people thinking she's not smart. "No, I don't think we should. It's probably on purpose..." Her face brightened with an idea. "This must be a shortcut!"

That actually made sense. In certain spots we'd passed while floating along the river, trees gave way to sandstone formations. A footpath like the one we were on wouldn't be safe on a low cliff. (Especially in water shoes.) It would make sense for someone to have cut a path through the forest to meet up with the river again at a less-rocky area. "I think you're on to something."

Alex offered me a small smile. "Carry on," she said. Even though she was already facing away and hurrying ahead, I grinned back at her. *This is just the kind of bonding experience we've needed...*

As we walked, I counted in my head. If the shortcut veered away from the river for more than five minutes, we should reassess our plan. Especially because our families still thought we were on or near the river. *One one thousand, two one thousand...* If I got to *three hundred one thousand* and there was no water in sight, we'd turn back. Too bad I didn't have a watch, and Alex's drowned phone couldn't tell the time anymore. She cradled it in the crook of her arm, like she hoped it would suddenly sputter and cough up a bunch of water and riverweed and then be okay. I was surprised she hadn't tried to give her phone mouth-to-mouth or something.

We moved along the path to a soundtrack of our loud breathing and the crunching of our feet hitting the carpet of needles and cones, damp leaves, and fallen branches. Punctuated by Alex's flip-flops slapping against her heels. I closed my eyes for a moment and savored my next inhale: pine, fir, and maybe cedar. The scent reminded me of the afternoon we pick out a Christmas tree and set it up in the living room, when all of a sudden our house becomes a forest wonderland. Then I opened my eyes again, because this really wasn't a hike to attempt without sight. There was so much to see. All the wildlife and plants I'd learned about for my TAG project on the national forest—now was my chance to spot them. *What if I stumble on something super rare, like the four-toed salamander? Better yet, what if we come across a wolf?* I lowered the tube for a second to pat the side pocket of my backpack, to make sure my camera was still there, easily accessible. Too bad the binoculars were somewhere at the bottom of the Wolf River.

A light breeze tickled my limbs, and I was thankful for it, because ever since we'd left the river, I hadn't been mobbed by flies. Maybe that was also thanks to the spiders in the forest—there were webs everywhere, glinting in the sunlight. Cool, but also creepy.

One hundred sixteen one thousand. Still no sign of the river, and I couldn't hear its rushing water anymore. But there was still plenty of time for the path to weave back to it.

Alex was really charging ahead; "walking with a purpose," as my mom would say. I did my best to keep up behind her. Because she was so confident in her movement, I didn't look closely at the path itself. I just followed along, even though there did seem to be a growing number of obstacles in our way: tree roots perfectly positioned to trip a hiker, large rocks sticking up out of the ground, sunken holes in which you could twist an ankle.

Two hundred thirty-four one thousand. A bead of sweat dripped from my forehead directly into my eyeball, and the sunscreen stung. I couldn't wipe the rivulets away because I was holding up the inner tube again. The breeze had disappeared, and it felt muggier than it had along the river. I heard a whiny buzz by my left ear—a mosquito. I shook my head back and forth because I couldn't swat at it with my arms in the air.

"Ow!" Ahead of me, Alex stopped short and then pitched forward, landing on her palms. Her phone dropped onto the ground.

"Are you okay?" I tossed the tube aside and hurried to squat next to her.

"No!" She clutched her big toe. "I just, like, stabbed my foot on something."

"Let me see." I scooted around and bent close to her mud-covered feet. She pointed at her purple-polished big toenail.

Below the edge of the nail, where the polish was chipped, was a spot of bright red. "Yeah, I think you got a scrape."

She groaned. "I'm probably going to get rabies now."

I held back a laugh. "Uh, not likely. Rabies is from animals, like raccoons. Maybe you mean tetanus, which can be in dirt." She gave me a horrified look. "You've been vaccinated. It's fine. Once you wash off your toe, put on some ointment—nothing to worry about." I stood up slowly. "Did you bring any Band-Aids?" Her bulging tote bag, after all, was like a pop-up drugstore.

She shook her head. "Just makeup and stuff." So I guess only the cosmetics aisle.

"Wait! I still have a mini first aid kit in my backpack." I worked the straps off my shoulders and pulled out the kit. Opening it, I realized the kit had already been used. Only two bandages were left inside, no ointment. But I did have a few remaining squirts of hand sanitizer. Better than nothing. "Here. Use this stuff."

"Thanks," she said, taking the tiny bottle and bandage from me. She squirted a big blob of sanitizer out and doused her toe with it, wincing.

I tried to remember what number I'd been at when I'd stopped counting—287, maybe? Close enough to three hundred, and we'd definitely been walking for more than five minutes. I turned in a slow circle, taking in our surroundings. Trees and ferns as far as my eyes could see. No river. I strained to listen, only hearing the sounds of the forest: the drone of insects, bird calls, rustling branches. And Alex, squirting more of the sanitizer gel for her hands. I think she used it all up. Then she crumpled the bandage wrapper and handed it out to me, like a little kid does with their mom. Or a princess would do with her handmaiden.

I still took the crumpled wrapper and stuck it in my backpack pocket because I didn't want to risk littering in a national forest.

"Maybe we should head back to where we came out of the water," I said. "We've been walking for a while, and there's no sign we're going to hook up with the river again." I was slightly worried that in the meantime, while we'd been in the woods and out of view, our families had made it back upstream and now they couldn't find us. I closed my eyes again to better listen, to see if I might hear them calling. Nothing. How long had it been since they'd made the turn, and we hadn't? Probably more than an hour. I thought about the life vest that had floated downstream. *Mom must be totally freaking out.* I felt really bad for her, and everyone else. Especially poor Lucy, who had been told to keep an eye on us. Yes, she'd done a terrible job of it, but in her defense, she probably didn't think we'd lose a phone, capsize our tube, exit the water, ruin the tube, and then have no way to return. All those Swiss cheese disaster holes had lined up. Our situation wasn't the fault of one person.

Well, except maybe me. I'd bounced the tube, after all.

Alex sighed. "We've already walked this far. Does it really make sense to turn around?"

"What if they're back there? Looking for us?" Imagining my parents and Nolan anxiously waiting on the riverbank made my chest tighten. When Nolan had gotten separated once at the Fourth of July fireworks, I'd panicked. In the fourteen minutes it had taken for my dad to find him, patiently waiting on a nice older couple's picnic blanket, I had curled up in a ball on ours and bawled. The idea that something bad had happened to my little brother was unbearable. I really hoped our families weren't feeling like that about us right now. Especially because we were totally fine. Just a bit off-course.

Alex swatted at a fly—a horsefly, the bigger ones you find in the deep woods. The bugs had come back with a vengeance. The mosquito buzz surrounded us like radio static. "Would the others even know where we got out of the river?" Alex made a good point. It's not like there was a sign or anything, only a small natural cove, and we'd left nothing behind—not even footprints in silt. Unless my binoculars washed up, there'd be no trace of us.

"I just wish we knew this path was heading where we actually need to go." I stared ahead, like I was hoping to see a marker tacked to a tree, telling us that we were on the scenic Blah-Blah Trail, and in only one quarter of a mile, we'd be back to the banks of the Wolf River. But this wasn't a trail like that. I turned to look at the way we'd come.

All I saw were trees, tall and dense and overgrown. Their branches crossing one another like the silk strands in those spiderwebs. I didn't see any kind of recognizable trail. Which didn't make sense, because we'd followed one to this spot. At least, I'd thought we had, as I'd followed behind Alex. I stared down at my feet, studying the ground, then zooming out a bit, to find the edges of the path. The forest floor was indistinguishable. Dainty, long-stemmed white-and-yellow wildflowers filled every space that wasn't covered in moss. There wasn't even a faint line to help us know which way to walk, to stay on the path. Because there wasn't any path. Not anymore.

"Alex," I said slowly, even though my heart was starting to pound. I'd been so focused on watching exactly where my feet were, to avoid tripping, that I hadn't paid much attention to anything around them. I'd just assumed that to Alex, in the lead, the trail had been clear. "Which way did we come?"

She turned and pointed with such total confidence that my shoulders relaxed. "That way." My eyes followed her outstretched arm—and saw just a bunch of nondescript pine trees surrounded by curlicue ferns.

"Are you sure?"

Her mouth wavered with the beginnings of a frown. "Yeah... well, I think so." She scratched at her elbow.

"So where's the trail now?" I asked, trying to sound very calm and not at all judgy, but my voice was rising higher with each word and I couldn't tamp it down.

Alex stayed silent, staring past the trees. Her mouth hung

open a bit, then closed, like she was about to say something but realized it wasn't quite right. "Huh. It's really hard to tell... It got kind of tricky back there, like, I didn't know if we should go left or right at one spot..." Her voice trailed off.

"Why didn't you stop then?" I asked, incredulous. "When you weren't sure?" Once the path faded, we should've turned around and traced it back to where we started. Not guessed at where it should go next. That's how you get lost.

She shrugged defensively. "It's like on a standardized test—if you're not sure, you make an educated guess. I made a couple of educated guesses. When in doubt, always choose C. Like Mr. Macht used to say in science class."

I squeezed my eyes shut while I sucked in a deep breath. "Alex—those weren't actual instructions. He was making a joke." I opened my eyes and stared at her.

She looked wounded. "Oh, and I was too *dumb* to know that." She grabbed at a nearby twig and twisted it anxiously in her hands. "Why are you acting like this is such a big deal?" she asked, but in a way that told me she didn't want an answer; she wanted me to stop acting like it was a big deal. To make her feel better, regardless of the situation.

But I couldn't do that. The worried look on her face told me I didn't have to say what I said next, that she already knew, but I said it out loud anyway.

"Because now we're lost."

EIGHT

THE FOREST CHANGED SWIFTLY to match our unease, once we became aware of our predicament. The gentle breeze, which had felt so refreshing, slinked away, and the air became still, stifling, and muggy. The trees leaned in, crowding us, watching to see how we'd deal now that we'd realized we weren't on a path at all but just standing in some random spot in the middle of the deep Northwoods. I don't think I ever understood all those ominous fairy tales about kids being lost in the forest until I realized that I'd become one of those kids. And the vibe shifted immediately. You know how sometimes it looks like the knots in tree bark are faces? Suddenly they were all sneering and laughing at us.

I shook my head back and forth to release some tension. I told myself: *Stay calm. Five minutes ago, you weren't worried about being in here. There's no reason to be worried now.* We'd walked only a short distance from the river. It couldn't be that hard to find our way back there, even if we'd lost the trail. We just had to march in the direction from which we'd come. We'd probably catch up with the path right away.

Well, I wanted an adventure to bring Alex and me closer together...

Alex, though, freaked out.

"What do you mean we're *lost*?" Her voice was high and tinny, practically a helium voice, and she sucked in air before and after speaking like she was about to do the penny dive at the pool party. Not that she'd participated in that this year. "How can we be lost? I don't want to be stuck in the woods." As if to make her point, she frantically slapped at a fly. The big deer- and horse-flies in this part of the forest had proven just as persistent as the littler blackflies by the river, and their bites stung harder. Alex gave up trying to shoo the fly away, snatched her tote and the now-empty ziplock dry bag, and started running in the opposite direction from me.

"Alex, wait! Where are you going?" I scrambled to gather my stuff and readjust my water shoes on my feet. The shoes were shrinking as they dried, becoming uncomfortably tight and scratchy where the elastic met my ankles.

"Out of here! I want to get out of here!" Her flip-flops slapped madly against the ground.

"I don't think you're heading the way we came!" I called after her.

Alex jerked to a sudden stop.

I jogged to catch up, the totally deflated inner tube slapping one of my sides and my half-on backpack flapping against the other. After we'd stopped, when Alex had scraped her toe, we'd turned around several times. Before that, I thought we'd been heading in the direction of a gnarled tree that was now a few feet to my left. But I wasn't positive. Maybe I'd noticed the tree when I'd scanned the area for signs of the river. Or maybe when I'd turned to look behind me. Or maybe I hadn't noticed the tree at all, and I was misremembering that now, only because it was one thing around us with a very distinctive look.

"Do you see the trail anywhere?" I asked, stopping next to her, panting.

Her eyes flitted nervously around the forest. "No," she said, her voice managing to be both angry and quietly ashamed.

I took a deep breath. "Okay." I took another breath, slower. "Don't freak out. This is not a huge deal. We can't be too far from it"—*depending on how far you marched us away while you were in the lead for some reason*—"so let's just calmly walk back."

"But which way?" she asked, hugging her bag to her chest like it was a stuffed animal.

"Um…" I squinted through the treetops, trying to figure out where the sun was. After noon, it tracks west in the sky till it finally sets. Had we exited the river on the east or west bank? I had no idea. *I should've paid attention to that, except how was I to know that we wouldn't be getting right back on our tube and floating away?*

Next to me, Alex breathed faster and faster, like she was working herself up into hyperventilating. I had to make a decision, and walking in the direction of the sun just seemed right. "That way." I pointed. "Let's try walking that way."

Alex nodded. "Okay." As she stood up straight, I spotted a big mosquito on a bare patch of her shoulder, above the neckline of her cover-up. I slapped it, leaving a smear of Alex's blood on her skin and my palm. At least, I assumed it was her blood. The mosquito could've already bitten me.

"Ouch!" She whirled to face me, furious. "What the heck was that for?"

I raised my palm to show her. "I got him? But too late, unfortunately."

The old Alex would've laughed at that or thanked me. This Alex just glared and wiped the gross remnants of the mosquito off her neck. "I hope at least *you're* happy. Being trapped in the forest like this. It's probably your dream come true."

My stomach flipped as I thought about how I had, honestly, been longing for one-on-one time with Alex on this trip. Without her phone and the constant Laura texts. Now we were alone in the woods. I had actually gotten exactly what I'd hoped for. Just maybe not quite like this.

We weren't trying to walk quietly through the forest, and that was a good thing, because flip-flops and water shoes make a ton of noise, slapping and squeaking with every step. We also weren't moving carefully at all, blazing our own trail of snapped branches and jostled leaf piles and crunched wildflowers behind us. I felt really bad about those crunched flowers— thinking of all the "Please protect plants and wildlife by staying on the trails" signs I'd seen on hikes in the university arboretum back home, at Devil's Lake State Park, and every other natural place I'd ever visited. Now I was in the national forest—a superspecial and protected environment—and I was stomping all over it.

I was also slightly wary of the green leaves and plant tendrils that brushed against our limbs as we moved, because the forests of the Northwoods are home to plenty of dangerous and irritating plants, like poison ivy, poison sumac, and wild parsnip— which sounds like something you might even want to eat, but it actually creates severe blisters if it so much as touches your skin. I wondered why the person who named that plant didn't go with *poison parsnip* or something even more descriptive, like *DANGER DANGER BLISTER WEED*, to make it abundantly clear that you should look, not touch. Unless you're wearing thick gloves and long pants.

There's a reason the hiking-clothes section at sporting goods stores is full of shoes with thick treads, quick-drying pants, and breathable layers. They don't sell slippery thin soccer shorts and regular swimsuits, and definitely not skimpy two-pieces and loose caftans like Alex was wearing. We were reminded of this as soon as we started hiking in search of the river.

I tried to maneuver around the branches and twigs, but it was hard to avoid them in the overgrown, untouched forest. They tickled and poked my arms and legs, which soon became covered in a pattern of angry red scratches. At least my clothes stayed pretty close to my body, though. Alex's flowy cover-up was like a magnet for bare branches.

"Ow!" she squealed.

I turned to see her stopped short, her body still leaning forward into a stride but her cover-up holding her back. She tugged to pull it loose, but it wasn't budging. "I'm caught on this stupid pine tree!"

I dropped the inner tube—gladly, because it was starting to feel really heavy, and gripping the handles made my palms sore and sweaty. I bent next to the branch where the cover-up's thin fabric had caught. "I have no idea how this is so stuck in here," I said. Gentle tugs did nothing to loosen it. The fabric was covered in bead patterns, and one beaded flower was snared in the branch. "Is it okay if I rip it? Otherwise, I think the only way you're going to get free is by wiggling out and leaving it here." To be honest, the cover-up was so flimsy that I don't know how much protection it was really giving Alex from the elements. If it was only going to keep getting caught, she might be better off without it. "You could wear your beach towel," I suggested.

"I'm not leaving this in the woods! Laura loves it."

"It's hers?"

Alex nodded, wiping sweat off her forehead but leaving behind a line of dirt. "I borrowed it for the cabin. Because, you know, I thought I'd be, like, relaxing by the lake. Good photo op." She smoothed the fabric on her arm. "It's Laura's favorite, but she loaned it to me anyway because she's that nice—and these are my colors. I'm a summer palette." Alex pointed to the swirls of peach and turquoise blue. "I promised her I'd take care of it." There was a waver in her voice, like she knew now that she would most likely be breaking that promise. And I felt a little bad for Alex, because I know how it feels to be scared of making a friend mad at you or of doing something to make her not want to be your friend anymore.

I *really* know how that feels.

I tugged again. The beading was stuck tight. "I'm going to have to rip it, but I'll be as gentle as possible."

Alex let out a deep sigh and braced herself. "Okay."

I pulled, and she winced as the fabric made a tearing sound. "You're free now," I said, examining the part that had been stuck. Beads had fallen off, but the damage was minor—definitely something that could be mended. That made me feel less guilty because part of me had secretly enjoyed shredding Laura's clothing, even just a tiny bit.

"Ready to keep moving?" I asked.

"Sure." Alex sighed. "How much farther?"

Like I know. We'd been walking for fifteen, maybe twenty minutes? The only thing that could help us tell the passage of time was the light and the temperature. It couldn't be that late in the day, because the sun was pretty high in the sky and the forest was still warm-ish. But for daytime in August, it was surprisingly chilly in the woods. The shade and dampness kept things really cool. "Ten minutes, maybe?" I guessed. If we were heading in the right direction, toward the river, we couldn't be more than ten minutes away.

We kept on walking, only now Alex was protectively clutching the fabric of her cover-up with one hand. Around us, the trees and plants grew tight. Scarily dense, like it might be impossible to escape their maze of branches. I felt a tug on my hair and let out a yelp, throwing my free hand up to feel if something was now on my head. Possibly something from one of the spiderwebs. My fingers landed on the prickly spines of...a burr. I yanked it out of my hair and threw it onto the ground. I ran my hand over my head again, picking off two more.

It was getting harder and harder to walk in my water shoes. The elastic edges dug into my skin, which had been rubbed raw. I wanted so badly to pull the shoes off, even for a few steps. But walking with bare feet would be risking injury, and probably even more painful. I couldn't believe how much the shoes already hurt. We hadn't been out of the water for that long.

Like she could hear me thinking, Alex whined, "How much longer?"

My spine prickled with annoyance. *You* just *asked me that.* "How should I know?" Was she turning into Nolan? I felt like my mom when we're in the car and Nolan asks every five minutes, "Are we there yet?" But I stopped to wait for Alex to catch up. My right foot pulsed, and I scrunched up my toes inside the water shoe, giving my sore heel a moment of relief.

I heard the slap-slap of her flip-flops as Alex, huffing, came up next to me. I'd felt so superior earlier, not having worn sandals for the tubing trip. But now I eyed hers with envy. Sure, she had a few scratches, and her feet were completely covered in mud, but Alex didn't have throbbing blisters on the backs of her heels. Who was the smart one now?

"I need a freaking break," she said, shading her eyes. "Where is a rock or a log or something we can sit on?"

"Why do you keep asking me where everything is?" I sniped. "It's not like I'm in charge."

"Oh, really? It's because of *you* that we're wandering the woods."

Wait, what? That was 100 percent her fault. Alex had been the one to dive out of the tube to rescue her phone. She'd been the one to insist we head off on an unknown trail instead of staying put in the cove. And she had also been the one to keep plowing forward in the forest when the trail disappeared, without telling me that she no longer knew where she was going but was *educated guessing*. All I'd done had been giving the tube one tiny, frustrated bounce. And I was pretty sure she wasn't aware I'd done that.

"Um, this is not my fault. I don't want to get into blaming or whatever, but you were in the lead, and you didn't notice when we went off the path."

"But you're the nature lover! With your whole talented-and-gifted project on this dumb forest." When she said "talented-and-gifted project," she adopted a mocking British accent. "I thought you knew everything about it."

"Sorry to disappoint," I told her.

"Whatever. You're the one who wanted to come on this trip." Then Alex muttered something, and I could only pick out a few words: *boring, rather, Madison, Laura, parents, no.*

"What did you say?" I asked, uncertain I wanted her to repeat it, because when I strung those overheard words together in my head, the sentences I made up were not things I wanted to hear. Other than "no" and "Laura."

"Nothing." Alex brushed a bunch of leaves into a pile on top of some green plants and then plopped down on it. "I'm sitting here and taking a break. By myself. I'll let you know when I'm done." She stared at her phone, like if she just gazed at it long enough, and with healing love in her eyes, then it might come back to life.

I blinked a few times, then moved to sit on top of a large, moss-covered log a few feet away. For a moment or two, my anger still ran hot enough that I wondered why I'd ever felt bad in the first place about what had been going on with Alex this summer. The blip. The shift. The...friendship breakup?

Because I'd felt really bad. There'd been an ache in my chest ever since I saw Alex the day she'd come home from camp, waiting in line at Michael's Frozen Custard with Laura. She'd lied to me when she'd texted that she was too tired for the pool. Even though I'd been counting the days. I'd written her letters. I'd even skipped swimming in solidarity—and two of those days, it had hit ninety degrees! I'd thought the sacrifice was worth it because Alex was my best friend. *But am I still hers?* That question felt scary enough to swallow me whole.

Maybe because the temperature was dropping in the shady woods, my anger cooled fast. Then I just felt lonely, even more alone than on registration day, when I'd stood in that bright fluorescent hallway all by myself. Lonely, even though my once-if-not-future best friend was barely an eagle's wingspan away from me.

ALEX

THE DOG DAYS OF SUMMER

I SILENTLY PANICKED THE WHOLE ride from Michael's Frozen Custard to my house, and it wasn't because of Zack's driving. As soon as I got out of the car, I texted Jocelyn. Before I even walked inside. Then I pressed to call her.

It didn't go straight to voicemail, so I knew the flip phone wasn't turned off. She was ignoring me. Or she'd given the phone back to her mom.

Next, I tried her landline. "Hi, is Joss there?"

There was a muffled pause, and I could hear her mom's ring smacking the phone as she covered the mouthpiece to mute it. "She's...busy right now, Alex—um, in the shower." The satisfaction in her voice, for quickly thinking of an excuse, told me she was lying. "Can I have her call you back?"

My stomach was dropping like I was on one of the bungee thrill rides that line the tourist strip in Wisconsin Dells. "Yes, please. Thanks."

It wasn't until late that Joss actually called me back, and that was after I texted her a different emoji about every forty-five seconds, even though I didn't know if she still had the flip phone with her anymore and whether it can actually show a full range of emojis. I took a deep breath and pressed to answer her call.

"Hey, Jallard!" Nicknames always show you're trying to be friendly, right?

"What's up," she said, her voice totally flat.

"I'm super sorry I didn't call earlier. There's, like, so much I need to catch you up on, but for starters, Laura Longbottom ended up being my cabinmate. That's wild, right? And she needed to...run some important errands after being stuck at camp for so long. I thought that since you were doing yard work anyway, it wouldn't be a problem for me to quickly help her out, once we got back." I crossed my fingers because of the white lies embedded in my explanation.

"Wow, important errands like eating frozen custard." She paused, waiting for me to say something, but I didn't have a response to that. She was right. Joss continued, "I was waiting for you, waiting to go to the pool. You knew that from my texts. But you told me you were too tired. Not that you were running errands." Her voice sounded strained from being so mad. "Why did you lie to me?"

"I..." I squeezed my eyes shut, struggling to think of an excuse. There really wasn't one? I sighed. "I made a mistake. And I'm sorry. It was just a lot, the end of camp and the bus ride back and everything. I guess I needed a minute for...recalculating."

Like the GPS in the car always says it's doing when someone takes an unplanned turn.

Joss was quiet for so long, I wondered if she'd hung up. I cleared my throat. "Anyway—wanna have First Day at the Pool tomorrow?"

"No," she said, her voice clipped. "It's not the first day anymore." My eyebrows scrunched. Jocelyn had a right to be mad, but now she was just being petty. Cutting off her nose to spite her face, like the saying my dad always uses.

Then she let out a sigh. "But I'd like to hang out tomorrow. If you're free." Her tone was softening. "Maybe ride bikes or something?"

I picked up on the smallest nervous tremor in her voice. So subtle that if I weren't her best friend, I never would've noticed. "Yeah! Definitely. I'll be over by eleven."

"Okay," she said. Another awkward pause. "Welcome home."

"Thanks." I flopped back on my bed, reassured. Things were going back to normal. Other than the texts from Laura that had been buzzing in my ear the whole time Joss and I were talking.

———————

Afterward, Joss and I settled into a routine of seeing each other a few times a week—but not every day. That was a huge change from every other summer. She never asked what I'd been up to when we weren't together, and I definitely never admitted that

I'd been hanging out with Laura, who became like an elephant in the room—because if I'd mention something cool that Laura wore, Joss would shoot me a judgy look that made me feel bad for liking it. Or I'd start to tell her a story from camp, and even if I stopped myself, Joss would stiffen up. Like she could tell it would've been about an experience Laura and I had shared, and she was jealous.

Still, some days it felt like nothing had changed. In the evenings, we sat on my porch in the glow of my phone and her school tablet, listening to Mateo and the younger kids on the cul-de-sac playing Ghost in the Graveyard. The way Jocelyn stared at their flashlights bobbing through the yards, I could tell she wanted to join in. And honestly, I did too. But neither of us actually suggested it. We were too old, and it kind of seemed like the days of "Team Alexelyn"—what we'd always called ourselves when playing neighborhood games like that—were past.

Jocelyn had become a different person since I came back from camp. Or maybe that's not the right way to put it. She was exactly the same, but I was different, and so the way I saw her had changed. Sometimes it felt like I was inhabiting Laura's body and seeing Jocelyn through her eyes instead of my own. Laura would think Joss's T-shirts were all so baggy, her shorts so long. Sometimes I considered offering to do her hair before we left the house, but I didn't want to make her, like, self-conscious. Joss never wore a stitch of makeup, not even lip gloss, and when

I suggested maybe going to the beauty store for makeovers on a rainy day, she rolled her eyes in a way she never used to. I mean, that kind of girly stuff—makeup, hair braiding, masks—had always been part of our sleepovers. I almost always suggested it, but it's not like Jocelyn hated it. But now if I said I wanted to go buy some sheet masks, her mouth would twist up into this angry little frown and she'd come up with some reason why that wasn't a great idea.

We'd gone from being two peas in a pod to two peas in a low-key food fight. We couldn't even agree on where to pedal off to on our bikes. Two weeks before registration day, Laura was visiting her grandmother in Milwaukee, so it was the second afternoon in a row that Joss and I had hung out. I could tell she was in a great mood by the twirl she did on her bike as she pulled up to my house. For once, I was ready, waiting on my front steps with my legs stretched out and my bike propped up next to me. I stood, slung my bag over my shoulder, and walked my bike to meet her at the curb.

"Look, I got us some reading material." I reached into my bag and pulled out a glossy magazine.

"Back-to-school stories? Don't remind me," Joss pointed to the "Back to School, Back to Wardrobe Basics" cover line.

"Whatever—you know you love school." Jocelyn is: a straight-A student; a teacher's pet; an overachiever; D, all of the above. "I'm the one who should be dreading it." Last year, I struggled for all my B's. The extra credit that gives Joss pluses on her report card just keeps me above water.

She shrugged. "Yeah, but I like summer more. Being outside and all."

"Me too. I'm not ready for fall. Among other things, I still haven't gotten rid of my racerback tan lines." Something Laura—who was maybe a little obsessed with her tan—often pointed out.

"Tanning is horribly unhealthy, you know."

"Thanks, *Mom*," I said. Actually, Joss sounded like *her* mom, who was constantly coming at us with a bottle of SPF One Million and a lecture. Probably because she works at a dermatologist's office. "So where should we go? There's a nail-polish color I saw in here"—I flipped to one of the folded-down pages of the magazine—"that I really want. Maybe the drugstore has it."

Before I could show her, Jocelyn blurted out, "I don't feel like shopping." She never did anymore. So how could she blame me for going to the mall with Laura? "But we haven't been to the zoo all summer."

That's because there isn't anything to do at the zoo. Sure, the red pandas are ridiculously cute, and the lions and tiger are cool, when they're not sleeping. But they're all usually sleeping.

I had plans to see Laura the next day, and I wanted to get the new polish so if we went for pedicures, I could use it. But I couldn't tell Jocelyn that. I sneaked a glance at her outfit for the day. She was wearing a faded gray T-shirt that read SAVE THE EARTH, IT'S THE ONLY PLANET WITH CHOCOLATE and shorts with tiny dolphins embroidered on them. Which were cute, but they also reminded me of Shark Boy and his Great White button-down at the dance. I was wearing a new fitted tank and the shortest shorts my mom would allow, both of which I'd picked out with Laura when we hit up the Fourth of July sales. We'd run into a few kids that day, friends of Laura's, and for the first time, I'd gotten to be in her spotlight-of-sunshine around people we knew from Walden. It was so unlike when I'd be out with Jocelyn and we ran into classmates—unless they were Houa and Kate, we either pretended not to see them or were ourselves ignored.

"Fine, let's go to the zoo." We'd only see anyone from school there if they'd been dragged along with younger siblings.

I kind of hated myself for thinking about how I could avoid being seen with Jocelyn.

We biked down the quiet, leafy streets of my neighborhood and past our old elementary school. Like always, once we hit our "secret shortcut" (the bike path parallel to Monroe Street), we raced each other to the end. Joss was beating me, so I tried to trick her into slowing down—calling out that I saw an abandoned baby raccoon alongside the path, but she didn't fall for it, because I'm sure she could hear the laughter in my voice. (Anyway, she knows too much about animals to believe me—like that raccoons are nocturnal. At least I think they are.) When I caught up with her at the end, I admitted defeat, promising to pick up our snacks at the zoo. We took a break then, resting on some sun-warmed boulders, with our bikes off to the side.

I fiddled with a blade of grass. "Are you nervous about going back to school?" It wasn't until I said it that I realized maybe I felt that way.

"Not really. Except for figuring out what my TAG project should be this year. I'm thinking about focusing on the Wisconsin wolf population. And I guess the eighth-grade state tests make me a little anxious."

I shook my head. "Come on, Joss. You never have to worry about a standardized test. You're always in, like, the one hundred and first percentile." I don't know if that's even a thing. I paused, searching for the right words. "I meant, like, socially. If you're nervous about that."

Joss shrugged. "It's not like we're going to a new school. I know what the deal is at Walden."

I pressed the backs of my legs harder against the rock, which was the perfect almost-too-hot temperature. "I guess you're right... But I haven't always *liked* the deal."

Joss stayed quiet next to me. We were talking like we used to—meaning, honestly—before everything got weird. Since that day at Michael's, every conversation felt like we might be on a patch of thin ice. So we'd glided along on the surface, sticking to the safe edges, most of the time. Now I'd steered us right out into the middle of the frozen lake.

Finally, Jocelyn said, "Maybe we can change things up. We already did." There was an extra stress on that word, *we*. "Like going to the dance?"

Which had been fun, I guess. But I still wanted the next one to be different. I wanted to be out on the dance floor. With Laura.

In the past, Joss and I could have fun together in any situation, as long as we were together. But I didn't know if that were still true. If being besties with Jocelyn was enough for me anymore. I'd always secretly wished we sat at a different lunch table, the one with Laura and all her cool friends. Now maybe I could be sitting there, *would* be sitting there. Yet Joss...I couldn't picture her sitting next to me. It felt terrible to admit that.

She was still waiting for me to reply. "You're right. The dance was something new." I dropped the blades of grass I'd been braiding and stretched my arms over my head. "Anyway, I just hope eighth grade isn't too hard." I meant it in all the ways: academically, socially, whatever.

"Cosigned." Joss stood up. "I'm hot. Let's go. The red pandas are waiting. Did you know they're not related to pandas at all? They're in a superfamily with raccoons and otters."

(What did I say about her knowing all about raccoons?)

"See, this is why *you* don't ever need to worry about school."

We took the bike path alongside Lake Wingra to the zoo. The golden late-summer sun shined down on us. I wasn't thinking about Laura or nail polish or whose lunch table I would be sitting at in September, but only the breeze on my face and the weedy smell of the lake and whether we'd see any turtles sunning themselves and the friend pedaling next to me. It felt, blissfully, like old times.

I think about that bike ride a lot because of how everything unraveled afterward.

NINE

THE FIRST TIME MY stomach rumbled, it was so loud I thought something was in the woods with us and that it was growling. I startled, raising my hands protectively in front of my chest, before I pressed one down to my belly and felt the rumble. Breakfast had been hours ago, and bagels and fruit only last you so long. At least I'd globbed on the peanut butter with abandon. By that time, we should've been eating our picnic in a park alongside the river. I pictured the spread Mom had packed for our families: deli sandwiches on thick sourdough bread, lots of potato and pasta salads that she'd whipped together in the days before we headed up north, because it's cheaper to bring your own food than to buy it at a café meant for vacationers. And Mom had even made her no-bake cheesecake with the graham-cracker crust. I'd watched her load everything into the trunk before we took off from the cabin for the Wolf River. It made me weirdly sad to think of all the food going untouched, and I wondered how long it could last on a late-summer day before spoiling. Because it was unlikely anyone was eating it—they would be frantically looking for us. The potato salad, I'm sure, was a goner. All that mayo.

My stomach groaned again, loud enough that Alex, still sitting on her leaf throne, could probably hear it. I had to eat something.

I yanked open my backpack and dug around, one-handed, because I was crossing my fingers on my other hand. *Please, please, please let me find a granola bar or something in here.* I shoved my neatly folded beach towel out of the way, and my hand landed on more fabric—my sweatshirt. *The* sweatshirt. I was glad I had it, but at the same time, I hoped we'd be out of the woods before it got cold or buggy enough for me to need to put it on.

It seems ridiculous to think that a sweatshirt played some part in what had happened on registration day, because it's not like Alex hadn't seen me wearing my favorite sweatshirt before. But I remembered feeling like there had been a bull's-eye on my chest, at least because of how Alex had stared at me. When I'd glanced down, thinking maybe I had spilled juice or gotten bike grease on myself or something like that, all I saw was the familiar, faded image of a wolf, midhowl.

Underneath the sweatshirt, though, was my backpack's jackpot: not one, not two, but *three* plastic-covered rectangles. Energy bars I'd thrown in as emergency snacks. And in the side pocket of my backpack, I had my water bottle too.

I pulled out two of the bars and stood up, stretching my legs.

As soon as my weight went back into my feet, the water shoes tightened and clamped down on my heels. The gouges from the shoe fabric rubbing against my skin really stung. I limped toward Alex, then stopped. I slipped one bar back inside my backpack. It might be a long time before we would be back at the cabin, eating whatever was salvageable of lunch. Maybe it would be safer to start by splitting one energy bar, just in case.

Sharing food reminded me of the day I'd run into Alex and Laura at Michael's, and how they'd split that single junior-size dish of frozen custard. No toppings, even. The only way it could've been sadder would've been if they were sharing plain vanilla instead of chocolate. (No disrespect to vanilla, but it is made for toppings or mix-ins.) I wondered whose idea it had been to share, and I guessed it was Laura's, because every time Alex and I went to Michael's, we got our own treats. And if I didn't watch mine like a hawk, she'd sometimes even snag a few roasted pecans from my turtle sundae when I wasn't looking. To be fair, I pulled the same trick with her. As best friends, it was our right to pick off each other's plates.

I stopped a few feet away from Alex's leaf throne. She was hunched over, her back to me, inspecting the torn part of Laura's cover-up. I cleared my throat, but Alex didn't turn to face me.

"Are you hungry?" I finally asked.

"Yes!" She whipped around immediately. "You brought food with you? Please tell me you did."

"Yeah," I said, holding it up. I tore open the shiny wrapper and split the bar in half, then placed Alex's share in her outstretched palm. "I have two more in my bag."

"You're amazing," she said, spraying a bit of the bar out of her mouth as she chewed. "Anything to drink?"

"Got my water bottle," I said, then walked back to where my backpack was sitting atop the inner tube. I decided to carry all my stuff back to her leaf throne, now that Alex's alone time was over.

"Here." I passed her the bottle. She started chugging from it, so quickly that I could hear the glug from her throat. "Whoa, don't drink too much."

She stopped, panting. "Why? Not?"

"Well, we don't know how long we're going to be out here, so we should probably ration—"

She shook her head before taking a huge swig, then said, "Seriously, if we're in the forest for more than another hour, I'm going to lose it." She looked like she was about to take another gulp, and I reached out my hand so she'd give me back the bottle. *Guess I was smart to keep the other bars from her.*

Alex finished eating, licking the sticky remnants of the bar—mostly melted carob—from her fingertips. Then she stood, scratching various bites as she rose up. "Let's get moving. I wanna be back in the cabin and taking a shower so freaking bad." She paused. "I mean, what I *really* want is to be home, in

Madison, but I'm trying to be reasonable with what I ask of the universe."

I nodded. I didn't exactly disagree. The forest was awesome; being lost in it wasn't. And that's what we were: totally lost, with no idea how near or far the river was. I didn't know it was possible to feel claustrophobic when you're out in the wilderness—that's the opposite of an enclosed space. But trapped is exactly how it felt, being in the woods and not knowing how to get out. We might as well have been locked in a closet; it felt just as tight and oppressive. If I thought about it too hard, my breaths got short and my pulse began to race. I closed my eyes and listened to the rustle of the breeze, the buzz of cicadas, and the chirps of birds, and I pretended I was back in Madison, taking a walk in the arboretum or something. Any place with really well-marked trails, where it would be hard—maybe even impossible—to get completely lost.

"Which way were we walking?" Alex asked.

I blinked, trying to remember a landmark to guide us. Why hadn't I picked out a specific tree or rock, or something, so we'd know which way to go when we started walking again? I guess when we'd stopped, I'd been too frazzled to think. A mosquito buzzed my ear, like it was criticizing me for not having planned better. I swatted it away. A mean deerfly immediately took its place and began circling my head like it was taunting me.

We could keep following the sun, though. Which was much

lower in the sky, but its rays still poked through breaks in the evergreen branches. "That way," I said, pointing in its direction. West. At least if we kept walking in one consistent direction, we wouldn't end up going in circles. That was something.

Unless, of course, west would only lead us deeper into the wilderness. The Nicolet National Forest covers 664,822 acres. To put that in perspective, a football field is a little over an acre. Once on a school trip, they let us onto the field at Camp Randall, where the University of Wisconsin Badgers play. We got to run the whole length of the playing field, which felt superlong. So the forest was something like over half a million times bigger? If we were going in the wrong direction, we could keep going in the wrong direction for a very, very long time. There are roads and ranger stations and campsites and fire-lookout towers in the forest, and nearby towns, but you can still walk miles without seeing another human.

So I really hoped following the sun was right.

I managed to roll the inner tube into a long cylinder so I could tuck it under my arm instead of having to drag it on the ground or hold it overhead like an umbrella. My arms were too tired to keep doing that.

We began walking again, this time with me in the lead. Every step I took, I felt the edge of my shoes rub deeper into the cuts above my heels. They hurt so much, I just wanted to stop. Instead, I gritted my teeth and kept going. I pictured sitting on the pier, once we were back at the cabin, dipping my heels into the cool, comforting water of Buttercup Lake. Imagining that soak made me feel a tiny bit better.

This time, I paid attention to the landscape we passed, in case later on I needed to remember where we'd been. One tree tilted across another in the shape of an X. Two boulders next to each other reminded me of the slow, dust-covered tortoises at the zoo. I wasn't sure if I'd be able to pick out those landmarks if I needed to in the future. *I have a camera, though.*

As I stopped to fish it out of my backpack, Alex bumped into me. "Jeez! What are you doing? I almost fell onto that rock." She pointed at a jagged stone sticking up to her left.

"Sorry—I thought I should start taking some pictures."

Before I could explain why, she interrupted me. "Oh, because we want to remember this wonderful hike so much."

Even though she couldn't see me, I rolled my eyes. "Actually, no. So we can recognize where we've already been."

Alex shut up after that, and I snapped a few photos.

We kept walking, even though my feet felt like they were slowly being sawed off, and Alex kept exclaiming every five steps that another branch had stabbed her toes. The flies and mosquitoes surrounded us, like our sweat and grime and worry had mixed into the opposite of bug repellant—bug attractant?—and now we were irresistible to them. We were bugnip, like catnip. Or maybe the insects were coming out in full force because the sun was sinking lower and lower in the sky. Now it hid behind thick tree trunks, not just their spindly upper branches. Every part of me ached: the curve of my shoulders, where my too-small swimsuit straps dug into my skin and collarbones; my calves, from all the hiking; my head, from the worries that kept racing through my brain. All that walking, and I didn't know if we were any closer to the river, or an actual trail, or anywhere we might find people.

I took pictures any time we passed something unique, but there was a sameness to the landscape. The trees blended together. I feel bad saying that because they were all beautiful, with their brown textured trunks and fringe of thick green needles, which waved at us like beckoning fingers. Rich green moss climbed up their sides, like they were all wearing cozy sweaters. There were white cedars and red pines and tamaracks and hemlocks and sugar maples and aspens and balsam firs and paper birches. A smorgasbord of native Northwoods species. If we weren't lost in the woods, but hiking, I'd want to capture them all in carefully composed photographs. But right then, I just wanted to plant one aching foot in front of the other and move forward, hoping we were getting closer to the river and my parents and Nolan and food and going back to the cabin.

We walked until I couldn't see where the sun was in relation to the tree line anymore because it had gotten so low. It was dusk. I had been hoping that at some point Alex would suggest we rest, but she hadn't. So I finally broke the silence. "I think maybe we should stop."

"For another break?" Alex asked, her tone both hopeful and annoyed.

"No, like...for the night?" I couldn't believe the words as they came out of my mouth. *We're going to be lost in the woods overnight. In our swimsuits. Without a tent or anything, just a busted inner tube and a really big ziplock bag. Alone, except for the coyotes and bears and bobcats and bats and spiders and, yes, wolves. How is this real life?*

"Are you *serious*?" She was only a few notches below shouting. "Like, where would we sleep? In a tree house? Are we going to *build* a tree house?"

"Of course not," I shot back. *Why is she acting like* this *is what I want us to be doing?* Maybe Alex was hangry. "But we should just stop here. Or wherever we can make some kind of a shelter. It's getting late—look how much the sun has gone down. Eventually it'll be dark. And it's already getting colder." I wasn't sweating at all anymore, and now that we weren't moving, I felt goose bumps forming on my limbs. It might've reached eighty degrees in the sunshine at midday along the river, but even in August, temperature lows in the Northwoods can drop to the fifties. That's why we wear sweatshirts and pajama pants while we stargaze and roast marshmallows, and why sometimes we even use the potbelly stove in the cabin's living room on a particularly chilly night.

In the dark, in the cold...we couldn't just keep walking. We might stumble on something and fall, twist an ankle or worse. We needed to rest and hope that the people looking for us—*They must be looking for us, right?*—would find our shelter spot.

"If we haven't found a way out by the time it gets dark, we're not going to during nighttime. We're better off using the daylight we have left to set up a shelter. We can keep heading toward the river first thing in the morning."

"No. We should keep walking," Alex said, crossing her arms over her chest, pouting slightly. "Until we literally cannot."

"Fine. I *literally cannot* anymore, okay?" I raised my right leg and pointed at my heel, which was smeared with mud and blood. "My shoes are *literally* killing me." I swung my leg down quickly, before I fell over. Maybe it was just having my backpack on, but I felt super wobbly. I crumpled to sit on the nearest rock.

Alex's eyebrows scrunched in either disgust or sympathetic agony; I couldn't tell which. "For the record, I think stopping is a dumb idea," she said. But she still dropped her stuff to the ground. Then she let out a small sigh of something like relief as she plopped down next to me.

Maybe we should've held out for a half-hidden cave or a collection of fallen logs in the shape of a makeshift fort. Maybe we should've tried to dig a hole like a burrow that we could've curled up in and covered ourselves with big ferns. We could've even made a double-seater leaf throne. But we were exhausted, and daytime was disappearing. Back home, summer days seem long when the light lingers after sunset. But in the woods, the canopy of trees snatched twilight away. So instead of getting creative with our surroundings, to make a shelter fast we simply did the best with what we had: the damp beach towels in both of our bags, the deflated inner tube, and the extra-large Ziploc. I spread the tube flat on the spongy, moist ground and placed the dry bag at the top. It made the covered surface just long enough that one of us could stretch out onto it and neither feet nor forehead would be on the dirt. My thin life vest—which I'd still been wearing all afternoon, like it might somehow help us divine the direction to water—was perfect for a stand-in pillow. Well, if you consider smelling foam that has marinated for years in river mildew perfect.

"We can cover up with the beach towels to keep the bugs off," I said. The mosquitoes got even more persistent at dusk. The buzzing around my ears was constant. I still had those two bug wipes in my bag, and I was glad I hadn't used them yet—we would need repellant to protect us while we slept.

I was on the tube, cataloging what supplies I still had in my backpack, and Alex stood next to me, wary of sitting. "Do you have anything in your bag that could help us?" I asked.

Alex shook her head, looking ashamed. She'd dragged her

tote around the forest all day, but nothing in it was useful. Unless it turns out you can survive by eating lip gloss. Then her eyes brightened with an idea. "Well, maybe we could use my magazine for something?"

"Actually, yes! Hand it over." She yanked it out and tossed it to me. I spread the glossy rectangle on the ground right next to the ziplock bag, then arranged my life vest across both. "Now we both can lie flat and share the vest pillow."

"Great."

I was about 90 percent sure Alex was being sarcastic. But then she sat down next to me and tested lying flat, and I knew it felt better to have something relatively clean and human-made under her head and neck, instead of pointy twigs and slimy leaves. And whatever was living under the slimy leaves. Possibly the broad-banded forestsnail. Which actually lives in its beautiful amber-colored curlicue shell.

"What now?" Alex muttered, staring up at the darkening sky and not me.

For the first time, I wondered if it was dark so early because of the cloudiness that had slowly overtaken the sky. *What is tonight's forecast?* I guessed we'd find out.

"Dinner?" I asked, reaching for my bag.

"Please tell me you have a cheeseburger in your backpack. Maybe some fries?"

I ignored the fact that I don't eat cheeseburgers, and she knows it. I also refrained from snarking about how this went against Alex's extreme pickiness about the healthiness of her food. That was a new thing, and definitely a *Lexie* thing. Instead, I answered, "I have another energy bar, and we can drink more water."

"WATER," she begged, making grabby hands.

I tossed her the bottle. "Only drink a little—for real, this time." Alex understood that we had to ration now, because she took only two dainty sips.

I dug in my backpack for another energy bar. *Should we eat half of it and save the rest? Now that this is going to be an overnight... adventure.* But, surely, tomorrow we'd be going home. How far could we possibly have wandered? They'd probably even find us tonight. I pictured Alex and me asleep on our tube bed as a spotlight shined down on us—from a helicopter or something? I wasn't sure what rescuers up north used to find lost people. Anyway, then we'd be bundled up in blankets and whisked back to Buttercup Lake.

I split the whole bar in half and handed one piece to Alex. There was still an untouched bar left in my backpack, after all. Along with a single squirt of hand sanitizer, maybe two globs of sunscreen, a bandage, one bug-spray wipe (because we'd broken down and applied the other), my camera, and my sweatshirt.

We ate slowly and in silence. But the forest around us wasn't silent. The ambient noise shifted as the light dwindled. The drone of insects grew louder. The breeze had strengthened, and above our heads, the branches groaned and leaves rustled like maracas. The air held the sweet scent of incoming rain, which worried me. Occasionally, we'd hear the sharp crack of a stick breaking or a crunching sound, and I'd stiffen, wondering if something was heading in our direction. I didn't see any other creatures around. But that didn't mean they weren't there. Forest animals are good at staying hidden. I wondered what might have already seen us, followed us. I shivered. I'm sure I was just imagining it, but I felt watched. The growing pit of fear in my stomach made it hard to eat.

I couldn't stop shivering, so I couldn't avoid my sweatshirt any longer. I reached into my backpack and pulled it out. The fabric was deliciously soft on my sun-baked, bug-bitten, mud-covered, scratched-up, goose-bumped skin. Putting the sweatshirt over my torso felt like wrapping myself in a hug, and till then I didn't know how much I'd needed one.

Alex glanced at me. She licked her lips, trying to get every last crumb of the energy bar—but maybe also from envy of my sweatshirt. She curled inward, arms crossed, and her knees tucked into the cover-up as much as possible. She rocked back and forth slightly, like the motion was helping keep her warm. I met her gaze, feeling a tiny bit vindicated that my sweatshirt— this particular sweatshirt—was really coming to the rescue.

Alex nodded in the direction of its wolf illustration. "I hope none of those find us tonight."

I sighed. "Wolves are generally not dangerous to people, Alex." In normal encounters, wolves shy away from humans. They certainly don't try to hunt them.

"But we're, like, two weak and stranded humans. You can't tell me that any predators that come across us are just going to prance away and try to snag a measly rabbit instead. We're sitting ducks."

I shivered again, despite the sweatshirt. I couldn't tell her that predators would leave us alone, because I had no idea what would happen if something found us in the night. There have been cougar sightings in the Northwoods, although biologists think they don't breed in the state, just pass through. But there were also plenty of coyotes, bobcats, and bears.

"Let's not go there," was all I said, my voice wavering a little. An image of the cabin flashed into my mind, warm and cozy and inviting, and I wanted to be there so badly, my heart actually hurt. Like Nolan had accidentally kicked me dead center in my chest while splashing in the pool.

The last rays of dusky sunlight hovered below the tree line. Kind of like having a night-light on in a bedroom. I slept with one on in my room till I was nine—I didn't like trying to go to sleep in total darkness. I felt that way again, for the first time in years. I wondered if I'd even be able to rest once darkness really overtook the woods. Probably not. The longer we sat in the waning light, the more scared I felt.

"I'm going to try to sleep." I lay down on the inner tube and pulled the beach towel over my body, right up to my chin. I don't know how it could possibly still be damp, but everything was, even though it had been hours since we got out of the river. I turned my head to one side, my nose centimeters from the ground. You don't realize that dirt has a smell until you're in a place like this, where it doesn't have to compete with all kinds of other scents. (Well, except for Alex's stinky-mango body spray.) I turned my head again, trying to find a position where nothing sharp was digging into my skull.

"Already? It's not nighttime," Alex said.

"I'm not going to be able to fall asleep when it's totally dark," I mumbled. Then it hit me, so suddenly: the wave of fear and sadness, a tsunami of feelings. I couldn't believe the situation we were in—it was real danger. I couldn't believe how alone we were. I couldn't believe how alone I felt, even with Alex beside me.

An owl screeched nearby. The noise made us both startle. Even after I realized what it was, and that a screech owl wouldn't hurt us (although owls' talons *are* extremely sharp), my pulse kept pounding. Every muscle in my body was tense.

Alex lay down next to me. "Um, yeah. I don't think I'm going to be able to fall asleep in the dark, either."

Even though the tube was small for two people stretched out across it, and our heads were sharing a life vest for a pillow, our bodies curled as far away from each other as possible, like we were making the shape of a wishbone. Alex draped her towel over herself, but because she's taller than me, it only covered from her calves to her shoulders.

There was so much I wanted to say to her right then—mostly how freaked out I was. Instead, I whispered softly, "Good night."

I didn't think she'd heard me until I heard her whisper back, "Night," in a quiet voice that sounded equally terrified.

Somewhere, off in the distance but close enough that we could still hear it, something howled.

TEN

A COLD DROP HIT MY face. Then another and another. When I blinked open my eyes, a droplet splashed right into my eyeball.

With a gasp, I sat up. My fingers wrapped around the top of my towel, drawing it up with me. I wiped the water off my face. In the darkness, splashed out of sleep, I was disoriented. For a second, I wondered if we'd actually found the river. If we were by a waterfall or something. I couldn't see anything around me, not even my hand in front of my face. Not Alex next to me.

Of course when I realized it was simply raining, I felt like an idiot.

The drops were picking up speed. I wrapped my towel around my shoulders and scooted closer to Alex. I wondered if I should wake her, even though there wasn't much we could do other than hope this was a quick passing shower and try to keep our bags dry. So I silently groped for the Ziploc beneath my half of the "pillow" and shoved my backpack and Alex's tote inside.

Lightning flashed, and for a moment, everything was

illuminated. I saw the outlines of all the trees and rocks and plants, and the silhouette of Alex's sleeping body next to me. Then the darkness returned, and seconds later, thunder clapped in the distance.

You know what is scarier than sitting in the forest in total darkness? Sitting in the forest in total darkness, then suddenly getting a lightning flash to show all the creepy unknown things—or creatures—surrounding you. A glimpse of sharp, gnarled branches pointing like fingers, just long enough for you to remember you're not safe in a shelter somewhere but totally exposed and totally unaware of your environment—and what else you might be sharing it with. I swear I saw a set of glowing yellow eyes as the darkness returned.

"Alex!" I hissed, nudging what I think was her shoulder but could have been her backside. She mumbled, and then I sensed her adjust to sitting up.

"What's going—"

Another flash of lightning interrupted her. Alex's eyes shined wide, scared, in the momentary light. This time, the thunder clapped much more quickly after the flash.

"Thunderstorm," I said. A cold front moving through brings them. Sometimes, they can be really severe: high winds, hail, flooding, and even tornadoes. Back home in Madison, tornado sirens warn you to get to a basement. And the Channel 27 News weather team even tells you the exact minute the storm cell is going to pass over your street. Out here, alone in the woods—there was no Bob Lindmeier, chief meteorologist, to warn us.

What if the forest flooded and we got swept away?

What if lightning struck us? Or hit one of the nearby trees, and then it fell onto our tube bed?

What if a tornado came barreling through and sucked us up?

The raindrops pelting my face mixed with my silent tears. I didn't want Alex to know I was crying, even though I was pretty sure she was also crying. Either that or shivering really violently next to me. My teeth chattered uncontrollably.

"C-curl up like during a tornado d-drill," I stammered.

We moved onto our knees and tucked down to kiss the ground, protecting our heads with our arms. It was a position we'd practiced since kindergarten. There was nothing else we could do but wait.

The only good thing about summer storms is that they usually move fast. The worst part probably lasted for ten minutes, but it was a really terrifying worst part. With all the lightning, it felt like being at a rock concert or on an amusement park ride with a strobe effect. You could almost smell the sizzle of the lightning strikes, feel the electricity in the storm clouds. My hair became staticky from the charge. Maybe because there was no roof or walls to dull the sound, the thunder clapped louder than I'd ever heard it. Each time it cracked, Alex screamed next to me and covered her ears. Sometimes I plugged mine too.

With every flash of light, I squeezed my eyes shut. I didn't want to see what was in the darkness surrounding us. I didn't want to see those yellow eyes again. I just wanted to pretend we were safe and dry, up in the cabin's aerie, where because the walls are thin, and it's right under the roof, storms can seem pretty intense. But never like this.

Eventually, the lightning died down. When thunder sounded, it was a low rumble, faraway in the distance. The forest went back to being pitch black, the sky without even a single star. I wished I could look up and see the constellations. There would be comfort in them, knowing that the same stars and shapes visible at the lake and at my house in Madison were there for me to see in the forest. To know that even if we were lost, at least we were still under a familiar sky. But instead it was just darkness, nothingness, nowhere.

The cold rain continued to drench us long after the wind and thunder died down. When it finally stopped, Alex and I, exhausted, lay back on the tube, which was wet as a Slip 'N Slide. I thought back to the time we'd camped at Echo Valley and our tent flooded, so we'd played in the rain till dawn. Alex and I had managed to make that fun, an adventure, just by being together. But here in the forest, we curled closer to each other only out of necessity. Neither of us spoke. There was nothing fun about our situation. It was a nightmare. Underneath my soaking-wet towel, I shivered and begged for sleep that I didn't think would ever come.

My everything hurt.

I opened my eyes, and even though I couldn't see my reflection, I could tell my lids were thick and puffy, like after I've been crying. The inside of my mouth felt like I had been sucking on those silica packets that come in a new box of shoes to keep out moisture—not that I have ever tried that, but the extreme, aching dryness is what I imagine that would feel like.

The night before seemed like a strange and unreal dream to me, as I lay on the tube, whose plastic was sticky and chilly, and blinked painfully at the bright morning sunlight. After the storm had passed, I'd woken up dozens of times from a noise or the cold. It had been unbelievably cold: bone-chilling cold, teeth-rattling cold, ache-in-your fingers cold. The thin, wet beach towel had barely helped at all. I had curled myself into a tiny ball, and then I'd wrapped my sweatshirt around my head for warmth and to block my ears. Noise was the most terrifying part of the forest at night. Every time I heard a rustle or the crack of a branch somewhere, I held my breath, wondering what was heading our way. If those yellow eyes I might've seen or might've imagined during the storm belonged to it. Whether it had claws. If it was hungry.

I was hungry—as night had dragged on, the sensation both gnawing and hollow in my stomach had been harder to ignore. When I'd tried to fall back asleep after startling awake, my stomach's churn had kept me up. Now, in the early light, I finally felt safe enough to find food. Or safe-ish, because I could at least see anything that approached us. And it wasn't raining. If I weren't so incredibly hungry, I'd lie back down forever, but thinking of the one energy bar left in my backpack gave me the will to sit up.

Moving was painful. Slowly, I lifted myself off the tube. My sweatshirt wrap flopped off my head, and the towel unraveled from my upper body. For the first time, I saw my skin. It was horrifying.

My arms were covered in bug-bite welts, the round lumps so close to one another that it looked like I was made out of bubble wrap instead of skin. Red bubble wrap, because the big bites were super irritated, and despite wearing sunscreen, I'd still managed to get burned. I pulled the towel off my legs and saw that they were just as red and lumpy. Everything itched so, so badly. I reached my hand down and scratched my calf. Then I couldn't stop scratching, even though my skin turned the color of a maraschino cherry.

I had to wrap the towel around myself again so I would stop. Also, because it was just after dawn and still so cold, especially with morning dew coating everything in the forest, including us. Rain puddles were everywhere. We were never going to dry off from that storm.

Next to me, Alex's eyes were still shut, although not in the peaceful way she normally looks while sleeping—I've seen Alex snoozing a lot over the years, at sleepovers and in her backyard hammock and on long car rides, like the one to get to the cabin. Her expression was a grimace, her brows knitted together and her eyelids squeezed, like she was in pain or trying very hard to shut out the world or something.

Alex doesn't sunburn easily like I do, but her skin was still kind of blotchy and red. The bugs had definitely feasted on her. She'd shrugged her towel up to cover her arms and chest, but below her cover-up, her legs were bare. Welts and scratches coated her calves. Her feet were so swollen that the plastic of her flip-flops pressed down into the tops of her feet, like a cookie cutter into rising dough. Just thinking of her trying to walk through the woods made me wince. I inspected my own feet, still in their tight water shoes. They were puffy too, and my heels were crusted with dried blood. When I wiggled my toes, the fabric rubbed harshly against blisters. Maybe we should've taken off our shoes to sleep. But if we'd needed to run for our lives in the night…

"Alex," I said, softly at first. Then louder. She made a snuffling noise and moved her head to the other side. I didn't want to take my arm out from underneath the towel, but I needed to get her up. Shivering, I stretched out my hand and lightly tapped on her shoulder. "Wake up," I rasped.

"Don't want to," she mumbled.

"It's morning." Sunrise was around six and sunset at eight. The day would be long, but it might take hours to wend our way out of the forest, especially in our condition. I didn't want to spend another night like this. I didn't know if we *could*. "We need to start walking."

"I can't move," she said, moaning.

"Try." I reached for my wadded-up sweatshirt, ignoring the ache in my arms. A mosquito landed near my elbow, then another by my wrist. I slapped at both, gasping at how much the impact stung against my poor, pink flesh. Then I quickly worked the sweatshirt over my head. Protection from the bugs, and sun, was great, but the fabric—normally so cozy!—felt awful against my raw skin, rough like sandpaper. *I think there's one bug-repellant wipe left in my backpack.* We'd have to share it, but it would be enough to protect our legs while we were walking. At least for a while.

Alex was still lying down, on her back, but now her eyes were open. She blinked up at the sky above the trees.

"Are you okay?" I asked.

"Do I look okay?" she replied.

I couldn't tell whether she was being sarcastic or legitimately wanted to know. I scooted closer and peered down at her face.

Her eyelids were as puffy as mine felt, and her face looked like she was having a truly awful breakout of acne—but the bumps were bug bites, not pimples. Worrisome, though, were her lips. They were swollen, like the time we were hanging out in the backyard while Mateo and Nolan were playing with a boomerang, and Mateo accidentally tossed it right into Alex's mouth. Even though she'd iced it immediately, her lower lip still swelled up and bruised, and it stayed that way for a couple of days. *Bee-sting lips,* her mom had called it.

"Did you hit your mouth somehow yesterday?" I asked, trying to remember if she had. Maybe when we'd first dived into the river she'd bumped it on something.

She shook her head. "I don't think so. Why? Is my mouth messed up?" She brought her fingers to her lips and began gently pressing.

I bit down on my own chapped bottom lip, thinking. I didn't want to freak her out. "Well, it looks a little swollen..." Maybe she had bee-sting lips, literally. Maybe something bit her *mouth* while we were sleeping, and now she was having an allergic reaction. That was terrifying to consider. It's not like we had an EpiPen.

Alex dove for her tote bag, and after rummaging through it for a few moments, she pulled out a sparkly compact with a mirror. Once she flipped it open and saw her reflection, she shrieked. "Oh my God! What's wrong with me?"

Freaking out wouldn't help us. "It's probably just dehydration or sunburn—your legs are kinda pink." Although the redness on her legs appeared more rashlike than a sunburn. "Does your throat feel normal?"

She swallowed hard. "Yes?"

That was reassuring.

"We really should start walking," I said, even though I couldn't think of anything that sounded worse considering how much my feet hurt, how much the rest of me ached, and how woozy I felt from being cold, sleep-deprived, and hungry. *Hungry.* I'd been going for the energy bar before I woke up Alex. I unzipped my backpack and pulled it out. It had gotten smushed or had melted at some point, and the bar had flattened into the shape of the wrapper.

"Oh, food," Alex said, with something in between a sigh and a growl. She moved to her hands and knees to scoot toward me, grimaced, and then sat back, holding out her palm.

I gripped the bar in my hands, staring like if I looked hard enough, it might magically multiply. This was the last bit of food we had. Should we eat all of it? We needed energy to walk. But what if we didn't find our way out in the next couple of hours and had to spend another night... "We should ration this."

"Ration it? It's one little bar. That's, like, what you would eat when food is already being rationed."

"Yeah, but this 'one little bar' is all the food that's left. I had three in my backpack. We ate the other two yesterday. After this, nothing."

"I'm eating half of that. I don't care what the consequences are." She opened and closed her palm.

Sighing, I unwrapped the bar. I broke off half, then thought better of it and tore that in half again. I placed her portion in Alex's palm. "Start with that." I wrapped up the rest of the mushy bar and squirreled it away in my backpack, because if it stayed out, I didn't think I'd have the willpower not to gobble it up.

Alex chewed furiously, then broke into a cough as she swallowed. "Water?" she croaked.

I understood when I tried to swallow the tiny bite I'd been savoring. My throat was so parched, the food wouldn't go down right. I grabbed my water bottle, which felt distressingly light. Either half full or half empty, and considering our situation, "half empty" was the one that fit. I took a tiny sip, then passed it to Alex.

"Ration that too," I croaked.

She took a long sip and only stopped when I reached to pull the bottle away.

"Are you okay to leave?"

She shrugged, then winced at the movement. "I guess. I mean, unless we should stay in one place, if that's a better strategy for them to find us?"

I wasn't sure. Everybody knows that if you're lost, you shouldn't keep walking or you might get more lost. But we were already so deep in the forest, and we didn't have enough supplies to comfortably—or safely—wait where we were. If we were near fresh water and some kind of food source, like blueberry bushes, maybe we could hang out till rescuers got there. But we weren't. "We should at least find drinkable water. Otherwise, we're going to get really dehydrated." There was always the rainwater pooled on leaves, if we got desperate.

Alex nodded, and I was relieved—it seemed like every other idea or suggestion I had, she'd fight me on.

"Then let's get moving," she said, rising to her feet.

She shoved the plastic dry bag in her tote and the wet magazine too. I rolled up the tube, pausing to inspect the torn spot. The jagged hole really wasn't that big. If only we had something we could patch it with. Leaves? They'd fall off in the water. The one bandage? Too small and it wasn't the waterproof kind. Pine pitch or some other kind of tree sap? Maybe we could use that to get a big maple leaf to cover it...

"Are we walking or not?" Alex shifted back and forth, wincing every time her weight moved from one foot to the other. The swollen tops of her feet bulged out from the straps of her flip-flops. She slapped at a mosquito, waved away a fly. Then she shivered and tried to hug her cover-up tighter, but there wasn't much to hug.

"Try wearing your towel to keep the bugs away. And to stay warmer." I'd rolled mine around my waist like a skirt. With that and my sweatshirt on, the bugs could only swarm around my head. Fewer to swat, at least. I'd reconsidered using the last bug-repellant wipe. The insects were the worst around dusk. I really hoped we'd be found by then, but if we weren't—I needed to save the wipe to get us through the night.

Alex draped her towel, which was covered in pine needles and leaf remnants, around her shoulders. I shrugged on my backpack, then tucked the rolled-up tube underneath my arm. The first full step took my breath away because the pain in my blistered heels was so bad. But I gritted my teeth and took another step anyway. And another.

I paused for one last look around us, at the spot that had been our home for the night. In daylight, it was pretty: a sun-dappled clearing in the middle of a cathedral of pines, the ground softened by moss and needles. It smelled fresh and clean, like cedar. On any other day, on any normal hike, I'd say it was a perfect spot to linger and drink in the Northwoods atmosphere. Listen to the warblers serenade us. But today, I just wanted to get far, far away.

I needed to do more one thing before we could go: make some kind of sign. I've absorbed enough movies and TV shows and books about people lost in the wilderness to know that, sometimes, they end up walking in circles over and over. I didn't want that to be us. I had my camera, but I couldn't photograph every landmark we passed. The better thing to do would be to leave something very noticeable behind, like one of our towels. The thing was, we needed pretty much everything we had except the soggy magazine, but I didn't want to harm the forest by leaving human stuff in it. That was like littering, even if it had a purpose. The rules in a preserve or park are simple: carry out what you carry in.

If others were looking for us and came across this spot, I wanted them to know that we'd been there. I could do that by making a cairn.

"What's the holdup?" Alex asked, her voice as irritated as it was weary.

"We should mark that we were here. I'm going to make a cairn."

"Which is...?"

"A human-made stack of rocks. Sometimes people use them to mark trails or to show which is the right, or wrong, way to go."

"Are we trying to lure someone here?" She snorted.

"No, but it might be helpful to mark that we've passed through. Because people are looking for us. Hopefully."

"Why don't we just spell out 'Help! We're lost' in rocks and twigs, then?"

That wasn't a bad idea, but it would take a lot longer and might be less noticeable to people stomping through the woods, considering how busy the forest floor was. Squirrels and chipmunks could carry our writing away. "This is faster. Hand me any rocks you see." I bent down and grabbed a few smooth stones and one that was rough like a geode. When Alex brought me a few more, I sorted them in order of size, then started stacking. It was harder than it had seemed when I'd read about it in some book. The stones, especially the rough ones, didn't fit neatly on top of each other. The mossy ones were slippery. But I managed to make a short, lopsided tower that stretched up almost past my knee. I stepped back to admire my work. I looked at Alex, expectantly. She shrugged.

"That's good enough, I guess. Follow me," I said to Alex. She picked up her tote bag, and then we were off into the forest, with nothing but half an energy bar to fuel us and only hope to guide us.

ALEX

POOL PARTY DAY

T HERE ARE ACTUALLY TWO Official Pool Holidays that Joss
and I celebrate each summer: First Day at the Pool, and
then Pool Party Day, which usually happens right before registration for the new school year. It's a family party, where the
moms and dads who were too busy all summer long to hang out
at the pool come with their kids to eat burgers, compete in the
water-balloon toss, and chill in the deep end while a DJ blasts
oldies across the PA.

But our parents were either at or heading to work, so the plan
was for Lucy to drive us before her shift at the zoo. From upstairs,
I heard Joss ring the doorbell, then my mom welcomed her inside.
"I haven't seen enough of you this summer, Jocelyn!" I felt a pit
in my stomach. A pity pit. Or maybe a guilt knot. Well, I thought,
they'll get to see each other every day, up at the cabin.

Whatever Joss replied, I couldn't quite hear. Then she
bounded up the stairs and knocked on the door to my room,
lightly, like she wasn't sure she could still barge in, which made
it even harder to ignore that guilt knot/pity pit in my stomach.

"Come in!" I hollered. I was struggling to tie the bikini I'd bought with Laura. If only she were there—she'd be able to figure it out. Tying the suit's strings was more complicated than braiding friendship bracelets at camp. Joss was always good at that kind of arts-and-crafts stuff. "Can you give me a hand with this?"

"W-what happened to your old suit?" Joss stammered. She was still wearing her turquoise one, which was faded and pilling.

I'd only worn my new bikini when I went with Laura to her pool at the country club. I avoided the suit otherwise, partly because of the complicated straps, and partly because my mom probably would not be okay with me wearing something skimpy. So whenever I went to our neighborhood pool with my family or with Joss, I wore an old one-piece. But today was a party. It was special, and now that everyone was coming home from trips and camps in time for school registration, more Walden kids might be there—Laura's friends. I needed to look like I belonged with them.

I shrugged. "It was time for an update." Then I did a twirl and shook my hips, the way Laura would while modeling something in a dressing room.

"Has your mom seen it?" Jocelyn asked, one eyebrow arched.

I stopped twirling. She was making me second-guess wearing it. "No, but she won't care." That was about as likely as her allowing Mateo to move into a bouncy house in our backyard (which is an actual thing he has asked to do).

Joss adjusted and readjusted the straps that cut into her shoulders, leaving red marks. "Maybe I should get a new swimsuit..."

Laura's voice popped into my head, from when she had called my identical suit a fashion "Don't" at camp. I didn't totally agree—it was an athletic cut. So, a "Do" for actual swimming. But I also understood Laura's point: that unless you're going to the pool to swim laps, wearing something more stylish makes a statement.

"I could help you pick out something new." Joss nodded but looked skeptical. "Anyway, help me double-knot this, so we can get going."

She walked over and quickly secured all the straps so I wouldn't have a wardrobe malfunction. I threw on a sundress, then bent down to grab my overstuffed tote bag, which was still stocked from the last time I went to Laura's pool.

"Holy moly, Alex. Are you running away?" Joss snorted. "What've you got in there?"

Why did she always have to act so judgy about this kind of stuff? "The *essentials*, Joss. Makeup case, some hair things, a magazine, body spray, nail polish for touch-ups." I shifted the bag onto my shoulder. I had to admit it was really heavy. I glanced at her backpack. "You've got a bag too."

"Yeah, with sunscreen, a towel, and a book."

We walked down the hall, and I banged on Lucy's closed door.

A muffled "*Go away, I'm reading*" came from inside. I banged again.

"We can ride our bikes," Joss said. "Or walk."

"I don't want to get all sweaty." I'd spent a lot of time making my hair look right—a high ponytail like Laura's. Also, I didn't think biking in my bikini, even with the sundress on, was such a great idea. "Lucy, we need our ride to the pool. Now!"

The door flung open, and Lucy stalked out, scowling. "Yikes, did a unicorn poop all over your face? You're so...bedazzled."

Next to me, Joss stifled a laugh. But Lucy's comment stung. All I'd done was put on a bit of gloss, and some highlighter... It was a party, after all.

"Mom!" I yelled, "Lucy told me I look like I have poop—"

"What did I tell you?" Mom hissed from the landing of the stairs. "You need to BE QUIET. Stop squabbling and go before you wake Dad." My dad—he's a pilot—was napping before he had to leave for a long flight. "Lucy, can you please just do me a favor and drive them?"

Lucy followed us downstairs, grumbling about being so close to finishing a chapter. Maybe it was a good thing that we had argued, because my mom didn't pay any attention to what I was wearing.

Once she started the car, Lucy said, "Please tell me I don't have to pick up Longbottom."

"No," I answered quickly and nudged at Lucy with my elbow,

because with Joss in the back seat, this conversation was making me uncomfortable. "It's just us going to the pool today." Like old times.

She ignored my nudge. "Laura's kind of a bubblehead. Don't you agree, Joss?" Lucy and I both glanced in the rearview mirror.

Jocelyn's face pinched, like she was stifling either a smile or a sneeze. She glanced up and saw me watching her. Finally, she said, "I'll neither confirm nor deny."

"That's very diplomatic of you," Lucy said, slowing for a stop sign.

I rolled my eyes at both of them. They were the ones acting like mean girls. *So do they think I'm a ditz now too?*

The pool deck was already crowded when we got there. I spotted a few kids we knew from past years of water ballet over by the diving well and waved hello. A bunch of high-school girls were lying out near the deep end, and next to them, the DJ was setting up his speakers. A cluster of Laura's friends from Walden—Monique, Bidisha, and Frannie—hovered nearby.

I'd talked to Bidisha one day when Laura and I saw her at the mall, and she was pretty nice. Most of Laura's cool friends were, once you actually talked to them. So I took a deep breath and rolled back my shoulders. "Let's say hi!" I pointed to the girls. By then a couple of Walden boys had joined them.

"Why?" Joss scratched at her elbow.

"They're Laura's friends." I pulled my sundress over my head, careful not to mess up my hair as it came off. A nervous flutter started in my stomach.

But Joss didn't budge. "Earth to Jocelyn?" I waved a hand in front of her face, the metallic flecks in my nail polish glittering with sunlight.

"We should grab a spot before all the lounges are taken." Joss lunged toward the row of chairs. My skin prickled with annoyance. It bothered me that she wouldn't even try to get to know them. After a second, I followed her, after one last, longing glance at the crowd.

We chose two lounge chairs close to the shallow end. Jocelyn pulled out her tube of sunscreen and started smearing it all over her arms and shoulders.

"Don't you think you've sunscreened enough? You're starting to look like the undead." It was the mineral kind that doesn't rub in easily, so her skin was ghostly white.

"Good! I don't want to get burned." She held the tube out to me. "Here. Coat yourself."

I shook my head, refusing to reach for the tube even though she was shaking it at me. "I'm good."

"Please tell me you're not trying to turn yourself orange like *some* people."

I knew who she was talking about. "Jocelyn! Laura's skin is not orange. That's mean."

She mumbled something I couldn't quite hear, other than

"tangerine." Then she pulled on a swim shirt with a zebralike print. It really clashed with her old turquoise suit. At least she wasn't covering up with her wolf sweatshirt, though.

We settled into our chairs. I flipped through a clothes catalog. "Hey, what do you think of this tank top?"

Joss nodded at it with barely a glance. "Isn't that brand pretty expensive?"

I folded down the edge of the page. "Yeah, but it's something I could wear on a date. Maybe with Kelvin." We'd been texting since camp, with increasing frequency. Laura was coaching my responses, and she was sure he was going to ask me to go out.

"Um, who's Kelvin?"

"Wait, I didn't tell you about him?" Joss shook her head, biting her lip. I guess there was a lot about Tierra de los Lagos I'd never talked about because it all involved Laura, and I didn't want to rub that in Joss's face. "Oh. Well, we went to the camp dance together. Or, we danced together at it. He held my hand." I smiled at the memory, even though his palm had been sweaty in a mildly gross way. "Anyway, we've been texting, and Laura thinks..." *Oops*. I'd brought her up again.

"She thinks what?" Jocelyn's tone was completely neutral, which was weird, because normally if your friend tells you that a guy might be interested in her, you act, like, excited for her. Or at least show some kind of happy feeling.

"That he might ask if I want to go out." I couldn't hold back my grin. Even if "going out" was not a literal term, considering he lived all the way in Minneapolis. Still.

Jocelyn blinked next to me. "Um, wow? You never told me you had a crush."

Have I really not told her any of this? I nodded. "He's so cool. He plays soccer, and he's really good at Spanish. And he spent half of camp flicking french fries at me, which sounds annoying, but it was actually supercute, and it sort of became our thing." That was true. He gave me a cup of fries at the dance. Or, handed them to me while he tried to win the limbo contest. Same difference.

Jocelyn looked skeptical.

"Maybe you had to be there," I explained.

"Probably." She nodded, looking away.

Our conversation stalled after that. There was a lot I wanted to talk about with Jocelyn, like how cool it would be to start eighth grade with a boyfriend—even if it was long distance— but the way Joss was sitting with her arms crossed over her chest, and a hat pulled low to shade her eyes, it seemed like maybe she didn't really want to talk. As if to make that even clearer, she pulled a huge hardcover book onto her lap.

"What is that, a dictionary?" I laughed.

She sighed. "Haven't you ever heard of a 'beach read'?"

"Aren't those usually lighter? Like, literally." That got me a half smile from her. "You know, we're going to be up to our eyeballs in books once school starts. Now's the time to relax."

I glanced toward Laura's friends, still huddled near the high-schoolers and the DJ. None were reading.

A few minutes later, the crackly speakers started blasting oldies. "I love this song!" Joss exclaimed. The music seemed to ease the bad mood she was in. She closed the book, hopped up from her lounge chair, and began dancing as she pulled her goggles around her neck. "Let's get in the water! It's too hot not to." She waved her arms over her head frenetically. The only place I'd ever seen dancing like that was my mom's Zumba class. Maybe I'd been lucky when Joss had refused to do anything other than sulkily sway at Walden's end-of-the-year dance.

"Joss, *please*." My eyes flitted toward the cluster of kids by the DJ, who were too cool to dance to this cheesy music. I glanced back at Jocelyn. "Stop doing whatever that move is."

"You mean the 'Electric Slide'? My dad taught me at my uncle's wedding."

"Just, no."

She lowered her arms. "Don't you at least want to get in the water?" she asked quietly. "I can't take another minute on deck."

The pavement was sweltering—if my toes touched it for even a second, they burned. Cooling off did sound nice. "Sure, fine, whatever." I pulled myself up from my chair, adjusting my bikini to make sure everything was covered. Then I plopped down at the edge of the pool, dipping in a toe. "Never mind, it's too cold!"

"Whatever, it'll feel great once you get in." Next to me, Joss leaped off the edge of the pool, cannonball-style, shrieking as she hit the water. Her huge splash drenched me. "*Argh!* It *is* cold!" she yelled upon surfacing.

"Joss! You got me all wet." I huffed as I wiped the beads of water off my goose-bumpy arms and legs. She'd even splashed my hair. So much for my perfect styling. "Stop flailing around!"

She swam to the edge. "What's your problem? It's only water. And in case you haven't noticed, we're at the *pool*." Then she swam a few feet away to practice our old water-ballet moves. Ballet leg, pinwheel, clamshell. I sat on the edge, dangling my legs in the water while twiddling the strings of my bikini bottom and glancing around the pool deck warily. My gaze lingered on the group by the DJ. They'd never noticed us. Maybe that was for the best.

"Aren't you going to get in?" Joss paddled in front of me, splashing like an otter.

"Nah. I'm going back to the chairs." I sprung up and hurried back to our spot, where I lay down in the sun. When Jocelyn came back a few minutes later, I pretended to be asleep. I think she knew I was still kinda mad.

The DJ announced the start of the contests, first the penny dive. Prizes were stuff like logo towels, last year's swim-team shirts, and six-packs of can soda. Jocelyn and I always worked as a pair—good ol' Team Alexelyn—and split all our prizes. I peeked an eye open to see if Laura's friends were going to participate. They were still just sitting around on their towels. I turned my head the other way and went back to pretending to nap, so Joss wouldn't ask if I wanted to.

Eventually I had to sit up because I could tell I was getting too fried on that side, and I needed water. I glanced over at the Walden group, who were beginning to pack up their stuff. *Now or never.* I cleared my throat. "Hey. So...let's go say hi to them, before they leave?" I motioned to Laura's friends.

Joss started biting her bottom lip. "Let me just finish this chapter." Which meant she really didn't want to. Joss twisted a stray curl around her index finger, the way she always does when she's scared. "Four pages left." They were already slinging backpacks over their shoulders. In two pages, they'd be gone. She knew that. Jocelyn tucked her chin and turned her attention back to the huge tome in her lap. She is a fast reader, but those four pages seemed to be taking her an eternity.

Maybe it was for the best. If we'd gone over there, and she was feeling nervous, Joss probably would've clammed up. Like at the dance—when she'd tried to dash out as soon as we got inside the gym.

I sat back in my lounge chair and studied my best friend, with her (slightly dorky) swim shirt and her faded turquoise suit's saggy butt and a small swipe of un-rubbed-in sunscreen smeared across her cheek and that humongous "beach read."

Then I looked away from her and down at my shiny pink toes,

which still matched Laura's. In that moment, I realized that no part of me matched Jocelyn, which gave me the same kind of melancholy feeling as the day the swimming pool closes for the season.

She sneaked up a glance to see that Laura's friends were already walking toward the exit. "Okay, I'm done."

"It's too late. They're all heading out."

"Oh, sorry. Next time, I guess…"

I think we both knew that sounded hollow.

We didn't stay at the party much longer. When Jocelyn's mom picked us up on her way home from work, we climbed into the back seat without a word.

"Too much fun in the sun?" Ms. Allard asked.

"Something like that," I replied.

The ride to my house was super quiet, like we'd had a fight. Or worse—like we were strangers in a car.

ELEVEN

WITHOUT THE BEACH TOWELS, I think we would've died.

I'd actually debated leaving mine behind. We'd be getting wet on the river (that was kind of the whole point), so I wouldn't need a towel until we were done tubing and on our way back to the cabin. Also, my dad is very picky about getting the seats in the car wet, which I understand because they do start to smell funky—like a wet dog—after a summer of riding home from the pool with a damp suit. So I would need a dry towel after our river adventure. But at the last second I'd shoved mine into my backpack and reminded Alex to bring hers along too, which she grudgingly did.

If my towel were still in the car, I would have been eaten alive by mosquitoes and/or tortured to death by the flies. Even with the towels protecting our bare skin, the bugs were awful. Tiny gnats swarmed our heads, buzzing our ears and hovering in front of our eyes and even getting dangerously close to flying up our noses. Three times I had to spit out something that flew into or onto my lips. I kept my mouth shut in a tight line and narrowed my eyes to a squint. It was hard to keep swatting away the pests while using one hand to keep my towel-skirt fastened together and the other to hold on to the rolled-up inner tube. Yesterday, I'd wondered whether we should leave the tube behind. Now it was our only shelter—our house, portable like a turtle's shell.

The towels protected us in another way: from the cold. I'd bet it was only in the low fifties. Fifty-five degrees, tops. Even for hardy Wisconsin kids, that's not "shorts weather." (Everybody knows that sixty degrees is the cutoff for shorts weather. It's probably in the Wisconsin Constitution. As soon as the red line of the thermometer outside my kitchen window hits the sixty-degree mark, Nolan and I flip out, immediately change into our favorite pairs of shorts, and yell, "It's shorts weather!" That's what happens to a kid after a long, cold Wisconsin winter, I guess.) Though I had my wolf sweatshirt on, it was old and thin, and my legs were bare but for my soccer shorts. Alex, with that tissue-thin cover-up over her bikini, was in worse shape. Even with our dirty, damp towels wrapped tight, and even though we were walking as fast as we possibly could, we both shivered uncontrollably. My skin looked mottled and shriveled. I'd never fully dried off, even though it had been almost a day since we'd left the river.

"Hang on," Alex called from behind.

I stopped, immediately having to shoo away bugs. That was the other benefit to fast walking—insects didn't swarm us quite so much while we were on the move.

Alex, panting lightly, caught up to me. "You don't have any bandages left, do you?"

I shook my head. The last one, Alex had already reapplied to her stabbed toe. And if I had any others, they'd be protecting my shredded heels. "Nope."

"I'm bleeding all over from these bug bites." As if to make her point, she scratched hard at her elbow, leaving behind an ominous red trickle when she took her hand away.

"You have to stop scratching," I said. "It'll only make them worse."

"I don't understand why they don't like you as much as me." She shuddered from another involuntary shiver.

Maybe they're friends of Laura. I caught a whiff of mango as she moved her arm to swat something. "Did you put on more of your body spray?"

"I thought rubbing it in would make me feel warmer, and that it might help with the itching."

I sighed. "Alex. You're attracting bugs with that stuff. It smells like sugar—no wonder the flies are tormenting you." And also me, because the scent of mango—even fake mango—made me even hungrier.

She swatted frantically at something by her shoulder. "Or maybe it's because I'm not wearing that sweatshirt."

I felt like I'd been stung, and not on my right leg, where I definitely had just been bitten by something. Did Alex mean "that *sweatshirt*" because without one, she was more exposed than I was? Or did she mean "*that* sweatshirt" because it was... dorky? Therefore making even insects reject me?

I pushed those thoughts out of my head and followed her. Alex was walking with a purpose again, and I didn't want to get separated. Although sometimes I wondered if being alone in the woods would actually be better than being lost with her, the way she was acting. The way things had been all summer.

Walking behind Alex, I could clearly see the damage on her arms and legs. Her bites had started out as small, pink spots on her skin, but they'd grown into large, raised, swollen circles. Most were topped with a smear of dried blood—whether from scratching or from the bite itself, I didn't know. But even the parts of her that weren't bitten up looked much worse. Her skin was covered in a fiery rash, especially from her feet to her calves. Gross little blisters had formed all over.

I knew what that rash was from: poison ivy. I'd seen pictures of it before, both what the plant looks like and what your skin looks like after you come into contact with it. Poison ivy has three green, almond-shaped leaves, and it grows all over the place in forests, as a shrub and even sometimes a vine. You have to be really careful to watch out for it while hiking. When we first took a break yesterday, Alex had grabbed a bunch of leaves and underbrush and made that little throne for herself to sit on. I hadn't thought to check the plants she was collecting or the area she'd dumped her leaf pile onto. If poison ivy had been in the mix, she'd basically coated her whole lower body in it.

She reached a hand to scratch furiously at the backs of her legs. When she stopped, the streaks looked even redder and angrier. *Yup. Poison ivy.* In a few places, her skin had even broken open and was weeping.

"You have to stop scratching," I said again. "You're starting to bleed."

"Seriously?" Alex stopped, stretching around to check out her poor, suffering legs. "What the heck kind of bug bites are these? I'm covered in them."

I shook my head sadly. "That's not just from bug bites. I think you sat in poison ivy."

"How could you let me do that?" she wailed.

"I didn't know!" Exasperated, I threw up my hands, causing my towel-skirt to drop to my feet. I bent to pick it up from the dirt, seeing that in addition to my own bites, I had several deep, bloody scratches. But at least no blistery rash. "And it's not like you were even speaking to me when you sat on that pile of leaves."

Alex didn't apologize, but she also didn't seem mad at me anymore. She stared anxiously at her oozing legs and rubbed at a spot of dried blood. "I'm bleeding, and we don't even have bandages." She began to whimper. "Bears can smell the blood. They'll come for us!" Her breathing was becoming loud and rapid, like she was getting hysterical.

"Um, I don't think that's true," I said, even though I wasn't entirely sure. "Anyway, your body spray is probably masking the smell of blood. Let's just hope bears don't want mangoes." I reached out a hand to pat her shoulder, out of friendship muscle memory. How many times had Alex started sniffling about something and I'd been there to give her a hug? Like the time that Laura had gotten our whole class to start calling Alex "A ledge" after the substitute messed up her name during attendance. Alex had acted like she didn't care, but as soon as the bell had rung, she'd bolted for the bathroom. When she came out of the stall, her nose and eyes were telltale red. I never liked Laura after that.

Memories like that are why I just didn't understand how, no matter how popular Laura might be, Alex abandoned Team Alexelyn for Team...Laurex, or whatever. (That sounds like a name for toilet-bowl cleaner.) The only explanation was that something was very wrong with me. Or at least that's what Alex thought.

Alex stiffened under my touch. "You know what would make me feel better?"

It was my turn to tense up. "What?"

"The rest of that energy bar. I'm starving." She paused. "You know being hungry always makes me super emotional."

"You mean hangry." That was true. When we were little and Alex would start crying about something, the first thing her mom would always ask is, "Are you hungry?" And Alex would say no, but then her mom would offer a snack, Alex would eat it up, and pretty quickly afterward stop her meltdown.

That half of a bar was all we had left. If I gave it to Alex, we'd be out of food. But if I didn't give it her, she'd probably get even hangrier. It was a tough call.

"No, we need to save it. We don't know when our next meal will be—"

"Just give me my half-of-a-half, please!" she begged, reaching for my backpack.

I took a step backward, shaking my head. "Let's wait until midday, at least."

She grumbled something I couldn't quite hear and then stomped away from me, into the forest. I followed.

It didn't take long before she stopped at a patch of green plants and started ripping the leaves off their long stems.

"What are you doing?" I dropped the inner tube to the ground and kneeled on it, wary of rubbing against anything that might be rash-causing.

"Getting my own food," Alex muttered, clutching a handful of greens. They didn't look that different than the lettuces and herbs sold at the farmers' market on the capitol square in Madison—some of the market's bagged salad greens look an awful lot like the weeds I help Mom dig out of her garden. The difference between what they sell, though, and what Alex had in her hand was that the farmers know what their plants are. And that they're safe as food.

"You can't eat that."

"Watch me." She opened her mouth, moving the handful of green stuff toward it.

The website for the national forest—which I'd spent tons of time on for my project—had mentioned poisonous plants other than poison ivy, oak, and sumac. Hemlock—the weed, not the tree—grows all over the state, and it's toxic to people.

"That plant could kill you! It could be poison hemlock! Do you want to die like Socrates?"

"Socrates?" She pulled her hand away from her mouth. "You mean Nolan's stuffed sock monkey?" That was its name.

"No, I don't mean his stuffed sock monkey! I mean a real person! The philosopher! He drank a cup of hemlock, and then he *died*." At least, I thought Socrates was real and not a character. Sometimes, with ancient figures like him, it gets confusing.

Alex dropped the green stuff. "Fine. But there has to be something we can eat in here. Fruits of the forest are a thing, right? We'll gather berries. I think it's just the bright red ones you have to worry about."

I shook my head, exasperated. "No, there are other ones too. Deadly nightshade berries can be dark." I'd read that in one of my mom's gardening books.

Alex turned to me, crossing her arms. "You know everything,

don't you? And I'm the village idiot. Or forest idiot. Well, fine. If you don't want me to eat the next berry I find in here—no matter *what* color it is—then I need my portion of the energy bar. Now."

Slowly, I worked my backpack off one shoulder and unzipped the front pocket. I pulled out the wrapper, folded neatly over what was left of the smushed bar. It had been cold and shady enough that the bar had re-hardened, and now it broke easily into two. I held out half to Alex, who snatched it and pushed it into her mouth immediately.

She made the same kind of face she used to make when the waitress would set the plate of doughnuts in front of us at Paul Bunyan's Cook Shanty. Or when she'd take that first bite of a Buttercup Lake s'more.

I shoved my half into my mouth too, trying to eat slowly and savor it, but I couldn't help myself. I was too hungry. The bar tasted better than anything I'd ever eaten. Better than a Michael's turtle sundae. And in seconds, it was gone—leaving us all out of food.

TWELVE

F OR A WHILE AFTER we ate the bar, navigating the forest felt easier. Alex and I were sort of getting along, or at least not snapping at each other for every little thing. The sun finally peeked out as we walked into an area that was like a clearing, although there were still tons of trees around. I had the idea that we should lay down the tube and rest for a few minutes, letting the sunshine warm us. I even took off my dew-dampened towel skirt, to let it air dry by hanging it on a nearby branch.

As I stretched out onto the tube, next to Alex, I had a weird flash of déjà vu. It was just like when we'd been at the pool party, lying on the lounge chairs. Except there was no oldies-playing DJ, no shade from umbrellas, no grown-ups in the grill area frying up burgers and dogs and restocking the coolers with ice cream sundae cups, the kind you eat with a tiny, flat wooden spoon. The only thing that was the same, really, was that Alex was stretched out next to me, so close I could hear her breathe, yet we weren't really interacting. I turned on my side, facing her back. Something else had changed between the two scenes—the bloody scratches, bug-bite welts, fresh bruises, and blistering rash all over her body, and the tangles of burrs and pine pitch in her hair. Last night she'd abandoned her ponytail; she said wearing her hair down felt warmer.

I kind of wished we could go back to the pool party. Not just so we wouldn't be trapped in the forest, starving and slightly injured. But because I think I'd act differently than I had. When she asked to go over and say hi to those girls—Laura's friends— I'd suck it up and do it, even though they intimidated me and I wasn't sure I had anything to say to them. And when Alex told me about her crush from camp—Kelvin—I'd be more encouraging. Like a supportive friend. I'd just freaked out a little when she'd brought him up. I was nowhere near having a boyfriend. I wasn't sure I even wanted one. If Alex was sure—she had leapfrogged ahead of me, and maybe I wasn't going to be able to catch up. What was going to happen to us? If she became one of those girls: the cool ones, with their fancy clothes and their boyfriends? I'd wanted to ignore what she was telling me and hope that all her new interests would fizzle away. Sometimes I'd even snarked about them, to make myself feel better. If I actually wanted to stay best friends, though, I at least needed to stop judging. And try to meet her halfway. It was sort of on me that so far, I really hadn't.

"Alex?" I whispered. She didn't answer, and from her deep and relaxed breathing, I could tell she'd fallen asleep in the few minutes we'd been lying down. I understood. I was exhausted too. Whatever sleep I'd stolen the night before hadn't been enough, and we were still so hungry and thirsty.

I let my eyes close. Yes, we needed to cover a lot of ground, but being well rested would only help us walk faster—and safely. Plus, the sun felt so good on my chilled skin. Maybe it would finally dry my hair, or my towel. Just a catnap…

I have no idea how long it had been when I woke with a start. The noise, still faraway, was the first human-made sound we'd heard since we'd left the river. The familiar hum of a plane's engine. You don't hear that much up in the Northwoods, and it was getting louder, closer. *People looking for us?* It had to be. We'd been missing for a full day. What had started as a tubing mishap had turned into something serious, scary, a crisis. By now, our parents would've started a rescue effort, like the kind you hear about on the news. We might already have been on the news, which was strange to think about.

"Alex! Wake up!" I nudged her arm, careful to touch only the covered-up part and not her painful-looking bare skin. "Do you hear that?"

"Wha—?" She blinked and sat up, looking confused about where we were.

"A plane! It must be people searching for us! It could even be your dad!" He didn't have a plane, but he was a pilot.

I've never seen her move faster, and that includes all the

times we were sitting in her backyard and heard the passing jingle of the ice-cream truck slowly driving down the street in the front of her house.

"Help us!" she screamed, her voice raspy. "Help us! We're lost! Here we are!" Birds in the trees, who maybe had been enjoying a midmorning (or late morning, I had no idea what time it actually was) nap, cawed angrily and flapped away from the racket she was making.

People up in a plane wouldn't be able to hear us, but I didn't think yelling could hurt, either. "Here! We're here!" I waved my arms and tried to bounce on my toes, but my feet hurt too much from the water shoes digging into the backs of my heels again. I tugged them off and threw them onto the inner tube. I started doing a move like jumping jacks—my bare heels still stung, but I ignored the pain. Anything I could do to get the pilot up there to notice our movement. *Wait... Maybe some of the useless stuff in Alex's bag isn't totally useless.*

"Get out your phone! Whatever's shiny!" I shouted. Alex fumbled around in her tote bag and pulled out her sparkly mirror compact and dead phone.

"Why?"

"We'll use them to flash the plane!"

She tossed me the phone, and we waved both objects around, catching the sunlight.

We still couldn't see anything up in the sky, but any moment, the plane would pop out above the tree line and the pilot would spot us in the clearing. I knew it. I kept jumping and waving the phone, even though every part of me ached. I rejoined Alex in screaming at the sky.

The buzz of the engine grew even stronger, like it was just beyond the treetops. I held my breath for a moment, preparing for the loudest shout yet, the biggest jumping jack. But the sky above remained still. Only the rows of light, puffy passing clouds like cotton balls drifted toward us, then away.

The engine's drone softened. It became faint. Then I couldn't hear it over Alex's continued shouts. "Shh, for just a minute." When she stopped jumping and screaming and waving, she doubled over to catch her breath. I strained to listen.

The plane was gone.

The pilot hadn't even flown overhead. Rescuers hadn't seen us. They wouldn't know we were here.

Alex stood again, cupping her hands around her mouth. "Come back," she croaked, waving her mirror at the empty sky. Then she started to cry.

I wanted to cry too. It had been so close. But I swallowed the lump in my throat and tried to focus on the positive. "Hey, at least we know they're looking for us. Next time, they'll spot us."

"Next time? What if there isn't a next time?" Her voice was panicked again.

"They're not going to give up." At least, I hoped not.

We both sank to the inner tube, which had grown hot in the sun while we'd been jumping around. It felt good to be warm again, but now my skin was tight and itchy, like it was being stretched too thin. My lips were chapped and dry. Either from dehydration or all the sun exposure.

"Are you thirsty?" I asked Alex, turning for my backpack.

"Dying," she said.

"Maybe don't use that word." I meant it as a joke, but it fell completely flat.

There was only a quarter of the water left in the bottle. I took a tiny sip, which tasted as good as an Oreo shake, or strawberry lemonade, or hot chocolate when you come inside from sledding.

I passed the bottle to Alex. "Slake yourself."

"Huh? Is there a snake?" She pulled her knees toward her chest.

"No, *slake*—it means to quench your thirst. It was a dictionary word..."

Alex frowned, and I trailed off. Looking up weird words in the dictionary had once been our rainy-day-at-the-cabin activity.

She took a sip—only a small one, not enough to slake at all. When she pulled the bottle away from her lips, I noticed that they were more swollen than earlier and really chapped too. Her lower lip even had the start of a painful-looking split. I scanned Alex's arms and legs. Her rashy skin was swollen tight and bleeding wherever she'd been scratching, which was pretty much everywhere.

Being exposed in the clearing was only going to make it worse, especially because we were all out of sunscreen. "We should get back in the forest, where it's shadier."

"But it's so cold in there, and if the plane comes back, nobody is going to see us through all the trees." She had a point.

"We can't just wait here and hope they do another flyover. We need to keep walking. We're going to run out of water soon, and we need to find something, maybe berries, for food."

I wobbled to standing and, as soon as Alex reluctantly joined me, rolled up the tube. I wished it were any color other than pine green, especially something neon. Blaze orange, a color that people might spot through the tree canopy. Instead, except for Alex's bright cover-up, we camouflaged perfectly. Even our towels were muted forest colors. I almost forgot mine, still hanging to dry on the branch. I pulled it off and wrapped it around my lower half again. For whatever reason, the bugs had mostly left us alone in the clearing. Maybe we were all out of unbitten skin for them to feast on. *Do mosquitoes double-dip?*

The worst part was when I had to squeeze my feet back into the water shoes. It hurt so much when the elastic met my heels that tears formed at the corners of my eyes, and I gasped.

"What is it?" Alex asked.

"My water shoes are too tight now that they're dry, and they're cutting into my heels—it really stings." I carefully pulled the backs of the shoes away from my feet and folded them down so I could step on the heel pad. It wasn't a great solution because the shoes didn't want to stay on my feet that way. They were like too-small house slippers. Also, the open wounds on my heels were at risk for getting dirty and infected. But it would have to do.

Alex raised an eyebrow. "Guess flip-flops aren't so dumb after all."

"Did I ever say that?"

"Maybe not, but you sure side-eyed them."

Fair enough. "Your feet are covered in scratches. I think we can call it a draw."

She nodded. "Now which way?" She pointed left, then right.

My stomach sank. I didn't know. I hadn't remembered to pick out a landmark when we walked into the clearing, so we'd know which direction we'd come from. The trees didn't all look the same, so I could trick myself into thinking that yes, we'd definitely walked past that tilted pine before, or around that scraggly tree that had knots in the shape of a scowling face.

I didn't want to tell Alex that I wasn't sure, though. "This way," I said, pointing in the direction the plane's noise had come from. Why not walk toward wherever it had flown from?

"Are you sure?" she asked. "I thought..." She scratched at her arm and stared into the trees.

Alex hadn't been paying attention to anything. Not since we'd gotten lost, and not on the trip till that point. She was the one who walked us right off a trail. The only thing that captured her eye was her still-dead phone and her now-destroyed pedicure. So I thought nothing of telling her, "Yeah, I'm positive." Then we started walking again.

With the backs of my water shoes folded down, the cuts on my heels stopped slicing deeper. Unfortunately, it meant the shoes slipped off about every four steps, and their footbeds became covered in pine needles, which tickled my arches and occasionally stabbed the bottoms of my feet. As a result, I was walking painfully slow.

Even though we'd dried off while resting in the clearing, it didn't take long before we began to shiver again, once we were deep in the woods. They still hadn't dried off from last night's storm. Everything glistened with moisture, from the mushrooms dotting the forest floor to the leaves dangling from trees. I wrapped my towel tighter around me. Alex had hers rolled around herself like a strapless maxi dress, her cover-up still on beneath it. We both looked ridiculous.

To force myself to raise and lower my feet for each step, I pictured the things I hoped we were walking toward. First I focused on the things I most craved: a can of bug spray. A bottle of fresh, clean water. Fried cheese curds from Culver's. Band-Aids and socks and thick-soled shoes to protect my feet. Then I started picturing the people I wanted to walk toward, in the most loving scenes I could imagine: My mom with her sweaty arm hugging my shoulder as we gazed at our finished hard work in the garden. My dad, leaning down to plant a kiss on the top of my head and gently pry the book from my hand, after I'd fallen asleep reading (and he always knows to mark my place). Nolan giving me one of his drive-by hugs, when he practically collides with my stomach and squeezes tight while his legs never stop moving. Alex and I lacing our fingers together and stretching our arms overhead, whooping and smiling as we jumped off the pier and tucked our knees to cannonball into Buttercup Lake together.

It was so weird to be longing for Alex while she was right beside me. It didn't feel that way, though: She was a million miles away. If the person grunting next to me was even still Alex at all. Maybe she'd left the chrysalis of her childhood self and had been transformed into a butterfly, a creature totally new. Maybe now she was *Lexie* all the time.

My stomach panged from hunger. I'd never been this hungry, not even the time I tried to join Alex in fasting on Ash Wednesday, for solidarity. Even then, I'd eaten a good breakfast, had plenty of water to drink, and planned on an early dinner. I'd gone without food for maybe ten hours, most of which I'd spent sitting like a lump in my desk at school. I hadn't even had to run around during gym period since it was a library day. Now we'd been tramping through the forest for over twenty-four hours, and except for the energy bars, we'd eaten nothing since bagels yesterday morning. *Why didn't I glob on more peanut butter?* I wanted to throttle Past Jocelyn and tell her to take a second bagel, why not, you're on vacation? But Alex had been so picky about "healthy" eating, nibbling on whole-grain toast and some fruit, only after she'd confirmed it was organic. I'd felt conspicuous going for seconds. Like she'd judge me for that too.

Our hunger made me anxious. At some point, we'd run out of energy to keep moving. We'd be at risk of fainting—which Alex had done once, during music class in third grade, when we were singing while standing on the risers. It was because she'd locked her knees, according to our teacher, Mrs. George, who made sure Alex hadn't hit her head and still called the nurse so Alex could get checked out afterward. What would I do if Alex passed out again? What would *she* do if I did? What if we *both* fainted?

All the worrying only made my stomach feel tighter and emptier, and my head lighter and foggier. I focused on taking slow, calming breaths. Sometimes my dad listens to nature sounds while he's trying to meditate, like recordings of babbling brooks or gentle rainstorms or birdcalls. He only started meditating last year, when he got downsized and was suddenly home all the time, on the computer searching for a new job. I didn't really get why he seemed so much more stressed out than when he had been at work late every night—until I found the stash of bill statements that Mom was keeping in the cupboard.

It was thick as a chapter book. I flipped through them, and while none of the bills warned that it was a "final notice" or anything, several were past due and had late fees tacked on.

Anyway, the nature sounds seemed to help Dad relax and think clearly and deal with the situation. Eventually, he got a new job. It wasn't permanent, and it paid less, but his contract was already renewed and he seemed to like it. At least, he was happy when he came home from work. And the bill stack shrank. The last time I was in that cupboard hunting for a binder clip, there were only two unpaid statements and neither was overdue.

So I tried to pretend that the sounds around me in the woods were a soothing nature soundtrack, to keep me calm. *Inhale, exhale.*

"Wait." Alex reached out and grabbed my arm, jarring me to a stop. I stepped on a twig, and it loudly snapped, like end punctuation to her command. "What. Is. That."

Sometimes the shifting light in the forest played tricks on us, appearing like a moving creature. Although it could be a real creature—we weren't alone in the woods. *I hope it's a wolf.* Alex's voice didn't sound like she'd noticed anything that would help us, such as a building in the distance or a signpost or even a glimpse of the river, swiftly flowing somewhere beyond the trees.

My muscles tensed. "What is what?" This is getting existential, I thought, almost laughing. I was feeling kind of loopy, maybe from the hunger, or maybe from the lack of sleep.

"That pile of stones?" Her voice rose in disbelief. "That's not the stack *you* made, right?"

I blinked. Then I blinked again, hoping that when my eyes fluttered back open, the cairn would disappear. Maybe it was a mirage. Maybe Alex was hallucinating. Maybe *I* was hallucinating.

It wasn't; she wasn't; I wasn't.

I knew right away it was my stack of stones because of how it tilted to the left, and because the biggest one on the bottom had some green gunk on it. Either moss or lichen (the difference between the two is that one is a plant and the other is a life form that's partly a fungus, although I had trouble remembering which was which). A couple of rocks had tumbled off, apparently, and lay on the ground in front of the remaining stack of stones.

Looking more closely at the area around us, I saw the indentation of flattened plants and leaves where we'd spread the inner tube last night. I kind of recognized a gnarled tree whose branches made the letter *Y*. The cluster of mushrooms that looked like they were "marching" in formation. My heart sank. We were back at our campsite. We'd spent half the day traveling in a giant circle, even though I'd tried to prevent that. We were no closer to being out of the woods or back to the river.

"Is. That. Your. Pile. Of. Stones." Alex's speech was stilted and sharp, like she was holding back a rock slide of rage.

"I think so," I said quietly. "I mean, yeah. I know it is. My cairn."

"So we're back to where we spent the night. We just walked. In a huge. Freaking. *Circle*." Alex was waving her arms around for emphasis, her voice getting louder with each syllable. The rage-slide was starting.

Why does she have to act like this? We both already knew what she was saying was true. But she still *had* to yell it at me, make this mistake *my* fault, when—really—I was the one who was doing most of the work of trying to keep us alive and get us out of the woods. And Alex was contributing...attitude? Near-constant whining? Occasional outbursts of hanger?

"Don't yell at me," I said, my voice quiet but firm.

"This sucks." Alex started kicking at the underbrush, sending clumps of needles and some of those poor mushrooms flying into the air. I winced, thinking of how she must be hurting her battered feet. "How could you let us do that?"

"Why is this *my* fault?" The skin on my face flushed with anger, and I dumped the rolled-up inner tube on the ground so I could wave my arms around accusingly.

"Because it's *all* your fault." Alex scowled at me. "The fact that I'm here."

"If you mean because I've kept us alive so far, then yes!" I wasn't yelling yet, but my voice was getting higher and tighter and raspier.

She snorted. "Barely. Look at us." She gestured at all the scrapes and bites. "Tonight—I can't believe there's going to be a *tonight* again—we'll probably freeze to death. Well, maybe you won't." She pointed at my sweatshirt, shaking her head and trying to curl her puffy lips into a snarky smile. Just like Laura had in the hallway. I winced.

"Why are you like this?" I crossed my arms over my chest. "Why are you being so *mean* to me?"

"*I'm* mean to you? You ruined my phone, on purpose!"

My stomach wrenched. "I—What are you talking about? You dropped your phone in the river. That wasn't something *I* did."

Her eyes narrowed. "Come on. I know you're soooo much smarter than me, but I'm not dumb about that. We didn't bump into anything, and there wasn't some sudden wave. I think you bounced the inner tube." She paused. "On purpose, so I'd lose my phone."

My mouth opened, but I had no words. *I never meant for that to happen.* Even if I'd been a teensy bit happy to see her phone sail into the water, it had still been an accident. "It wasn't on purpose."

"Nope, don't believe you." She crossed her arms over her chest and sized me up. "This"—she uncrossed her arms and motioned at the forest surrounding us—"is probably what you've been dying for. Trapping me in your precious woods, without even my phone. So you could have me all to yourself."

"What?" I sputtered. She was making me sound like a creeper, and it wasn't true. "I didn't want any of this to happen!" I'd *wanted* a fun morning on the river. An adventure, but the normal kind, where you see some cool wildlife and get splashed during the low-key patch of rapids, and take some pictures that you might actually print out and stick up on your memory board, and at the end of the day, you return to the cabin and eat s'mores together and then go to sleep on the aerie mattress in side-by-side sleeping bags, not on top of a busted inner tube with a blanket of bugs.

"You've been, like, so mopey all summer. Because you're jealous. You can't handle the fact that I have other friends now, like Laura, who is actually nice and fun, and doesn't always have to prove how smart she is. Hanging out with her is awesome."

And hanging out with me is… The implication cut like a knife. "I don't care that you have other friends, but I care that Laura is turning you into a clone of herself! Because she's the worst." We were both shouting by this point. "She doesn't even know that New Mexico is a state, not a country." That was a low blow, but it was true—last year Laura kept asking our social studies teacher whether Mexico or New Mexico shared a border with the United States. It seemed to astonish her that New Mexico, a state, shared a border with Mexico, the country. "She's too extra to even eat her own dish of custard. And she used to call you 'A ledge'!"

"Which she apologized for! Because normal people, like, grow up and change. At least now she doesn't wear a swimsuit that's almost falling apart. Or that." She pointed at my sweatshirt. "'Lupine lover.' I swear, Jocelyn, you act like such a dork sometimes, I can't even. It's embarrassing." She exhaled sharply, blowing her tangled hair away from her red face.

I just stood there, half stunned and half defiant. When she'd let Laura laugh at me in the hallway—when she'd laughed right alongside her—I thought nothing could feel more like a betrayal. But Laura wasn't even here to witness this. Suddenly, it was clear what had happened on registration day hadn't been because Alex was hypnotized by Laura or was performing some kind of obedience test. It had everything to do with how my best friend now felt about me. *Embarrassing. Dork.*

I felt the unmistakable prick of tears pooling at the corners of my eyes. The fact that I knew I was going to cry made me, at least temporarily, angrier. Alex had hurt me so much over the summer. She'd made me feel small and nerdy and uncool; most of all, she'd made me feel so lonely. I wanted her to feel as bad as I had.

Alex has always been sensitive about not being "smart" because Lucy is such a superstar. And, well, my report card is full of A's that—to Alex—seem effortless while she sometimes struggles. She's told me before that she always feels like "the dumb one" compared to Lucy or me. That's her Achilles' heel.

"You know what? I was wrong. You and Laura are perfect for each other." My voice was shaking as I spoke. "But I hate to break it to you. Even compared to Laura, you're still the dumb one." I paused to let my words sink in. "That's just who you are."

For a moment, Alex just stood there, blinking at me. She might've been blinking back tears. I opened my mouth, thinking I should take it back, apologize. But then she suddenly lunged toward the ground, picked up a handful of mud and leaves, and threw it at the center of my sweatshirt. It hit the wolf smack in its face.

It was obvious Alex hadn't thrown it to hurt me, because after years of dodgeball games and tossing a Nerf in the pool, I knew she could chuck something a lot harder than that. It was almost like she was trying to cover the wolf in dirt. Like she hated it. Or in that moment, hated me.

I couldn't believe she'd done it. It was weird and shocking and immature—ironic, since we were fighting about who needed to grow up. But I also couldn't believe what I'd said about her. I didn't even mean it. Yet I'd released those words anyway, and now they stained Alex. Like the clumps of damp dirt smudging the wolf on my chest—although what I'd said couldn't ever be brushed or washed away.

ALEX
REGISTRATION DAY

REGISTRATION DAY IS LIKE practice for the first day of school. You don't have to wake up so early or go to any classes, but it is the first time you'll see all the kids you haven't been hanging out with over the summer. The first time they'll see your new clothes, new shoes, new hair, new braces (luckily, I didn't have those to deal with). And your new friendships. According to Laura, registration is the real first impression. "Think of it as the soft launch," she said, which is apparently some kind of business term her mom uses a lot.

I'd only ever thought of registration day as when you get to pick up your schedule, while crossing your fingers that you're in at least one class with your best friend. For seventh grade, Jocelyn and I hit the jackpot: three classes plus lunch together. We'd shrieked with joy so loudly that my mom had startled and dropped her coffee, and then we had to help her mop it up with paper towels from the restroom.

But Laura is right. Registration is actually so much more than picking up a schedule. Especially this year. I didn't know if I could remake a first impression on kids I'd been going to school with for eight previous years—or longer, if we were in nursery school together—but I was hoping for a fresh start. This year, I'd be sharing Laura's spotlight. Everything was going to be different now that I was Lexie. Shinier. Cooler. Funner. I mean, more fun.

Even though the time window for incoming eighth graders to register was eleven to one, I got up at eight forty-five to start getting ready. When I was in the bathroom, styling my hair, Lucy banged on the door. "What are you doing in there? I have to get to the zoo. There are *three* day-care field trips coming in today."

"Just give me another minute!" I hollered through the door. "Use the downstairs bathroom!"

"Mateo's in it, and I'm afraid to go in after him!"

When I finally unlocked the door to let her in, Lucy did a double take. "Please tell me you aren't doing all that"—she motioned to my face—"for another trip to the pool."

"It's registration day, silly!" I pushed past her to get back to my room. I'd narrowed my outfit choices to four. Laura and I were going to videochat to pick out the final selection.

"Definitely number three," Laura said, after I modeled each outfit twice. "The tank looks great—that's a summer color." Laura's mom had "done my colors," which meant picking out a palette of my perfect shades.

"Awesome, thanks." I started to put the other outfits away.

"Hey, do you want a ride?" Laura asked. "My dad can drop us off on his way to play golf."

"Um, sure!"

"Great. We'll be there in twenty."

I danced around my room after we ended the chat. To be honest, I hadn't been sure how it would work, being back in the halls of Walden after everything that had gone down this summer. Laura had a ton of other friends. It's not like I was the only person she'd been hanging out with. I'd wondered if it would be the kind of thing where our friendship would fizzle once school began: We'd see each other in the hallway and nod "hey," or briefly hug and squee, but then go our separate ways. Instead, today we were going to be making a first impression together.

My phone buzzed. I grimaced when I read the emoji-less text: **Hey, what time do you want to go to Walden?**

Jocelyn. I placed the phone on my dresser, thinking of how best to answer. I didn't want to tell Joss that I was riding with Laura because that would obviously make her feel excluded. But this was not a situation where she could tag along with us—definitely not after how things had gone at the pool party.

Maybe I could text Jocelyn back once I was at school. Something like, **Just saw this! At Walden already.** And then add the school emoji or the smiley with the glasses or the pink hearts. She wouldn't be able to see them on the flip phone but the little question-mark-box icon would show I was trying to send her nice emojis. Or I could just write **xoxoxoxo**, like Laura does all the time.

I slipped my phone into my bag and skipped downstairs to wait. My mom wandered into the hallway while I stood by the front door, checking my outfit again in the big mirror.

"You look nice," she said, thankfully not commenting on how tight the tank was.

"Thanks, Mom." One strand would not cooperate with the rest of my ponytail, no matter how much I futzed with it.

"Do you want me to drive you to school? Or are you and Joss walking?"

Finally, my ponytail was perfect. I turned to face my mom. "Actually, I'm going with Laura. Her dad's driving us."

"Oh! Well, in that case, thank him for the ride." My mom paused, like she wanted to say something else. She cleared her throat. "I can't believe it's already school registration. And almost time to head up north."

The end-of-summer vacation we always take—with Joss's whole family. I think I knew why Mom was bringing that up, at this particular moment.

"I'll see Jocelyn at school," I mumbled, even though I kind of hoped I wouldn't. It would just make my reboot...complicated. "Mom, you know I have other friends besides Joss."

"And that's great, sweetie." She patted my shoulder. "You've always been a good friend."

I don't know why her compliment made me feel so guilty, like she'd caught me with my hand in the cookie jar or something.

My phone buzzed—Laura was outside. "Gotta go," I said, pressing into my mom for a quick hug.

"Good luck with everything!"

I wondered if she was referring to more than my schedule assignment.

When we got out of the car at Walden, Laura stopped me before I could start up the walkway. "Lexie, you're missing something," she said, her voice a singsong.

I froze, momentarily panicked, thinking that I'd somehow forgotten to put on my shorts or something nightmarish like that. Or that Mateo had pranked me by cutting a snowflake pattern into my shirt—which he did once, and then he had to use all his saved-up allowance to buy me a new one. I scanned from my polished toenails to the tops of my bare shoulders. *It must be my ponytail.* I felt for a strand out of place. "What?"

Laura grabbed my wrist and slid a shiny bangle on it. It was engraved with the letters BFF. Then she held out her own wrist, modeling an identical one. "Now we're twinning!" She looped her arm through mine and propelled us up the steps and into school for the "soft launch" of us as a duo. It felt like she'd put something else on me: a glass slipper. My Cinderella moment, as Laura guided me into school.

Except for the texting. Constant texting. Even Laura noticed the buzzing. "Do you need to check your phone? It's like you're hiding a nest of bees in your bag."

Actually, a hive. The correct word came to me in Jocelyn's slightly know-it-all voice, which left a stab wound of guilt in my gut. "No, it's cool."

"What if it's Kelvin texting you?"

I shook my head. "Pretty sure it's Jocelyn."

Laura's nose wrinkled. "Yeah, okay to ignore."

Another stab. So I did pull out my phone and quickly replied: **Sorry just saw this! At Walden already. Xoxoxoxoxoxo!**

The kids milling around inside seemed a little confused, but impressed, when Laura and I waltzed in together. Josh Haberman came up to us to say hi, and even though my heart still belonged to Kelvin, it beat faster with each step he took toward me. He leaned in to give Laura a high five, and then one for me too. "What's up, Lexie?" Super friendly and casual, like we'd always hung out.

By then, Houa and Kate had wandered into the hallway. I waved but didn't leave Laura and Josh to go over and say hi or anything. Neither girl made a move to come over toward us. In fact, even though Houa half-smiled and waved back at me, she then pulled Kate close to whisper in her ear.

Is it terrible that I'm pretty sure they were talking about how I was with the cool kids? Is it more terrible that it felt kind of... awesome?

By the time Laura and I made our way to the *A through M* line at the registration table, after so many high fives and what's-ups with people who wouldn't have even known I was alive in past years, my phone had stopped buzzing altogether. The office lady behind the table flipped through the stack of printouts till she found our schedules, then handed them over. Laura and I held them up, side by side, to compare.

"Oh, sweet! We have social studies and math together." Laura nudged me in my side. "You can help me do all the assignments." She smiled. "Because you're the smarty."

I smiled too, thinking about how weird it was that I was considered the smart friend, now. That might be kind of nice.

The longer we stayed inside school, the more it felt totally normal to be standing next to Laura, in her spotlight of cool. It felt like if things hadn't always been that way, then they should've been. Now I'd finally found my place. What exactly had been holding me back, all those years of lunchroom anxiety, of being invisible at my locker, of huddling by the snack table with Shark Boy at dances?

Jocelyn, I guess?

"I don't want to spend another minute in school before we have to." Laura shoved her schedule into her bag. "Let's get out of here. Do you want to pick up lunch at the juice place?"

"Okay." I didn't really want to leave—I would've been happy to soak up more of the attention. People looked at me differently now that I was with Laura. There was no way eighth grade wasn't going to be amazing. But Laura had a point. Every moment left of summer was precious.

We were slowly walking—strutting—down the long hallway that leads from the office when I saw her burst through the double doors. It was a record-scratch moment.

Jocelyn was wearing some kind of baggy athletic shorts and her gardening Crocs. And while that part of her outfit wasn't ideal, it wasn't horrible, either. Same with her topknot, which was escaping its hair elastic, like maybe she'd been running to get there. It occurred to me that perhaps Jocelyn had waited so long for me to text her back that when I didn't, maybe she freaked out about missing registration altogether and left in a total rush. Her parents were both working and she didn't have an older sister to drive her, so she'd probably either ran or biked to get to Walden in time.

What I couldn't overlook, though, was the sweatshirt. Her favorite sweatshirt, adorned with an illustration of a howling wolf standing proud in front of moonlit trees, with the caption LUPINE LOVER! She'd gotten it for her ninth birthday—the year we had a picnic at the Baraboo Zoo, where actual wolves live. (For some reason, there aren't any at the zoo in Madison. Lucy doesn't know why.) Joss had worn it on countless after-school bike rides, chilly nights on my porch, trips to Ski-Hi apple orchard, low-key movie marathon afternoons. She'd worn it so much, in fact, that the elbows were very thin and one had the beginnings of a hole.

The sweatshirt looked as hopelessly dorky as it sounds. And, I mean, I'd told Joss that! In a loving way, whenever she wore it when we were hanging out. Maybe she thought I was just teasing when I told her it was the best one to wear for the planetarium field trip because nobody could see it in the dark. But I was serious. It was the kind of clothing choice that nobody cared about when we were in elementary school, but once we got to Walden, most girls stopped wearing old oversize sweatshirts with howling wolves on them.

Joss stopped walking and stood in the middle of the hallway, like a confused animal in the road, watching us glide toward her. She nervously smoothed her hair, righting the tilted topknot. Then she forced a big, nervous smile across her face. Picturing it now kind of breaks my heart.

But in that moment, all I could think about was how awkward and frustrating the pool party had been. Joss hadn't even been willing to say hi to Laura's friends. She'd done the Electric Slide while wearing goggles and a saggy-butt one-piece. She teased me for wearing makeup. She brought a dictionary-size book to read.

Maybe that's just who she was. But did I still want to be like that? Did *Lexie*?

I glanced at Laura, next to me. Her eyebrow arched. What had she said when I told her the constant texts were from Jocelyn?

"*Yeah, okay to ignore.*" I couldn't do that. But I also couldn't stop for Joss, not when I was arm in arm with Laura. So instead I raised my free hand to give her a tiny wave. The BFF bangle, cold against my flushed skin, slid down my forearm as I did.

"Hey, Alex..." Joss's voice sounded nervous, tight. Confused. We were about to pass her by.

Before I could respond, Laura giggled and leaned in to whisper something in my ear, while looking right at Jocelyn's sweatshirt. But it was a stage whisper, loud enough for others in the hallway to hear. "More like lupine *loser.*" Then she giggled again. I was so shocked that I laughed too, because I didn't know how else to handle the situation. Joss remained frozen in place.

Seconds later we burst through the doors and were outside and it was all over.

My new best friend, at least according to the bracelet hanging like a handcuff from my wrist, had just called my former best friend a loser. Out loud. On registration day. In front of other people.

I hadn't defended Joss. Instead, I'd laughed, and then I'd walked away.

Which basically meant I had just publicly dumped my best friend.

I hated myself for it in that moment, and I still do. But I also kind of hated Joss, and her stupid sweatshirt. For giving me no choice but to do it.

THIRTEEN

I PICKED UP THE INNER tube, readjusted my backpack, and headed out in whichever direction I'd been facing. I didn't wait for Alex to gather her things. I didn't turn around to see if she was following me. I simply walked as fast as the half-on water shoes would allow. Which wasn't very fast.

I knew she was following, though, because after I'd walked a certain distance I could hear her flip-flops approaching behind me, staccato slaps that gradually matched my steady pace.

My heart was still racing from the fight. And my stomach was knotted up like a pair of earbuds. I couldn't believe she'd thrown dirt at me. The worst part, though, was that I *could* believe she'd secretly thought I was embarrassing and a dork. The fight confirmed what I'd suspected—no, feared—all summer.

And I'd called her dumb. One of the things that defines best friendship, what makes it different than all other friendships, is not that you know all the things that delight or annoy or inspire your best friend. It's that you know all their vulnerabilities, the things that they secretly worry or wonder about, the soft spots that are the most tender when bruised.

We'd bruised each other pretty badly, and now we were limping through the forest, in silence, single file.

I wanted to stop and tell Alex that I was really sorry, that I'd only said that stuff because I was hurt, and that she was never dumb. To remind her that she was always making me crack up, because she knew the funniest thing to say in any situation, and that you have to be really smart to craft jokes that land every time. And she was smart in other ways too—Alex always knows how to design an outfit because she can tell which colors and patterns work together, even the unexpected pairings. Her ruthless strategizing brought Team Alexelyn to victory again and again in cul-de-sac games of Capture the Flag. The way she interprets the ambiguous parts of books and movies is always super interesting. And even in terms of school, not getting A's doesn't mean you're dumb at *all*.

But equally, I wanted to run away from her as fast as I could and let her find her own way out of the forest, if she hated being in there with me so much. Although the water shoes were never going to let me run anywhere.

At least now I knew that this summer hadn't been a blip or a fight. It was an ending. A lifelong best friendship circling the drain, like when they empty all the water out of the pool at the end of the season. (Actually, I don't think they entirely drain the pool for the winter. That can make it crack or pop up out of the ground because of the pressure, so they leave a little water inside.)

In some ways, I felt more panicked now that I understood Alex and I were over than I did about being lost in the woods. Which sounds ridiculous. Except, if you think about it—what kind of life was I desperately trying to get back to? One in which I'd watch on the sidelines as my best friend further morphed from Alex into *Lexie* and flitted around school, laughing at the things that made me...me? Of course I wanted to be with my family again, but without Alex, I wasn't sure what my life was going to be like.

I tried to focus on the forest sounds again, to help my mind and heart calm down. I listened to the birds singing, the bugs buzzing by my ears, the underbrush crunching underfoot, and the water babbling nearby. *Wait, what?* I paused midstep so I could listen more carefully. Sometimes when the wind rushes through the pines, it makes a sound like a waterfall. It's very confusing when you're trying to locate water. I heard Alex stop behind me, keeping several feet in between us. I could sense her wanting to ask me why I'd stopped, but she kept silent.

If I listened very closely, while holding my breath, I could hear the trickle of water flowing over rocks. The burble was very faint, and I was already feeling kind of loopy and exhausted and emotionally overwhelmed, so maybe I was delirious and imagining it. Or being tricked by the breeze again. I opened my mouth to ask Alex if she heard it too. Then I closed it. I didn't want to be the one to break the silence.

Her eyes bored into my back as I stood there, listening and also scratching at a bug bite that had turned into a bloody welt on my forearm. I could tell Alex wanted to know what I was doing—I'd even cupped my hand around my ear to better hear, although I'm not really sure that works—but she would have to ask.

Without a word, I began to slowly walk in the direction of the babbling-water sound. Even if it was just the forest playing tricks on us. I was so thirsty and dirty—my feet and legs were caked in mud and blood. They were swollen too, either from so much walking or maybe all the inflamed bug bites. It would feel delicious to dip my toes in a cool stream, wash off all the gunk, and take a rest.

We hiked up a bit of an incline, making my thigh muscles ache. My hands hurt from gripping the rolled-up inner tube, which was much heavier than you'd think. The slapping of Alex's flip-flops behind me slowed again. I wondered if we should turn around. *Just five more steps, and then if I don't see anything, we'll turn back.* We were too weak to waste any unnecessary physical effort. At three steps, I reached the top of the incline, and then I saw it, a few yards away. I wanted to turn around and high-five Alex, do a little victory dance. But instead, I took off running, the inner tube awkwardly bumping into my side, until I reached it.

A stream. A beautiful, bubbling stream.

I dropped to my knees on the rocks next to the crystal-clear water. I cupped my hands and dipped them in, then pulled them up to my mouth. The water tasted amazing, better than iced tea on the hottest summer day, or steaming chai on the coldest winter day. I kept drinking and drinking and drinking.

Alex dropped her tote bag to the ground next to me. It took her a moment to settle herself onto the rocks—she winced as her shins pressed against the stone, and I sneaked a glance at the backs of her legs, which looked truly awful. Dots of dried blood covered them, overlapping with the fiery, oozing rash and big, threatening blisters. There were also a couple of strange dark spots on her calves. And her filthy feet were covered in scratches and sores.

She didn't dip her hands into the water but stuck her whole face into the stream, like she was bobbing for apples. That was actually not a bad idea. I took a deep breath, squeezed my eyes shut, and plunged my face into the water. It felt so clean and refreshing, and the coldness made my skin tingle, like the first time I tried Noxzema, which Lucy swears by for dealing with zits. I opened my mouth and took another big gulp before pulling my head out of the stream.

I kept drinking until my stomach felt really full, like after-Thanksgiving-dinner full. Then I unzipped my backpack pocket and took out the water bottle. I dipped it into the water to fill it, then screwed the top back on tight. I arranged my backpack behind me so I could lean against it, like it was a bolster or a stadium chair. Then I peeled off the water shoes, wincing at the crusty red marks left behind wherever the stretchy elastic edge had been pressing into my puffy skin. My feet were a mess: bloody, dirty, swollen, aching. Finally, I plunged them into the freezing stream. I gasped, because even though the water felt amazing, the temperature was such a shock.

A few feet away, Alex had hiked up her towel skirt so she could do the same, although she put her legs in up to her knees. Something in between a smile and a grimace spread across her face. It was funny because it reminded me of the pool party and how slowly she'd dipped in one painted toe, then rethought the whole thing and stalked back to her lounge chair. Here, she plunged right in without a second thought.

She reminded me of the old Alex, whom I missed so badly I could feel my heart cramp.

Finding the stream was good for a lot of reasons, most obviously that we needed water to stay hydrated. It would also help us clean off our wounds and ease the pain in our feet. Plus, there might be food sources growing along it—like those Wolf River apple trees I'd read about. I don't know if apples would even be in season, but fall wasn't that far away, so even if we found a tree with unripe fruit, we might still be able to nibble on the pulp.

A stream flows toward something, usually downhill to a

larger stream or river, or maybe eventually a lake. We couldn't be that far away from the Wolf—however far we'd walked in about twelve hours of slow movement, minus any time we'd spent walking in a circle. So it was possible that this little stream would lead us back to the river. That would make it a lot easier to find our way home.

For the first time that day, the muscles in my shoulders relaxed and unknotted. My feet and calves were chilled, but the water felt too good to pull my legs out. I leaned farther into my backpack for support, then let myself close my eyes. The gurgling water was such a soothing sound—I could totally understand why my dad likes listening to that stuff. Already I could think more clearly, like my emotions weren't overtaking me. I peeked one eye open to glance at Alex, quiet next to me. She was draped over a large rock, her legs still plunged in the stream.

Five more minutes. Then we should start walking again, following the stream's flow. It would be so much easier to travel now that we had something to guide us, and I wouldn't have the responsibility of deciding which way to go. Also the trees were less dense alongside the stream. I shut my eyes again, not to nap but just to rest them.

At first, I thought that Alex had fallen asleep, and that she was whimpering while dreaming. She does that sometimes—it used to wake me up when we were having sleepovers. Once, Alex even started talking in her sleep, mumbles that I could barely make out, but I definitely heard "caterpillar" and "muffins" at least three times. So at first I ignored the whimpers next to me, until I felt Alex's ice-cold fingers on my arm.

I blinked open my eyes, and her face was centimeters from mine, her expression stricken. It surprised me that she was so close and even touching me. I opened my mouth to ask what was going on—even though it meant that I'd be the one to cave on the silent treatment—but Alex quickly brought her index finger to her swollen and cracked lips, signaling for me to stay quiet. I knew then that something was very wrong. But I was thinking, like, a skunk had wandered nearby.

Seeing she had my attention, Alex slowly outstretched her arm to point upstream. My gaze followed, and when I saw what she was gesturing toward I would've screamed, if Alex's glittery fingernails hadn't dug into my skin to remind me to stay quiet, stay calm.

We weren't drinking alone at the stream anymore. Our party had been crashed by a large black bear.

FOURTEEN

WHAT DO WE DO?" Alex hissed.

"Stay very still," I said, my voice barely a whisper. I didn't think the bear had noticed us yet. It stood half in the stream, half out—soaking its paws, just like we'd been—while happily lapping up the water. I watched as it took a step in our direction. Even though its muscles were covered by a thick coat of black-brown fur, I could see how they tensed and contracted. With only a small movement, it showed its power. I forced myself to glance away—what if the bear could somehow sense me staring, and then it would look downstream and see us?

There are lots of black bears in the Northwoods—the Department of Natural Resources website estimates twenty-eight thousand throughout Wisconsin—though I'd never seen one in the wild before. The closest I'd come is the carved wooden figurine of a big bear that sits in a neighboring cabin's yard—the first time we drove by it, I gasped and grabbed for my camera because I thought it was the real thing. I'd seen signs that bears were around Buttercup Lake, though—and not just the literal signs reminding people to secure their garbage cans so they don't attract scavengers. Sometimes there were paw prints in wet mud. Once, a neighbor described having to scare one away from an uncleaned barbecue grill.

Bears are actually shy, according to all the books and articles I've read. Most of the time, if they realize they've gotten near humans, they'll scamper away. The problem is when you startle them while they're close by. That's when they get defensive, and people can get hurt.

A weathered old Northwoods guidebook back at the cabin had covered all this. Most people encountering a bear have the impulse to scream and dash to safety. Not a great idea, as bears can outrun a human, and a startled bear might charge. The guidebook said that to avoid surprising a bear, you should make sure it knows humans are around while you're still a good, nonthreatening distance away. By talking, laughing, and waving your arms. Once a bear realizes it's gotten close to people, it'll usually scoot off to a quieter part of the forest. Then you can walk away too.

Alex and I needed to make noise and laugh and move around while the bear was still upstream. Before it got dangerously close.

"Do you remember the words to 'Down by the Banks'?" I whispered.

"Why are you asking me about a hand-clapping game?" Alex hissed back. "There is a huge bear. Right over there. It probably smelled all our blood." *Could Alex possibly be right about that?*

"We're about to die." Her fingers laced together, and I wondered if she was praying.

I shook my head no. "Only if it feels threatened by us. We have to make sure the bear knows we're here. Just play along." I took a deep breath, then clapped my hands to start the rhythm. "Down by the banks of the Hanky Panky," I sang. My voice wavered. I locked eyes with Alex and nodded at her as I kept clapping to the beat, a little louder. I forced a really fake laugh.

She glanced toward the bear, who still hadn't noticed us. Alex also took a deep breath, then unlaced her fingers to join me in clapping. "Where the bullfrogs jump from bank to banky." Her voice was unnaturally high and tight-sounding, and out of tune—but Alex has never been able to carry one. Not even the "Happy Birthday" song.

"With a hip, hop, hippity, hop." I raised my hand so she could high-five me. The smack echoed through the trees.

"Hip, hop, hippity, hop," she repeated in a warble.

"Leap off a lily pad and go kerplop!" we sang and sealed with the loudest clap yet, and then we fake-laughed in unison.

The bear, which had waded all the way into the stream, suddenly stopped. Its ears perked up. It sniffed at the air. The muscles in its legs tightened. I held my breath, hoping that it would turn and move away, upstream. But it didn't. Instead, it looked downstream, right at us.

My heart seemed to rise into my throat as the bear's dark

eyes now locked with mine. *Okay, now it knows we're here. It'll leave. Any second now...*

The bear stayed in the same position, watching us, with its nostrils flaring.

"Next verse?" I said to Alex. We clapped another high five. The bear watched us. It opened its mouth, wide like a yawn. But I don't think it was bored or tired. I think it wanted to show us its huge, sharp teeth.

"I don't think this is working," Alex hissed in between lines of the song.

What else are we supposed to do? My pulse pounded in my head so hard that it was becoming impossible to focus.

"I'm going to make a run for it," Alex whispered, still next to me. "I'm not going to sit here like a little mouse, waiting to be eaten."

"No!" I grabbed her arm. "It'll run after you. Unless we convince it we're nothing like little mice." I paused. *That* was what I'd been trying to remember. "We need the bear to think we're bigger than it is. That we're the alphas here."

I looked around frantically. Behind us, the life vest lay on top of the unrolled inner tube. I grabbed the vest first, arranging it around my head like the weirdest crown you've ever seen. The inner tube I held up and sort of behind me, almost like it was a cape or wings. Then I slowly stood tall. With all that stuff on me, I must have looked a lot bigger. Hopefully in an imposing way, not just a ridiculous one.

You're supposed to speak calmly but loudly to a bear. You aren't supposed to show any fear. I don't know if they can smell blood from far away, but they definitely can sense fear up close. Then they know you're the beta, or worse: prey.

"Hi, Bear," I called to it, trying my hardest to sound relaxed, almost cheerful. "We are big, strong humans over here. Total alpha females. Just doing our thing."

I had hoped that the bear would suddenly turn and scamper through the trees. Instead, it rose to stand on its hind legs. It wasn't snarling at us or anything aggressive, though. Maybe it was curious? I really wished I'd done a TAG project on bear behavior.

I stood there long enough for my arms to burn from holding up the inner tube. I was now in the middle of a staring contest with a bear. *Okay, so what do you do if making yourself appear bigger doesn't immediately scare the bear away?* We were at an impasse...until the bear opened its mouth, let out a loud grunt, and took one slow, deliberate step in our direction.

"Oh no oh no oh no oh no." Alex whimpered next to me.

"Stay calm, stay calm, stay calm, stay calm," I whispered back. I raised my arms higher, even though my biceps ached. "Do you have all your stuff?" Alex shook her head. "Grab all your stuff. Our stuff," I added because my water shoes were still sitting on a rock near Alex's flip-flops and tote bag.

Alex frantically tossed the shoes into her bag and slung it over her shoulder.

I spoke quietly out of the side of my mouth. "Okay, I'm going to keep talking to the bear. You're going to stay behind me, and we're both going to walk backward downstream, slowly. And calmly." I didn't think we should dash for the woods, where we might not be able to monitor where the bear was in relation to us, and where it would be impossible to escape quickly because of the overgrown trees.

Alex became my shadow, standing so close behind me that I could still smell her mango body spray, mixed with her sweat. "Ready?" I asked.

"Ready," she replied.

"Okay, Bear, we're going to mosey on our way now. Enjoy your drink," I said, my voice sounding firm but friendly, like a kindergarten teacher's. "Don't mind us." I took two tentative steps backward, which was tricky with the flowing water and the slippery rocks below the stream's surface.

"Can you spot me?" I asked Alex.

"Uh-huh. Actually, I'll lead," she said.

"Good idea." She grabbed a fistful of my sweatshirt and gently tugged me along to follow her. The water splashed around our calves and up to our knees. My towel skirt was heavy from the bottom half being soaked. I felt the knot starting to unravel, but I couldn't lower my hands to grab it. The towel dropped into the water with a splash.

"Got it," Alex said, reaching her free hand to scoop it up.

The bear was still on its hind legs, watching us intently.

"See, Bear? We're not bothering you. You can go back to whatever you were doing. Taking a bath. Fishing. Having happy hour. It's kind of hard to tell."

Alex tugged me downstream again. My toes gripped the rocks and pebbles on the bottom of the stream. I wanted to lower the tube so badly. My arms were shaking, hard.

The bear made one last grunt, almost sounding exasperated. Then it lowered onto all fours. *Please let us go*, I begged. I held my breath, wondering if it was about to charge us.

Instead, the bear dipped its snout back into the stream for a drink. It wasn't even looking at me anymore.

It had worked.

We still needed to get out of the bear's sight, though. "Walk faster," I instructed Alex. She pulled me along. My eyes stayed glued on the bear. I could keep holding up the tube for maybe a minute longer before my arms would drop.

The stream curved to the left as it sloped downhill, and once we finished the turn, the bear disappeared from view. My arms tumbled down like strings that had been cut on a marionette. The inner tube made a big splash as it hit the surface of the water, soaking me. "Go, go, go!" I urged Alex, turning to face the same way. I grabbed the tube, and we began running, even though we were still in the stream. We made it only a few feet before Alex tripped and fell.

I whirled around to pull her up by her armpits. Her tote bag was mostly right-side-up, but it was all wet.

"Are you okay?" I asked, glancing back nervously to see if the bear had followed us downstream.

"Yeah, I think so—there was a branch or something underwater." She wiped her hair off her face, and I helped her resettle the tote bag on her hip.

"Maybe it's safe to go back to the shore now. I don't see the bear anywhere."

"Should we walk on the other side?" Alex pointed across the stream. "Because the bear came from the one we were on."

"Good idea."

We waded over and climbed onto the rocks. I checked one last time for the bear, craning my neck to see as far upstream as possible. It was gone, somewhere into the forest. We were safe. At least, for now.

FIFTEEN

FOR A FEW MOMENTS, we sat in silence on the rocks, like we had before the bear showed up, except this time without our feet and legs dangling in the water. Instead, we both had our knees tucked up to our chests, like we were giving ourselves hugs. We were shivering because the sun had disappeared under thick, gray clouds, and we were soaking wet again, and it wasn't as warm as it had been the day before, even when the sun did peek out. Last night's storm must have been part of a cold front—an early sign that fall was on its way. But I think we were also shivering from the adrenaline leaving our systems. We'd just escaped a *bear*, after all.

I started to laugh. Everything was so ridiculous and scary and strange, and laughing seemed like the only reasonable thing to do while sitting on rocks and logs, staring at your bug-bitten and battered limbs, lost in a national forest with your ex-best friend. Then I couldn't stop laughing.

Which confused Alex. "What's so funny?"

In between breathless giggles, I managed to choke out,

"Just...everything. Like, I was wearing a life-vest crown and an inner tube. To scare away a bear. By clapping and singing. And it worked! What is going *on*?"

Alex's furrowed brows slowly smoothed, and her mouth curled into a tiny smile. Well, as much as her swollen lips could smile. Then she started laughing too. "Now *that* was a fashion mistake."

That only made me laugh harder. Tears streamed down my face, and I'm not sure they were only from how hard I was laughing. I cried from relief too. Because we were being real with each other, and things felt natural for the first time on this trip. No, for the first time since Alex had come home from camp. Because if Alex was sort of making a joke about my sweatshirt, then maybe said sweatshirt wasn't going to totally destroy us. Maybe all this—getting lost in the woods and getting friend-dumped before we got there—was something we were going to be able to laugh at. Together.

As we shook with laughter, we leaned closer to each other till our shoulders touched, and then all of a sudden, we were hugging. It didn't feel casual and normal like it used to, when in every photo of us together our arms were slung around each other's shoulders and our faces pressed close and often one of us was secretly giving bunny ears to the other. This hug felt tentative and stiff, strangely polite, and it was short-lived. But we both really, really needed it.

"I'm so glad we didn't die," Alex said. "Thanks for making that not happen."

"It was a joint effort." I really meant that. I cleared my throat and wiped the lingering tears from my eyes. My stomach muscles were so tight from all the laughter that they felt like they might snap if I took too deep a breath. And somehow I still felt full, even though we hadn't eaten anything since the meager bites of bar for breakfast. Maybe it was from drinking all that stream water.

"So what do we do now?" Alex asked. She was rubbing her belly, like hers also hurt.

"Keep walking?" I said. "Alongside the stream, because if we're lucky, it could be a tributary to the Wolf River." She gave me a confused look. "*Tributary* means the water flows into a bigger body of water, like a stream into a river into an ocean. Anyway, if that's the case, we could follow the stream to the river, which would lead us to somewhere with people. Maybe to our families looking for us." It was possible they'd never figured out that we were far from the Wolf. We hadn't left much of a trace when we headed into the forest. The only clues they could've found were the things we'd lost in the river: Alex's life vest and my binoculars. That was worrying, both because of what they might think had happened to us—drowning—and because it meant search efforts perhaps hadn't moved deep into the Nicolet. If we wanted to be rescued, getting close to the river was key.

I tried not to think about how terrified and sad our families must be, especially if they thought we'd been lost in the water.

"Sounds good." Alex reached over for her tote bag and pulled out my water shoes. "Here you go." She tossed them to me, then pulled out one of her flip-flops.

I glanced down at my feet. My heels were no longer caked in mud, thanks to the stream, but they actually looked worse clean—bloody and raw. I couldn't walk through the forest without something protecting the soles of my feet, but the thought of the water shoes pressing against my open wounds was unbearable. I dipped the shoes in the stream, to at least loosen them up before squeezing my feet back inside.

"Um, I think we have a problem." Alex was frantically searching the tote bag.

My stomach twisted. "What kind of problem?"

"I can't find my other flip-flop."

Oh no. "Were you wearing it in the stream?"

She shook her head. "I took them off while we were resting. I tossed all the shoes into my bag when we escaped from the bear." She smoothed her hands through her hair like she always does when she's nervous—or as much as she could, considering how sticky her hair was with pine pitch. "I was kind of freaking out, though. Maybe I missed one sandal. Or it could have fallen into the stream when I tripped."

"Are you sure it's not in there?" I asked.

"Pretty positive." She pulled out her body spray and the wet magazine and swiped her hand around the bottom of the bag. "Definitely not in here."

Backtracking in the direction of the bear to find the missing flip-flop seemed like a really bad idea. "We can't go back for it."

Alex nodded in agreement, but she still looked worried. "Guess I'll have to walk barefoot…"

I shook my head no while pulling the water shoes off my feet. "Take mine."

"Are you serious?" She hesitated to accept them.

I nodded. "I can't wear them anyway—the backs of my heels are too cut up. So the shoes hurt like crazy. Because your feet are smaller than mine, they might actually fit you after they dry."

"Jeez, are all your clothes too small now?" she said with a laugh.

I was quiet for a moment. Then I blurted, "We didn't have a budget for new summer clothes this year. That's why I'm always wearing old stuff."

Alex's face blanched. "I'm really sorry. I had no idea."

I didn't feel very bad about it—clothes aren't that important to me. And anyway, because things were looking up with Dad's new gig, Nolan and I would have a little money for back-to-school shopping. "It's fine—you didn't know."

"I wouldn't have always suggested shopping if I had," Alex insisted.

I could tell she felt bad.

"Thanks, but I didn't take that personally. You love shopping—and that's okay."

She nodded, and we smiled at each other, almost shyly.

When Alex slid her feet into the shoes, they were a Cinderella-perfect fit. "Well, you can use my one surviving flip-flop." She tossed it to me, and I worked my right foot into it. We both stared at my bare left foot and its raw, blistered heel.

"Wait." Alex stood to unravel the towel from around her torso. Laura's cover-up, still wet, clung to her legs. She took a deep breath, then grabbed the section that already had the tear in the beading. Before I figured out what she was planning to do, she yanked her hands away from each other with a huge rip of the fabric.

"Alex?" I gaped at her. She'd made a pretty clean tear and was now holding a long strip of the material, which was similar to gauze. She balled it up and tossed it to me.

"Use that to wrap your foot, like a bootie. So at least it won't be bare."

I held the wad of fabric in my hands, shocked by her generosity. And feeling a smidge guilty about how satisfying it had been earlier to rip the cover-up, under less dire circumstances. "Isn't Laura going to be kind of mad—"

"It's stained and torn, so whatever. And I think she'll understand." Alex paused. "I mean, if we die in these woods, it's not like Laura's going to get it back, anyway." Her words hit me like a mallet.

"Thanks." I got to work, wrapping the gauze all around my foot, taking special care to cover the wound on my heel. I tied the bootie off with a firm knot, then took a practice step. It felt weird, like walking around with balled-up tights stuck to the bottom of your foot. But it was better than going barefoot.

"Are we ready?" I asked, bending to pick up the tube and then adjusting my backpack.

"We're ready," Alex said.

Walking alongside the stream was tricky because of all the rocks, which were slick with lichen (or was it moss?) and sometimes hidden beneath fallen leaves and brush. Also, the bugs had come back with a vengeance—mostly gnats and blackflies, which apparently also hang out by streams. Maybe also they were attracted by our scent, which was...pungent. Even though we'd been in and out of the stream, the dirt, sweat, natural body smells, and lingering mango spray were commingling into the kind of scent that normally does not exist outside of a locker room.

We'd been out of the stream for a while, but my hair refused to dry. Same with my sweatshirt, swimsuit, shorts, and towel skirt. The air was much cooler than the day before, and I longed for the sun to sneak out from the clouds and warm us. My fingers were pale and wrinkled, and I had a shiver that would not quit, no matter how fast we moved. Although we weren't moving very fast. After all the bear-encounter adrenaline faded, I felt more tired than I ever had in my life. Even more tired than the time Alex and I had stayed up all night during a sleepover, marathoning every season of our favorite baking-competition show, with only pee breaks in between. The next day I'd gone with my mom as she did errands, and while we were waiting in a long line at the bank, I'd actually fallen asleep standing up.

I felt like that now—groggy and a little disoriented. Sometimes I couldn't tell if the trees were swaying or if I was. Everything had a bit of a haze on it, the fuzzy look of old family photos people took before digital cameras—or the apps people use now to make their smartphone pictures look old-timey. My thoughts started to drift with the cedar-tipped breeze.

Maybe it was also the fact that Alex was wearing my water shoes, and I was wearing one flip-flop and a cover-up-fabric bootie, but we both seemed clumsier. At one point, Alex tripped on a log that was obviously right in front of her. I stepped on a flat stone, and although it wobbled only slightly, it sent me tumbling to my hands and knees, into a cluster of ferns.

"Ow!"

"Are you okay?" Alex turned slowly to check on me. Even her voice was slow; it sounded like she was pouring the words out the way you wait for syrup to drip from a bottle.

"Yeah, just unbalanced or something." Maybe it was because we were so cold—and so hungry. Moments passed, and I still hadn't stood back up. I wasn't sure I could. I really wanted to lie down flat, press my cheek onto the ground—even with all the dirt and sticks and leaves and grubs and webs—and take a long nap.

Alex melted to a seat next to me. "So let's just take a li'l rest for a minute."

"That sounds good," I murmured. Alex leaned against a tree trunk. I rested my head on a bed of ferns and needles, looking up at her. I watched Alex's eyelids start to flutter, and I don't remember anything after that.

SIXTEEN

I WOKE TO THE SOUND and vibration of my teeth chattering. My cheek still pressed against the forest floor; I could feel the prickly imprint of pine needles. I blinked my eyes open, expecting Alex next to me. But she wasn't leaning against the tree trunk anymore. I had no clue as to how long I'd been asleep, except it was still daytime. The sun had lowered a lot, though, and it was already dim in the forest.

"Alex?" My voice was rough and hoarse. I shifted and realized my stomach still had a strange, stabby, too-full feeling, despite us not having eaten anything lately. I winced and rose to my knees. "Alex?"

Then I heard her, off to my right. Throwing up. "Alex!" I staggered to standing and hobbled in her direction. She crouched on her hands and knees, a few feet away from the edge of the stream. I dropped down next to her and, instinctively, put my hand on her upper back. I could feel her shaking and shivering. "It's okay," I said, because I could tell that she was not. Her shoulders tensed, and I knew what was coming next. I pulled her matted and burr-strewn hair back, holding it in a gentle ponytail. I squeezed my eyes shut as she vomited again. With my free hand, I rubbed her back, like my mom always does when I'm sick, and made a comforting shushing noise. "It's okay," I repeated.

After that, she dry-heaved twice. When it seemed it was all over, she sat back on her heels, like she was doing child's pose in a yoga class.

"What happened?" I asked.

"My stomach," she moaned. "All I threw up was water."

Not surprising—there was nothing else in our stomachs to throw up. "Did you have *anything* to eat?" I was worried about what had made her sick and whether it would make me sick too. When the energy bar got hot and melty, had it gone bad? I pressed my hand to my stomach, which still felt off. It also could have been from drinking too much too fast, or from contaminated stream water...

"Only a nibble," she said very quietly.

"Of what?!"

She shrugged, then winced. "A mushroom. I couldn't help myself. You know I love mushroom pizza the most." She looked like she was going to start crying. "It was that or I was going to try to eat my body spray."

That probably would've been safer. But telling Alex that wouldn't help now. Neither would getting mad. "Hopefully you got it all out of your system," I said. "You'll be fine." But I didn't know that. She might've poisoned herself. "Do you think you can walk?"

Alex wiped her mouth with the back of her hand. Her whole body was speckled with bug bites, welts, and the rash—her skin was crusted with traces of blood. Her bloodshot eyes looked glazed. She nodded and attempted to stand up, wobbling.

"Careful!" I reached for her elbow to keep her steady. Then my stomach churned. I was really surprised that I hadn't thrown up too. Normally the sight or sound of anyone else vomiting makes me feel like I'm about to do the same.

We started off again. I had Alex walk next to me or slightly ahead, in case she was going to faint or something. If Alex passed out behind me, I might not notice until I was too far away to run back and find her. My head felt kind of spinny, like I was on the merry-go-round they used to have at the playground before it got removed for being too dangerous. It felt like my brain had been replaced by cotton balls. At least we had a stream to follow, because otherwise I had no idea which way to go.

"I'm still sleepy," Alex mumbled next to me. Her syllables blended into one another in a funny way—like when people are slurring in movies or on TV.

Sleepiness after waking up from our accidental late-afternoon nap—the second of the day—wasn't a great sign. "You didn't eat any other plants, did you?" I asked, listening closely to my own voice, to see if it sounded weird like hers.

"What? No. I wish." Alex was irritated again, but only because she narrowly missed tripping on a tangled root. "I'm still sleepy."

"You just said that," I muttered. It was kind of hard to get out the right words. My mouth was numb from the cold.

We kept bumping into each other, mumbling apologies at first, eventually giving up. My feet and fingertips ached like in wintertime. I didn't realize for several steps that my towel-skirt had fallen off again, till Alex stopped, scratched furiously at her arm, and then pointed at it crumpled on the forest floor behind us. "Your..." She paused, frowning while she thought. Hard. Finally her eyes flickered. "*Towel.*" She hadn't remembered what it was called.

I shuffled back to grab it, noticing on the way that there were strange dark spots on my legs, too. I bent, swaying from the dizziness of changing position, for a closer look. I ran my wrinkled, pruney fingertip over my calf, where one spot was. It felt like a bump. I bent even closer, despite the pounding blood inside my head.

"Oh no, I think I have a tick." The Northwoods are full of them—that's why long pants, tucked into socks, and plenty of bug spray are necessary while hiking. My mom even has a special scarf that was treated with permethrin, a repellant that lasts through many washes. She wraps it around her head to drive the bugs away when she's out in the garden.

That's when I realized the half-dozen dark spots on my legs were not scabs from bug bites or flecks of dirt. They were ticks, and they were literally eating me alive. I clutched at my stomach, the queasiness suddenly back and even stronger.

Get them off me. But you need tweezers to get rid of ticks—you can't just brush them away. They latch on tight.

"What's-going-on?"

The way Alex said it, it sounded like one long, sloppy compound word.

"I have a tick. A lot of ticks." I picked up the towel and shook it out, although I was too weak to make it snap. I didn't want to put it back around myself—I was afraid of what else might crawl up my legs to hide underneath it.

"Oh gross," Alex said.

I decided not to tell her that the spots on her ankles and forearm were also probably ticks, and who knows what was under her towel.

"You can't get them off without tweezers," I said, shuddering.

"Then you're in luck." Alex struggled to pull her tote bag in front of herself so she could dig around in it. "Ta-da." She held out a small hot-pink pouch. It was strange to see it in the forest, something so bright and plastic and unnatural. Everything around us was muted, organic, able to camouflage.

She tossed it to me, and I caught it but then immediately fumbled and dropped it to the ground. When I picked it up and unzipped it, I found a nail kit inside: clippers, clear polish, file, and a tiny tweezers. "Sweet."

"Always be prepared or whatever," Alex mumbled, with an attempt at a grin, but it looked more like a grimace.

I sat down on a smooth green log and moved the tweezers to one of the black spots. I'd seen my mom and dad remove ticks before, after gardening or hiking. The trick is you put the tweezers as close to your skin as you can get, and when you pull up, you make sure not to twist or jerk too much or you might break the tick while it still has its parts stuck in you. I shivered, whether from being cold or from the absolute grossness of what I was trying to do, I don't know. Probably both.

With a deep sigh, I yanked up with the tweezers. *Got it.* I found the next spot.

"Should we, like, keep walking?" Alex slumped on an adjacent log, still watching me, although her eyelids looked dangerously heavy.

The sun was sinking fast—it was definitely late in the afternoon. Alex was right. As horrifying as it was to walk around with parasitic bugs clinging to your legs and literally sucking your blood—and as dangerous as ticks were, in terms of stuff like Lyme disease—we couldn't afford to waste daylight. Once darkness fell, we'd have to face another night in the forest.

"I guess you're right," I said, putting the tweezers back in the case and zipping it up. I placed it back in Alex's tote bag, and then I shouldered my backpack, wincing as it touched me. I felt worse than the day after I'd gone on a rock-climbing trip to Devil's Lake State Park, which had been really awesome, but apparently I'd used all sorts of muscles that don't normally do much in my daily activities. The morning after climbing, my hip and butt muscles had been so tight that I could barely walk down the stairs to breakfast. After a day and a half in the forest, so cold and damp, everything from my pinkie finger to my jaw to the bottoms of my feet throbbed and twinged.

Alex stood with a groan. We stumbled through the trees again. I put all my energy into focusing on one foot in front of the other. Each step took everything I had.

The trees cast shadows on the forest floor—ones that confused us at times, when we mistook those shadows for branches and logs we needed to step over or around—and I started to have this strange sensation that we were being watched. That something was in the woods with us, at a distance. I'd stop momentarily and look around, thinking that maybe I'd seen a flash of brown or gray. Maybe it was a stealthy deer. Or a fast-moving squirrel. I wondered, though, if it might be a wolf. They were in these woods, somewhere. At the ranger station in Lakewood last year, they'd said wolf packs lived at Archibald Lake and Ada Lake. Both weren't far from where we'd started tubing. It had been my great hope that while we were on the river, I'd see a wolf. Now that we were lost—trapped—in the forest, it seemed only fair that I'd at least get my sighting out of it.

At points, the promise of a wolf was the only thing keeping

me walking. As much as I longed to find the river and a way back to our families, back to the cozy cabin alongside the starlit lake, it was starting to feel like that was never going to happen. Like we were in a new reality where those things didn't even exist anymore; only the forest around us did. The closer the sun dropped to the horizon, the more my hope of walking out of the woods faded with the light.

"Ow!"

Alex's shout startled me because neither of us had made a sound in the last half hour or so, other than the crunch of our footsteps.

She'd tripped on a root. Alex sprawled on the ground, her tote bag lying on its side. I dropped to my knees to gather her stuff. "Are you okay?"

She raised her palm, which held a fresh red trickle. "Sliced my hand."

I winced. "Ouch."

She stared at the blood like she was being hypnotized. "Is it going to attract the bear?"

"No," I said, although I'd shared the same initial worry. I grabbed her elbow to guide her back up. Alex wavered once we were both standing. I was wobbling too. Were those fireflies around us? I blinked again, only to realize that they were spots in my vision, from standing up too fast. Or maybe from not drinking enough water. I wanted a drink so badly. But I didn't think we should have any more stream water—including what was left in my bottle—because we didn't know if it had made Alex so sick and my stomach so stabby.

When I looked back down to the ground, I couldn't see well enough to distinguish the shadows from twigs and rocks. If we kept walking, we would trip and fall every few feet. It was too dim. "Let's stop for the night."

Alex let out a soft groan. I understood. We were going to be spending another overnight in the forest. Without food, without a real shelter, without proper clothes to keep us warm. Without drinking water, unless we actually started licking it off leaves.

We picked a random spot a short distance from the stream. I unrolled the tube and placed our bags next to it. Then we shook out our towels. My fingers were so numb it was hard to curl them around the fabric for a good grip. I could barely lift my arms high enough to flap off the needles and leaves. I struggled to pick off the burrs clinging to the tiny loops of terrycloth fabric. Eventually, I gave up. We silently crumpled to the inner tube.

Somehow the plastic was still damp, and it felt so cold against our bare skin. But kind of good on all the bug bites and scratches and welts—almost like an ice pack on a bruise. I'm sure we had plenty of those too. Alex and I lay side by side. Our heads rested on the life vest atop the dry bag. I stared up at the tree canopy, dark branches stark against the periwinkle twilight. Occasionally a bat flitted across the patch of open sky, and I debated whether I should protect my head with my towel, before deciding it was more important to keep it covering my body. I tried to ignore the hollow pangs in my stomach, the sharp aches in my legs and back, and the panic in my head, at the thought of another night spent like this. Cold. Defenseless. Hungry. Bleeding. Sick.

Lost.

SEVENTEEN

VEN IN MADISON, NIGHT only gets so dark. It's not a big city, like Chicago or New York, but it's big enough that there's plenty of ambient light. In summertime, during the Perseid meteor shower—which happens every August—you might be able to see a few shooting stars in the backyard or if you walk deep into the arboretum. You'd need to drive into the country, twenty minutes along Highway 12 or something, to really see the night sky and enjoy the show. Up north, night is deep-dark everywhere—the stars shine bright, especially against the mirrorlike surface of Buttercup Lake. When the water is still, you can stargaze without even looking up. Until a loon passes by, leaving a ripple.

The darkness in the forest that night was like nothing I'd ever experienced. It spread through the trees, shrouding everything in velvety blackness. The afternoon's puffy rows of clouds had never faded but grown thicker. I couldn't look to the constellations for comfort; the clouds tucked away all the starlight and even the moon. This was a darkness so intense, you could almost touch it, feel it. I imagined it having the same texture as the sea-foam candy my grandma used to make for Christmas—light but still solid.

The nighttime chill seeped into my bones. So frozen and numb, I didn't think I could move, not even if something jumped out of the trees and onto us. *Bobcats are nocturnal.* I worried about every crackle, every crunch, every whisper of the breeze, every...howl?

Not close to us, but somewhere in the not-too-far distance, howls carried softly but clearly through the trees. I managed to raise myself onto my elbows to listen, which shifted the towel that was covering me like a blanket. Next to me, Alex stirred.

"What is it?" she whispered. Her voice still sounded strange, soft and thick. "Oh my God, is that a wolf?"

"Shh." I shushed her both because I wanted to listen and also because I was kind of afraid of making our own noise, afraid of what it could attract in the forest at night. "Um, I think so," I whispered back. It didn't sound like a coyote. They bark and yip. Wolf howls are long and drawn out, like a song.

I know I'd been hoping to see a wolf. But the thumping in my chest was from fear more than excitement. I didn't want to encounter one like this, at night when I couldn't actually see it, and while we were lying on the ground, half conscious, and so totally vulnerable. Like a pair of sleeping baby bunnies. You can't blame an animal for acting on its instincts. And if it mistook us for prey...

Alex curled toward me and tucked her head underneath her towel. She was shivering as hard as the swimsuit-dryer machine shakes at the pool. I touched her shoulder. Like ice, even through her shredded cover-up.

I began shrugging out of my wolf sweatshirt, even though as each inch of my skin got exposed to the cold air, I had to fight the impulse to tug it back down and pull the fleecy fabric tight against my body. Once the sweatshirt was off, I lay down next to Alex and spread it equally over both our torsos. Alex snuggled toward me and mumbled what I think was a thank-you.

I was really happy we were back to being together.

The howling stopped. But there was another noise, a loud shuffling sound. Something moving through the forest. I held my breath, trying to decipher whether the something was coming toward us. It stopped, then started again. Stopped, then slowly faded away. I squeezed my eyes shut, afraid of seeing what it might be. Remembering those yellow eyes during the storm.

It was probably something small, like a raccoon. Or a possum. But I wondered—weren't bears nocturnal? Even if they aren't strictly active at nighttime, I know they root around in garbage—and pillage bird feeders—after dark, when there aren't humans to scare them away.

My heart beat faster. I curled closer to Alex. With my ear practically next to her lips, I could hear that she was muttering something in her sleep. *"Yesssss...doughnut. I wannanother doughnut. Mmm."* Then my stomach growled. It's not that I hadn't been starving before—hunger was a constant gnawing, twisting feeling. I understood why Alex had said she wanted to eat the mango body spray—by that point I would eat anything that remotely resembled food. It's just that other things, like movement sounds that could be bears or bobcats or even a transient mountain lion approaching our sad, slapdash not-really-a-shelter, made me sometimes forget that the hunger was there. But hearing the word *doughnut* seemed to activate the juices left in my stomach and brought the hunger roaring back so strong that it and food were the only things I could think about. I really would eat anything. I would eat meat, even though it goes against everything I believe in. I would eat caviar, even though the concept of fish eggs is extra disgusting to me. I would eat sweetbreads, which I'd once tried to order the single time Mom and Dad took Nolan and me to a fancy restaurant, when I saw it on the menu and assumed it was something like a cheese Danish or kringle—you know, a *bread* that is *sweet*. Dad had stopped me and explained that, no, sweetbreads are actually meat: the pancreas or thymus glands of a calf or a lamb. I was so shocked I dropped my fork onto the floor and almost knocked over my glass of water. I ended up ordering the one vegetarian option, which was a surprisingly delicious cauliflower "steak."

But I would, in all seriousness, eat sweetbreads right now. Anything the guy eats on that bizarre foods TV show: Hand it over. Gimme a fork. I was that desperately hungry. And the combo platter of hunger and the fear—of what was lurking around us, or what was happening to our cold and starved and dehydrated and tick-covered bodies, or what struggles we might face in the morning—made it really hard to fall asleep.

Next to me, Alex managed to rest, but fitfully. Every so often, she'd startle awake, let out a whimper, and then eventually her breathing would slow and settle, and she'd fall back into light sleep. I was kind of jealous that she was able to at all, but I also wondered if that was because she was worse off, physically, than I was.

Far away, I heard the howling again. I think. It's possible I might've been imagining it. I squeezed my eyes closed, even though there was barely a difference between having them open or shut. I couldn't see anything around me. It was too dark for my eyes to even adjust.

Suddenly, out of nowhere, Alex's right leg jerked and her ice-cube toes kicked my calf. I let out a muffled shriek.

Half awake, she flopped her hand over to pat my arm. "So sorry, accident," she mumbled.

"S'okay," I whispered back.

"Is it, though?" Alex said, still patting me.

"Huh?" Her voice had the same drowsy tone as earlier, and

I wasn't sure whether she was actually awake or still talking in her sleep.

"Like what I did...what I said...all that Laura stuff."

I was quiet next to her, just listening.

"Y'know, I didn't mean for things to get weird this summer."

She *was* awake.

I took the bait. "How exactly did that happen?"

Alex was quiet for so long, I thought she'd fallen back asleep. "We were in this tiny cabin together. The second I walked in, tired...homesick...Laura was super friendly. Then we were together, like, all the time. And kind of bonded? If it weren't for camp, we'd probably never be friends because she's so popular. But now we are." Alex yawned. "Funny how stuff works out. Thought that camp would ruin my summer."

"Yeah, I remember. Funny." It wasn't actually funny to me. But I was glad we were finally talking about it.

"Just wanted you to know," Alex mumbled as she pressed her face into the sweatshirt, which was mostly around her by then. "Not like I planned it. So I didn't really know how to deal. And I...feel bad. Just feel so, so bad."

A warm tear slid from the corner of my eye, and I quickly wiped it away. "Thanks," I finally said, my voice catching on the word. "I feel bad too. I didn't mean what I said; you're not dumb. I was just trying to say something that would...hurt. Because of how I've been hurting."

I'm not sure if Alex heard me or if she'd already drifted back to sleep. But her hand was still on my arm. I scooted closer because we needed to share body warmth. Last night, we'd slept far apart like parentheses. That night, we were double quotation marks.

EIGHTEEN

I T FELT LIKE A miracle that I ever fell asleep; even more of a miracle that I eventually woke up. I struggled to blink open my eyes—so swollen they were almost sealed shut, and the energy it took to lift my hand to wipe at them felt like the same level of effort the champions on those ninja-warrior TV shows have to use to scale a rock wall. My fingers were so puffy and numb, I fumbled in touching my own face.

The forest looked fuzzy, like someone had applied a filter with soft lighting, blurred edges, and a lot of haze. Apps should call it "fairy forest" or something like that. Everything seemed kind of dreamy, like I wasn't fully awake. I blinked hard, swearing that I saw something in the distance, a structure like a fire tower or a deer stand...but it was just another copse of pine trees. I pinched my arm—it was impossible to find a spot that wasn't already bruised, scratched, sunburned, or bitten—to make sure I wasn't dreaming. I felt the pinch, although maybe not as hard as I should've. All my senses were dulled.

Next to me, Alex lay on the tube, staring up at the sky. Her big brown eyes were wide and her mouth open—as much as her swollen, bleeding lips would allow. Burrs dotted her hair like they were barrettes. She stared without blinking, which was starting to freak me out.

"Are you okay?" The words came out in a whisper-croak, and forcing my mouth to form them felt like stabbing my throat with a sharpened pencil. I rubbed my neck and winced. The skin was sunburned, like everywhere on my body.

It seemed exceptionally cruel to be both freezing cold and also sunburned.

"Alex?" I croaked again. *Is she...* I swallowed hard, which stung.

Then she blinked and focused her gaze on me, or at least she tried to. Her eyes couldn't quite fix on me or anything else as she stared off in the distance like she'd been mesmerized. "Yeah?" Her voice had the same rasp as mine.

"Is morning," I said, then cleared my throat. "It is."

"Yeah," she said again.

"We should start walking," I said, even though the thought of standing up and moving around seemed impossible.

"Yeah." Her eyelids began to flutter, like she was falling back asleep.

"C'mon." I rolled to my side and willed myself to sit. It took three tries. The headache once I forced myself up was really bad; a pounding inside my skull like the thudding footsteps when Nolan and his friends play tag in the attic space above my bedroom in Madison. Times one thousand.

Slowly I began to shrug on my backpack while looking around. There was nothing else to gather; all my stuff was still in my pack. I just had to roll the tube and tie my towel around my waist. With my arms bare—Alex was still snuggled beneath the sweatshirt—I could see that they too were covered in bites, bloody welts, and a few more ticks. *Disgusting.* I avoided looking at my legs.

I stood up in stages, like when you roll up slowly in a yoga exercise, one vertebra at a time, bringing your head up last. I kept my eyes squeezed shut for a few moments, to avoid the dimming head rush I knew I'd get otherwise. When I finally opened them, Alex had managed to work herself into a cross-legged seat on the tube. Even though she was convulsing with shivers, she held out my sweatshirt to me.

"You can wear it," I offered.

"You're shivering too," she mumbled.

"We'll take turns," I said, before I took the sweatshirt from her and threw it on. I hadn't fully realized how frozen I was till the fleecy lining blanketed my skin.

When Lucy started driver's ed last year, she told us that the weirdest part was when they brought in "intoxication goggles," these science-lab safety goggles modified so they apparently show what it feels and looks like to be impaired by drugs or alcohol. Everyone in Lucy's class had to try them on, then walk from the back of the room to the whiteboard, stumbling and disoriented. She said when you had the goggles on, everything was blurry and warped and kind of like if you'd wiped hand lotion across your sunglass lens by accident. Not fun.

It felt like we were walking through the forest while wearing those goggles. I was light-headed and dizzy, and it was hard to follow the path of the stream, even when there wasn't much stuff in our way. And it was still cold, even if the sun shined brighter than the day before. I wanted to hug my arms across my chest, for warmth, but the only way I could do that would be to abandon the tube. *Do we really need it at this point?* I kept it, though, because if I'd already dragged it this far...plus the whole littering thing.

We'd stopped to rest on some large rocks when I spotted the green bushes only a few feet away. The berries hanging down were plump and a dusty deep blue, just like the blueberries I'd picked in the wild before when Nolan and I were visiting my grandma, who loves to go berry picking.

My stomach growled louder than a bear. I stumbled over to the bushes. The hunger in my belly grew stronger with every step. Seeing food—at least what I thought was food—was unbearable. I reached out my hand and plucked a fat berry from the bush. I rubbed the bloom off to inspect it more closely. Identical to the blueberries Mom buys in the cartons from the grocery store. It couldn't hurt to try one—even if I were wrong and it was poisonous, could one toxic berry kill me?

I mean, starvation could also kill me.

I took a deep breath, then popped it into my mouth. I bit down and blueberry flavor, full of overwhelming sweetness, exploded across my tongue. It tasted better than anything I've ever eaten in my life. I grabbed another, and another. "Alex," I croaked. "I found food."

She was next to me in seconds, grabbing at the bush. August is the tail end of blueberry season, so these were late bloomers, and the bush wasn't very full. We got only a handful each before we'd picked it bare. "Maybe there's another bush?" I wondered out loud.

Alex and I began wandering the immediate area, trying to find more. "Here!" she called after a few minutes. The second bush had even fewer berries dangling from its leaves.

"Don't eat too fast," I said. "Or you might get sick again."

"So hard not to," Alex murmured.

"We can pick off the berries, put them in the dry bag. Ration them, for the rest of the day." It was amazing how much easier it was to think with a quarter of a cup of berries in my belly.

We cleaned the bush of all the fruit, and then Alex carefully tucked the berry bag into her tote. We continued walking, with our heads slightly clearer. At least mine was. Alex, next to me, was awfully quiet. Except for her raspy breathing.

"Are you feeling okay?" A couple of flies circled her, and she wasn't even trying to swat them.

"So cold, so tired," she mumbled. "Can we go inside the house now?"

My stomach tightened, and it wasn't from eating the berries. "There's no house, Alex." I paused. "You know that, right?"

"Isn't that a house over there?" She limply pointed at a rock formation, the opposite direction from the stream.

"No, that's not a house." There are plenty of reasons why someone in our situation might develop confusion: dehydration, hunger, sleep deprivation, anxiety. But the one that worried me the most was hypothermia. I saw a science video about that once, and it was harrowing what hypothermia does to a person. It can even make you hallucinate, in later stages. I watched Alex closely to see if she was still shivering. When a very cold person stops shivering, that's actually a really bad sign—it means their body has quit trying to regulate temperature. Alex was perfectly still. So maybe she was hypothermic and hallucinating a house.

"Why don't you wear the sweatshirt for a while?" I pulled it over my head and helped her work her arms into it.

It was still funny, considering everything, to see her wearing the label "Lupine Lover."

"This is the best sweatshirt in the world," Alex muttered, and that's when I knew she was really in tough shape.

As we kept walking, the stream was fading to a trickle, going from a width we could cover in three big steps to one that we could hop across. Which made me doubt it was going to lead us to a larger body of water, like the Wolf River or a nearby lake. The stream seemed about to peter out in the forest. When that happened, we'd be without a plan again. And it's not like it was a trustworthy source of drinking water. We really were going to have to start licking leaves for their moisture. But what if we licked the wrong ones, like poison sumac...

"So, the stream is drying up," I said to Alex. "We have no idea if it's going to lead us to the river. I think we should go back to heading in the direction of the sun."

"Whatever you decide," she mumbled, dropping her tote bag to the ground while I stared up at the sky, plotting our next move. But I didn't know which was best. Follow the sun, or follow the stream? I was too exhausted to make a decision.

Something flashed into and out of my peripheral vision. I sucked in my breath, thinking about that bear. But when I squinted toward the movement, I didn't see anything but trees, endless trees. *The sunlight's playing tricks again.*

My stomach was back to aching. Whatever sustenance the berries had provided was fading, fast. I glanced at Alex. She wavered with the breeze. As I turned to look forward, my head spun. Then I glimpsed that flash of movement again. *I think that is an animal. Probably a squirrel. Or a deer.* I was surprised we hadn't seen more white-tailed deer in the forest. They're almost as common as mosquitoes up north.

I turned my head slowly, tracking the movement. Then I saw it. I couldn't believe my eyes.

A wolf.

It had stopped suddenly, its front left leg poised in a bend, and its head turned to stare at me. It wasn't gray, actually. Its fur was a beautiful blend of colors: downy white, soft nutmeg brown, and gray tipped with silver. Its ears were perked up, and its amber eyes watched us intently.

I held my breath as I stared, afraid that any movement from me—even a tiny exhalation—would send it running away. I let myself blink, hard, in case I was imagining it. If Alex was hallucinating, I could be too.

"Alex," I whispered to her. "Do you see that?" My heartbeat pounded inside my ears.

"See what?" She swiveled in my direction.

"The wolf." Afraid to point, I nodded at it.

"No?" she answered groggily, then squinted as she took a step toward me, cracking a stick beneath her feet.

The noise broke the wolf's stillness. It began to trot away, along the stream. *My camera.* I reached for the pocket of my backpack and pulled it out to begin snapping pictures of the wolf. I pressed and pressed the shutter button without even looking at what was on the display screen. I didn't want to take my eyes off the wolf. Even as it ran, it was still eyeing me, almost like it wanted me to follow. Like it was beckoning us. *Now or never, Lupine Lovers.*

I glanced ahead at what was left of the stream. I'd been ready to walk away.

Except the ranger had said the wolf packs lived near two lakes—where people boated, fished, and camped. Maybe the stream fed into one of those lakes. Maybe the wolf was following the stream home. In that case, it would be smart to stick by it.

The wolf hadn't approached us, so I didn't think it meant us any harm. I'd read stories about animals—including wolves— saving humans who were sick or hurt or lost in the wilderness. Maybe that's why it had paused and kept looking back at me, like it was saying, *"Hey, come along. I'm going your way."* Maybe it actually appreciated my sweatshirt. I pressed to take another photo, and my camera beeped. Out of battery. Its lights shut down, and the display went blank. The noise must've startled the wolf, because it was moving again. So far, the stream hadn't led us to the Wolf River, but finding an actual wolf seemed like a good sign. Good enough, anyway.

Decision made.

I grabbed Alex's hand so she wouldn't wander off or fall into another nap, and then we followed downstream.

NINETEEN

WE MOVED MUCH FASTER than before because I was trying to keep up with the flashes of silver and gray fur ahead. The shape of the wolf was a blur, and I really began to wonder if it was even there, or if I was too tired to distinguish a wishful daydream from reality. Maybe we hadn't gobbled up blueberries after all, but something else—some kind of psychedelic berry. If—when—we got out of the forest, my recharged camera would tell me if I'd even seen the wolf at all.

But we'd heard howling the night before. I knew wolves lived in the forest. That I was following the trail of a real, live gray wolf was a less-bizarre explanation than that I was chasing a hallucination through the forest.

Until, suddenly, it disappeared into the pines. We stopped beside the stream, which flowed much wider and faster at this spot. I was glad we hadn't abandoned it. Looking at the water, I licked my lips. I felt so thirsty—but still afraid to drink from the stream. I saw a maple leaf on the ground and picked it up. Three raindrops rested on top of it. Desperate, I licked them. Then I scanned the forest again, searching for a bit of silver-gray amid all the tawny cedar bark and fir green. Our wolf friend was gone.

I picked up another maple leaf, this one with four drops. "Lick this," I said. Alex did so without question.

"Where're we," Alex mumbled through a yawn. Her lips were even more swollen, which hardly seemed possible. She tilted backward, then caught herself by slamming her palm onto a nearby tree trunk.

Now that we were standing still, I felt woozy too. While we'd been walking fast, I'd been able to ignore the dizziness, the hunger, the thirst, and the worry. And the cloud of tiny flying insects surrounding us. "Alone in the woods, again," I finally answered. I closed my eyes, unsure what to do.

The wind in the trees was back to making that waterfall sound. Except—the breeze had died. The air was still. The noise continued, louder and stronger than our burbling stream. It sounded like the river.

"Do you hear that?" I asked Alex. I wanted to make sure I wasn't imagining it. I still couldn't see which direction the sound was coming from.

"Like a waterfall," she murmured, trying to lick her lips. "Yeah."

"Follow me." We continued farther downstream, stumbling over rocks and logs and around trees, fiddlehead ferns tickling our limbs. One branch almost impaled me after I bent to adjust the cover-up bootie still tightly knotted around my foot and then stood up without making sure nothing was in the way. The rushing-water sound grew louder—really loud, like we actually were approaching a set of falls. And then, through the trees, I caught sight of sunlight glinting on the surface of water. I brought my hand to my mouth, stifling a yelp of joy. I didn't want to jinx it. I didn't want this to be a mirage.

Just ahead, our stubborn little stream tumbled over a formation of smooth rocks, flowing into a frothy river the color of root beer. (That doesn't mean it's dirty—sometimes the water takes on that hint of reddish color in the Northwoods because tannins from cedar trees seep into the water.) I didn't know for sure that it was the Wolf we'd found, but it was definitely some big Northwoods river. Not one that would fade away.

Tears welled at the corners of my eyes. I glanced back at the forest, searching the trees for any movement. In a way, the wolf *had* helped us get here; I made my decision to keep on following the stream because of it. So I looked at the wolf on the sweatshirt Alex was wearing. *Thank you,* I mouthed.

"Are we there yet?" Alex asked, dropping to a seat next to me near the edge of a rocky outcropping above the water.

"Well, we found the river. Or *a* river," I self-corrected.

"Great. Wait here, them find us." She lay down flat on the rocks, then turned to press her face against the cool slab of stone. Her skin and lips must have felt as fiery and angry as they looked. The rash had spread farther across her legs, and all the sores either oozed or crusted. I studied my own limbs, covered in bites, cuts, and ticks. One flip-flop and one foot wrapped in formerly light-coral fabric now the color of red mud.

We were still in the middle of nowhere. How often would people pass by? We weren't near a trail or anything, as far as I could tell. It could be minutes before someone floated along or, I supposed, days.

"Let's rest for a while. See if anyone comes downstream." I sat next to Alex, spreading the inner tube out behind us. If only it didn't have that tear—we could blow it up to float to safety on our own. I ran my finger over the damaged part. It didn't need much to be patched—a generous square of duct tape would do the trick. But we didn't have that. If only pine pitch would work. It was certainly good at keeping leaves and needles stuck in my hair.

Alex handed me the dry bag, a handful of berries still inside. I grabbed a few. We'd been okay since eating them this morning (assuming the wolf wasn't a hallucination), so they were safe. I needed more food: my stomach was back to feeling hollow, my muscles weak.

We ate the berries slowly. Normally, when I pile blueberries into my breakfast bowl, I gobble them by the spoonful, paying no attention as my molars mash them up. I mean, who sits at the breakfast table and really contemplates the blueberry? Now, each berry was like a precious jewel. I would put one in my mouth, rolling my tongue around it, feeling the plumpness and the texture, eagerly anticipating the burst of flavor when I finally allowed it between my teeth to bite open. After the explosion on my tongue, I would chew maybe thirty times, until it was just blueberry juice I held in my mouth, before I would finally swallow. Then, repeat. It could take you half an hour to eat ten blueberries if you savored them that way.

Alex ate just as slowly, methodically. When she turned to face me, her eyes were clearer. The blueberries had restored her, or maybe it was the thrill of finally finding our way out of the woods. "If I could time travel, I would go back to the version of me sitting at the table at Paul Bunyan's, and I would eat a freaking doughnut. I would eat it *so hard*."

I laughed, spraying a bit of the precious blueberry mash out of my mouth, which was really a shame. "Yeah, that seems like an entirely reasonable time-travel choice." I paused. "I'd go back to Walden, registration day. I'd...I don't know. I guess I'd wear something different." My face flushed as I said it. I doubt Alex could tell I was blushing, though, considering how dirty my cheeks were.

She hugged her arms to her chest, rubbing the thin fabric of the sweatshirt. "Don't be stupid. I mean, I guess it's obvious that, like, I was..." It took her a long time to say the words. "A little embarrassed. Because it's important to me to look good. It gives me confidence. But what happened that day wasn't your fault. Or what happened the rest of the summer." She stopped, fiddling with the stalk of a maidenhair fern. "I just got caught up in being Laura's friend. Honestly, Jocelyn, I really do like spending time with her. We're interested in a lot of the same stuff, and she's actually super generous, and also hilarious." She paused again. "I know that's weird for you, so I feel bad saying it, but it's the truth."

"It *is* kind of weird. The you who is friends with her—Lexie—is different from the you who's friends with me—Alex."

"They're both me. I'm not, like, having a split personality."

"But you've changed," I said. "Even when you're not around Laura, you act different than you used to."

"So do you? I mean, we're all just figuring it out. Who we are, and who we want to be." Alex sighed. "I'm sorry if I hurt you. I think I needed to push you away a little bit to know who I am. But also to know that I *do* still want to be your friend. It's just...I want other friends too." She was quiet for a moment. "Do you think that could be okay?"

For so long, we'd been Team Alexelyn, a dynamic duo that didn't allow much room for anyone else. Not even shared friends like Houa and Kate. If I were being completely honest, I didn't really want Team Alexelyn to change. But it already had. So now rather than clinging to a ghost version of our best friendship, what I wanted was to still be friends—even if we weren't exactly *best* anymore.

"Yeah, I think it could be okay." I paused because my voice was rising with emotion and I had to swallow it back down. "I'd like that."

There was one big blueberry left in the bag. "It's yours," Alex said.

I shook my head. "No, you take it. You're probably still dehydrated from puking."

She rolled her eyes, which, honestly, was reassuringly normal behavior. "Don't be ridiculous, Joss."

I'd been "Jocelyn" to her since registration day. It felt good to hear her use my nickname again. She plucked the berry out, put it between her teeth, and bit it cleanly in half, one of which she held out for me. "Sorry, kind of gross, but what can you do?"

I laughed and popped it into my mouth, thinking of the day that she and Laura had shared the dish of frozen custard at Michael's. This wasn't gross. It was friendship.

We waited on the rocks, watching the river, for hours. Long enough for the blueberry fuel to run out and for us both to start shivering again, as the sun inched from directly overhead toward the tree line. The only creatures we'd seen in or around the river had been some birds—sparrows and a couple of turkey vultures I briefly misidentified (they're nicknamed "tourist eagles" for a reason)—and one shy white-tailed deer, stopping for a drink.

Most fishermen like to go out in the morning. Kayakers and canoers too. The odds of someone passing by were getting slimmer.

"Maybe we should walk downriver," I suggested. "At least to where we're level with the water's edge."

Alex startled—she'd drifted into sleep again. Then she nodded. We gathered our things and began climbing down the rock ledge. The surfaces were slippery, and my arms and legs all felt rubbery and weak. My fingertips trembled as I gripped lichen-covered stones to steady myself.

Alex was going first, focused on stepping carefully from stone to stone, and looking away from me.

"Hey, Alex," I called, when I noticed that the strap of her tote bag was sliding toward the edge of her shoulder. If she stopped, I could readjust it.

When she heard me, she looked up in my direction while still moving forward. And that's when one of her—my—slippery water shoes slid on a mossy boulder, and she fell.

It wasn't from a big distance—and it was more of a slow crumple than a fall—but she still landed hard. I heard something—hopefully her tote bag—thwack the rock surface. Followed by her shouting in pain.

"Alex!" My single flip-flop flapped against the stones as I scrambled to reach her side. "Are you okay?"

"I bumped my head," she said, reaching for it. Already her

temple was red. At least it wasn't bleeding. But head injuries can be really dangerous even if they don't bleed.

"Open your eyes wide." She did, and her pupils looked okay. *But do they get wonky right away if you have a concussion?* "Do you see stars or anything?"

"No, it's daytime."

I sucked in a breath. "In your vision—because you hit your head."

"Oh. Nope." She paused. "I whacked my knee too."

"Can you still move okay?"

"I don't know," she said through gritted teeth. "Help me up?"

I grabbed her elbow to lift her up from the rocks. She could stand at least. "Try taking a step."

She bent her knee, wincing, and moved forward to put her weight on that foot. She winced again, then took another step. "It hurts a lot."

I bit at my lip. "Do you think you can keep walking downriver?"

She put her hand on her forehead, like she had a headache. "Not very far." She sank back down.

We were trapped. Again. I threw the rolled-up tube against the rocks. "I'm so sick of dragging that useless thing around! If only it didn't have a stupid tear—we could tube our way back to civilization. But no." I kicked at it. "Instead we're doomed."

Alex stared at the tube. She blinked. "Wait." Her tone sounded almost excited. She pulled her tote in front of herself and dug around inside. I could hear her unzipping one of the interior pockets. Whatever her hand landed on made a huge smile spread across her face, despite the obvious pain that a smile caused her cracked lips.

"This." She held out a thin and glossy square of paper.

Except it wasn't paper—it was a sticker. A bumper sticker with a picture of a howling wolf in front of a moon, a lot like the one on my sweatshirt. Printed below was: I ♥ WISCONSIN WOLVES.

"Thanks?" I was really confused. *Is her head injury making her give this to me right now?*

"At Paul Bunyan's, when I was wandering around trying to find cell service or a Wi-Fi network, I saw it and thought it was so *you*, and I was still feeling super bad and guilty about stuff, so I bought it and put it in my bag. I guess it was going to be, like, an olive branch?"

This time, I couldn't fight back the tears welling in my eyes. *Thought it was so you.* The sticker was, and I loved it, and it felt so good that Alex had wanted to get it for me. Alex still knew me, she accepted me, and she still cared. That meant the world. I blinked, and tears ran down my cheeks, but I didn't mind that she was seeing me cry. "That's really nice."

Alex began crying a little too. "So yeah, I don't know why I was waiting to give it to you, but now is clearly the perfect time."

Sniffling, I started to unzip my backpack to put the sticker inside for safekeeping.

"What're you doing?" Alex asked.

I stopped, confused. "Making sure I don't lose it?"

She started to roll her eyes, until she winced and stopped. Her head must've really hurt.

"It's for the tube, Joss. A patch. So we can float the heck out of here."

TWENTY

I COULDN'T BELIEVE IT. Now we had a patch. Actually, we'd had one the whole time—I tried not to think about what would've happened if we'd known that on the first day, although when we set off on that footpath, we had no idea that we were going to wander so far from the river and get completely lost in the woods.

"I almost don't want to use it," I said, holding the sticker in my left hand while I used my absolutely disgusting towel to dry and clean the area of the tube where the puncture was.

Alex struggled to even pull a face at me. We were *that* exhausted, plus she was injured. "Please. I'll buy you 'nother." Her speech was still syrupy, and now I had no idea if it was for the same reasons as before or because she'd hit her head.

I used my ragged, dirt-caked fingernail to peel off the backing, and then I carefully placed the bumper sticker over the hole. I pressed it down and smoothed the sticker flat, so no air bubbles were left trapped between it and the plastic of the tube. "You're a genius. Seriously." Alex beamed with pride. "We'll just give it a minute to really stick."

I don't know how strong bumper-sticker adhesive is or whether it's waterproof. I do know that it's pretty hard to peel it off actual bumpers, which is why my parents have never allowed us to put stickers on our car. "What if you stop liking that slogan?" Mom always asks. Sometimes that's a ridiculous question, though—I'm never going to stop liking the environment. Or the Wisconsin Badgers. Or wolves. Still, I worried this sticker wouldn't stay put and we'd start leaking air on the river. Then I remembered what else was in Alex's bag.

"Hand me the nail kit?" I asked.

"Is this really the best time to tweeze off ticks?" Alex countered, although she reached for her bag anyway.

"Nope," I said as I took the pouch from her. I unzipped it to pull out the bottle of clear, glossy polish. Whenever my mom gets a run in her tights, she uses nail polish to cover the hole so it doesn't get worse. So I did the same, covering the sticker with polish to reinforce its hold.

"I guess you really were just being prepared," I said, "by bringing all this stuff along. I take back my snarking."

Alex smiled, still looking proud.

When I'd coated all the edges of the sticker, I capped the bottle and sat down. "How long does that stuff take to dry?"

"It's quick, but I always give it at least eight minutes."

We waited for what felt that long, although who knows if our sense of time was anywhere close to accurate anymore. "We can reinflate it now," I said, after running my fingertip over the shimmering polish, which felt smooth and dry. The inner tube, even though it was a heavy-duty one that the tour place had filled with a bike-tire air pump, still had one of those plastic valves that you can use to inflate by mouth. Being big enough for two, ours was going to take an awful lot of breath to fill up. And we both had been breathing kind of funny, like we were only capable of taking in shallow sips of air. "We'll take turns."

I flipped the latch off the valve and put my mouth on it, tasting a hint of minerally river water. I inhaled through my nose, deeply as I could, then started blowing, hard as I could, into the tube. My breath didn't even create a ripple in the thick plastic. I paused, covering the valve with my finger, and took in another breath. Then I sealed my mouth onto the valve again and pushed all my air out, until my stomach squeezed and it felt like I was going to collapse inward, like a deflating parade balloon.

Repeat. Repeat. Repeat. I kept going until my head spun. If I hadn't been sitting down on a wet log, I would've fallen over.

"Your turn." I could barely whisper.

Alex made it through only two exhalations before she clamped her finger over the valve and dropped her head between her knees. Without a word, I replaced her finger with mine and started again. With that bump on her head, maybe she shouldn't be exerting herself. And her lips were still so swollen, it must have hurt to use them.

The tube began to rise up, slightly. We can do this, I thought. It'll just take some time.

When the tube was about half full of air, I had to stop for a rest. I felt so dizzy I thought I might throw up. And I was dying of thirst too. Whether it was a good idea or not, I inched over to the edge of the river and scooped water into my cupped hand for a drink. I didn't think I could keep inflating the tube without it.

Alex insisted on taking another turn, but then she started coughing and couldn't stop. She hunched over, wheezing. Her face was cherry red.

"You're done," I said.

She tried to shake her head no, but that only made her cough harder. I wheezed in another breath and pressed my lips back around the valve. Even the gross taste of plastic made me hungry. I kept going until the tube was about three quarters full—it had the round shape of a doughnut again but like one that had gotten smushed in the box. If I pressed on the side of the tube, the plastic would sink. It wasn't firm and buoyant like it should be. But I couldn't bear to breathe into it any longer. My head ached, and so did my lungs. I felt like I was about to pass out.

The question was: Could we still float on the tube? It only needed to keep us above water, like a raft. Hopefully it was filled enough.

"Let's try it now," I panted to Alex.

She made a little nod, still holding her head, and reached for her tote bag, trying to drag it closer to herself. Her arm lacked the strength to swing it up to her lap.

I rubbed at my eyes. "The tube's not going to hold us *and* all our stuff," I said. "Too much weight. We have to leave everything behind."

"Everything?" Alex mumbled.

I nodded, biting down on my lip to stay focused. I picked up my backpack and set it on a large, flat rock a few feet from the river's edge. I didn't even bother to unzip it and look, one last time, at what was inside. Just my camera, which was dead anyway, and the wrappers of the energy bars and bug wipes and bandages. My water bottle. The used-up tube of sunscreen. The empty mini first aid kit.

I kicked off the sole surviving flip-flop and unwound the fabric from my other foot. I even untied my towel skirt and dropped it next to the backpack. I hated leaving our stuff in the forest. You're supposed to carry out what you carried in. Maybe, after we made it to safety, someone could bring us back to this spot so we could collect our things. I could recharge my camera then, and finally see if my wolf sighting had been real after all.

Alex handed me her tote, and I placed it next to the pile of my belongings. She pulled off her towel too. Then she raised her arms and worked her way out of the sweatshirt, handing it to me.

I held it in my hands, then pressed it to my chest, like I was hugging it goodbye. It was such a dumb thing, feeling sad about leaving a sweatshirt behind. For a moment, I considered putting it on. How much weight would it really add? But that would be foolish. We needed to be as light as possible if we wanted a chance of floating to safety. A sweatshirt would soak up heavy water. The only thing we could carry with us was the life vest, because that was itself a flotation device, and who knows if we'd need it to save our lives.

I folded it up and placed it next to my backpack, tracing the outline of the wolf one last time. *Lupine lover!* Dorky, yes, but I still loved that sweatshirt.

I would also be okay without it.

Next to me, Alex was saying goodbye to her phone. She pressed the home button one last time and then lovingly set it on top of my sweatshirt. It was oddly comforting that our two prized possessions were sticking together.

"Okay, let's go." I picked up one side of the tube, and Alex took the other. We slowly waded into the river. The water swirled around our ankles. Even though the sun was out again, we'd never warmed back up. My legs were already numb to the frigid temperature.

We walked until the river came up to our thighs, when the current began tugging at us. Even though we both were holding tight, we were barely strong enough to keep the tube from floating away. "Do you think you can climb on?" I asked.

Alex nodded. I tightened my grip on the tube. "I'll hold it

steady. One, two, three, go." She grabbed the edges and wiggled her way on top. The tube squeaked and sank an inch deeper into the water. Once Alex was in the middle part, I took a breath, then jumped to hoist myself up and over the edge. Without my feet planted on the riverbed, the current immediately snagged the tube and pulled us into the downstream flow.

I wasn't quite on; my hands clung to the side of the tube, but my lower body was adrift in the river. I squirmed, struggling to kick my way up. With me dragging one side down, the tube began to take on water. "Help!" I glanced at the bumper sticker, still stuck on tight but with the waterline creeping closer to it. If the sticker fully submerged, it might fall off despite the nail polish sealing it to the plastic. Then we'd capsize.

Would we be strong enough, then, to fight the current? If not, would the one life vest be enough to save us both?

Alex grabbed my elbows and yanked me upward. I kicked furiously, then pulled my knees up to my chest, until finally I was inside, curled up in the puddle of the sunken middle of the inner tube. We were barely afloat but still moving swiftly with the current.

I glanced back at the spot where we'd entered the water, and I watched the neat little pile of our belongings fade. It was another cairn, marking that we'd been there. That we'd made it out of the woods. Then suddenly the cairn was out of my view, and it was just us, alone with the river.

TWENTY-ONE

FOR A WHILE, WE huddled in the middle of the tube, taking turns shading each other's faces from the sun. I don't know how you can be so cold in blazing bright sunshine, but we were still freezing. I shivered like a wet cat, but Alex had stopped altogether. *Not good.* We clung to the life vest like it was a security blanket. Occasionally, I'd lift up my head to study the forest surrounding the river. Hoping that I'd see a cabin, or a hiker, or a sign. Maybe even the pickup point for a tubing trip. Instead, all I saw were tall grasses and endless birches, pines, and maples, dotted with the occasional sandstone cliff.

Alex had fallen asleep somehow, with her face mashed against the inner curve of the tube. At least—I think she was sleeping. Her eyes were shut, and when I accidentally kicked her shin, she didn't flinch or yelp or anything. "Alex?" I pressed my fingertips to her wrist. Her pulse was present but really weak. Although I wasn't sure that I was checking it correctly. Alex didn't budge even when I tried to recheck it by pressing on her neck artery.

When someone has a concussion, you have to keep them

awake. I didn't know if Alex had one, but she had a head injury, and I wanted to keep her safe regardless. So every few minutes, I'd poke her with my numb toe until she finally grumbled at me.

My stomach churned. The choppy river wasn't helping with that, either. Every few seconds, the tube would spin in a new direction. I leaned over the side and heaved, but for better or worse, nothing came up. The tube bounced and rocked in the current. Water sloshed into the bottom, keeping our lower halves soaked and cold. I couldn't feel my toes anymore, even when I used them to rouse Alex, so I shifted to rest my feet on the edge of the tube. Big horseflies landed on my outstretched legs, but I didn't have the energy to swat or kick them away. I just let them bite me, like some kind of human all-you-can-eat buffet. I doubted there was any unbitten skin for them to feast on, anyway. Considering all the mosquito bites and the ticks, it was a miracle I had any blood left.

As we floated and the afternoon dragged on, I felt sicker and sicker. My stomach really hurt, like when I had the stomach flu. Two more times I thought I was going to throw up, but the nausea taunted me just below that level. Occasionally the bottom of the tube would brush past a large rock or fallen log in the river, which would poke us. I crossed my fingers that the tube wouldn't get another tear. A hole we couldn't patch would be the end of us. I sank back against the side, where the plastic felt warm, or at least warmer than the river water. Alex's sunken eyes were still closed, her breathing regular but shallow. I nudged her again to keep her on the right side of the sleep-wake divide.

There was a strange noise from downstream—a roar, but not like a bear's. The roar of fast-moving water. *Rapids*. A sign we actually might be back on the Wolf River—its lower part has lots of spots where people do whitewater rafting when the water level is high. Even the part we'd been on for our "lazy river" tubing experience had one or two sets of baby falls. I pulled myself up to look. Sure enough, only a few feet ahead, the water churned. We were headed straight for the froth.

"Alex, hang on!" I shook her shoulder. Finally, she blinked up at me, her eyes struggling to focus.

"Rapids," I said, just as we hit them.

Water sloshed into the tube from all sides. I clutched Alex, and her hands seized my arms. I groped at the bottom of the tube for the life vest, in case we got knocked out—or capsized—and needed it to save us. Jagged rocks surrounded the tube, and I wished more than anything for a helmet, imagining what would happen if we whacked our heads, then went underwater. The tube jolted again, and I screamed, although the roar of the water drowned me out. Alex whimpered next to me. It felt like being inside of a washing machine, as the tube twisted and spun and we dropped along with the river. If there had been anything in my stomach, I definitely would've thrown it up. We bounced again, both screaming. I squeezed my eyes shut.

And then, suddenly—miraculously—the tube was floating lazily once again. Both of us still safely inside, although the middle was so full of water that we were submerged up to our belly buttons.

We sputtered and gasped, crying with pain as the frigid water swirled around us. My fingers, mottled with cold, stayed curled around the life vest, refusing to let go.

I spun to check the sticker. Still stuck on, but at least a third of it was underwater. The adhesive on one corner was beginning to peel off. We didn't have much time left before the sticker would stop sticking, and nail-polish reinforcement would be useless while everything was wet.

Alex and I huddled together. She kept closing her eyes like she wanted to sleep. And she still wasn't shivering, despite how cold it was now that we were drenched. I longed to have something to wrap around our shoulders. I wished we'd kept the towels with us, or at least my sweatshirt. But even if we had, that stuff would all be soaking wet and would probably only keep us that way. Alex groaned and rubbed at her temple, sporting a budding rainbow bruise.

How long could we keep going? At what point should we abandon the tube, try to get out of the water again? Our tube wouldn't survive another set of rapids, and after all the rain, the water level was high—there would be more ahead. But I didn't know if we would survive on land, either. We had no supplies.

We were in swimsuits, and I was barefoot. Like this, we wouldn't make it through another night. We'd die of exposure.

I lay back against the tube, letting tears roll down my cheeks. Next to me, Alex was limp. Her eyes were still closed, her expression pained.

I was so tired, so hungry, so thirsty, so cold. My thoughts became hazy. I didn't have a plan. The river was going to take us, wherever it wanted. I didn't know what to do other than give ourselves over to its flow.

TWENTY-TWO

W HEN I HEARD THE music, I thought it was inside my head. It had been so long since we'd heard any sounds that weren't from nature: singing birds, whistling breeze, crackling underbrush, howling wolves, churning river. The last human-made noise we'd heard had been that plane—which never had come back looking for us. Hearing a melody and lyrics, a sure sign of people, was jarring—but the music was so faint, I knew it must only be a memory. Especially because I was hearing an oldie, that same "Electric Slide" song the DJ had played at the pool party. That scene drifted back in my head, and it was so real, I could almost smell the burgers and hot dogs on the grill. Hear the laughter of kids doing the water-balloon toss. It was bittersweet to be remembering that particular day, which should have been such a good one but ended up being kind of a bummer. *Discordant* is a good dictionary word for it. Slightly out of tune. A lot of the summer had been that way.

The memory was only getting stronger. The sounds of music and laughter grew louder, although the "Electric Slide" had ended and the melody of the next oldie was unfamiliar. Can you even remember a song you've never heard? I blinked up at the blue sky above the river. The music and smells didn't stop when I opened my eyes. *I'm definitely hallucinating.*

The scent of food was killing me. I tried to focus on anything else that I could—the ice-cold water sloshing around my legs, Alex's labored breathing, the sea-sickening wobbliness of the tube as it struggled to stay afloat—but the scent wouldn't fade. It intensified. I didn't think I could take smelling it—even in my imagination—for one second longer. *Maybe this is what happens when people die of exposure. They go a little mad toward the end.*

I raised my head from the sinking edge of the tube, to see if I could find something to distract myself from the imaginary food smell. Nothing but trees to my left. When I looked to my right, I saw it.

The party.

A gentle bend in the river lay ahead, and alongside it was a low-lying area cleared of trees. Some kind of park or a campground. There were a few rustic picnic tables near the water's edge. A distance behind them, a barbecue grill.

I wasn't imagining the scent of burgers and hot dogs (and hopefully veggie patties). I wasn't imagining the oldies playing. I wasn't imagining the laughter.

A dozen or so people milled around, holding sweating cans of soda and plates piled with picnic food. They were smiling and dancing and enjoying the late-summer afternoon along the river. They hadn't noticed us yet, I didn't think.

"Alex!" I croaked, shaking her awake. "People! There are people?" *Unless I'm hallucinating them too.*

"What?" She rubbed at her eyes and struggled to sit upright.

"Hey! Hey! Over here!" I called. But my voice was so weak, and the breeze was strong enough to carry it away. The music drowned any sound we made. Our half-inflated tube hugged the opposite side of the river from the party. I reached my arms in the water, trying to paddle that way.

"Help us! Please!" Alex tried to shout, but she could only cough it out. I kept paddling. What if we passed by this park and they never noticed us, never came out to help? Nobody was looking toward the water—they were all focused on their food.

"We have to swim for it," I said to Alex. I grabbed the life vest and worked her arms into it, then snapped the buckle. She needed it more than I did. "Hold on to me." I reached for her hand. Our palms squeezed tight, just like when we used to do the lake jump.

I rolled off the tube and into the river with a splash. The current was strong, but I fought it, kicking my legs harder than I ever thought I could. Alex fell in after me with a louder splash. The life vest barely buoyed her above the surface of the water. She grabbed the stretched-out strap of my suit and clung to it, as I furiously kicked and did my best to propel us toward the people. She took a deep breath. "Help!" she screamed at the top of her lungs, her voice finally competing with the music.

A woman wearing a baseball cap suddenly looked up. Her burger dropped to the ground. She mouthed something like, *What in the world?* Then she pointed at us and turned to shout at the others, "Someone's in the water!"

The guy next to her climbed up on a picnic table for a better view. His jaw dropped. "It's those missing girls!"

Everyone else turned to gape at the river. Then it was like an official had started a race, and they all dashed toward the water, shouting instructions at one another. My legs were losing energy. I didn't know how much longer I could kick or tread. Our heads bobbed above the surface, dropping below every few seconds. I sputtered out a mouthful of river water. I clung to Alex. I kept trying to move us closer to them, but the current was dragging us away.

The baseball-cap woman and the guy splashed into the river, still in their hiking clothes and shoes. They began swimming toward us. "Hang on, girls, we're coming for you!"

I kept kicking, even though the water was pulling me down. Alex coughed and flapped her arms to tread. Her hand squeezed mine tight. I sank below the surface again. Underwater, everything was eerily quiet and murky. I wanted to kick myself back up. But I couldn't figure out how.

Then I felt Alex pulling me up. Fighting for us. I broke above the surface, gasped in a breath, and my legs started kicking again. The effort to help me had been too much for Alex, whose grip on my hand was loosening. I hooked my arm around her, to make sure she wouldn't go under now that I was up. Even with the life vest and with both of us treading furiously, we were barely hanging on.

But we were Team Alexelyn once again.

Then an arm appeared. It swooped around my chest, guiding me through the water with strong, confident strokes. A woman's voice said, "You're okay, girls. It's all going to be okay." I kept kicking; I couldn't stop till we were safe. The guy was next to Alex, helping her swim. Once we had help, we moved quickly toward land.

When I felt the pebbly shore beneath my bare feet, I knew it was true. We'd made it out of the woods, and out of the river. We'd actually saved ourselves.

I took one triumphant step out of the water. And then I collapsed.

TWENTY-THREE

WE DIDN'T REALLY HAVE a lot of last-morning-at-Buttercup-Lake traditions. Everyone was always busy cleaning the cabin and packing up the cars. I would take an extra minute in every space, from the aerie down to the living room, to soak up the musty cabin smell and the old family photos and the trinkets that represent years of family—and friend—memories. The last night's campfire scent would linger on all my clothes. I always wanted to bottle that up, take it home with me, so I could sniff it in the dead of winter when summertime seems so far away. By the time our parents would say, *"Pee one last time if you need to, and then everybody into the cars,"* I just walked out the door. (Well, after peeing. It's a long car ride.) I never wanted to glance back at the lake or Allard's Roost, not even for one farewell look, because that's a little too sad.

"There's always next year," Mom would say, and that was usually my comfort.

Next year isn't always the same, though—I know that now. Things, and people, can change. Will change.

Because we were still recuperating, Alex and I weren't helping with the cleanup or the packing this year. Instead, we sprawled on the Adirondack chairs on the patio. Munching on leftover doughnuts that her dad had driven all the way back to Minocqua to get us from Paul Bunyan's Cook Shanty. The cold front had passed, and it was summery warm again, especially with the severe-clear skies and sunshine. Of course, we were covered up from head to toe—my peeling sunburn and Alex's poison ivy rash were going to take a long time to fade and heal. Same with all the scrapes, bites, gouges on my ankles, and Alex's rainbow-bruised goose-egg bump on her temple.

Apparently that picnic spot along a branch of the Oconto River—we hadn't actually found our way back to the Wolf River but a mile or two east—is rarely used. You can't park right by it but have to hike in for half a mile along a secluded forest trail, so even though it's a very pretty area and there are grills (and even an outhouse), many days nobody is there. It is purely luck that we happened to be drifting by on a beautiful Friday afternoon when the extended Simpson family was having "Simpson Fest"—their unofficial family reunion to celebrate a relative visiting from Seattle. Karen Simpson was the baseball-capped lady who had spotted us and jumped into the river, along with her brother, Jack. Once they pulled Alex and me out of the water, and after we both fainted, they carried us along the trail to where their cars were parked. Then they called 911 to explain what had happened. (No cell reception in the picnic area.) By then I had regained consciousness, and apparently I kept apologizing for interrupting their party. It's all kind of a blur to me.

Karen was a nurse at a nearby health center, so she could tell we were both suffering from hypothermia. It doesn't have to be wintertime cold for you to get it—hypothermia develops whenever your core body temperature drops below ninety-five degrees. Which, after days and nights lost in the forest, wet and basically wearing only swimsuits, ours had. I don't remember much of what was going on while we waited for the first responders to arrive. I do remember Karen, and the other adults, clucking about "what rough shape" we were in. But also telling us how "amazing" it was that we had survived and found our way to safety.

Somebody, maybe the police, must have called our families. By the time we got to the hospital, they were already there. Both my parents were crying, and so was Nolan. We got to do a family hug before Alex and I were whisked away to be treated.

Amazingly, we were both okay—aside from the hypothermia, literally hundreds of bug bites (and their swelling), a dozen or so ticks, poison ivy rashes (mostly on Alex), sunburn (worse for me), the wounds on my heels (which were getting infected), a head bump and badly bruised knee (Alex), various other cuts, dehydration, and hunger. So maybe we weren't "okay." But it could have been much worse. Alex didn't actually have a concussion, although the doctor still ordered a scan to make sure her head was going to be fine. They kept us in the hospital overnight for observation. The next afternoon, we were both released with instructions to follow up with our doctors in Madison and to finish the courses of heavy-duty antibiotics they'd started us on.

We all stayed at the cabin afterward because our parents thought we should rest for a few more days before Alex and I tackled the long drive home. Most of that time, we hung out on the couch in the living room. Alex and I even slept in there, because we were so tired and achy, and it is a lot of steps up to the aerie. Everyone else, including Tampoco, hovered around us. Like they were afraid that if they looked away, we'd disappear again. Especially Lucy. Even though she still brought along her book while she kept watch in the living room, she couldn't seem to focus on the pages. She kept sneaking glances at us on the couch, making sure we were still there.

"We're not going anywhere, Lucy," I said, petting Tampoco behind his ears.

"Seriously—I don't think I can move," Alex added. "In fact, can you pass me my laptop?"

Lucy handed it to her, and Alex opened up her email. I think she still really missed her phone. We'd told the forest rangers about our cairn of belongings, and they promised to hike in to look for our things. I hoped they'd find them and I'd get my camera back, so I could see the photos I'd taken while we were lost. I'm about 95 percent sure the wolf was really there, although I'm also 95 percent sure it didn't purposely help us find the river. As much as that makes a good story.

It's funny, but I didn't really care about getting back my sweatshirt. It certainly had a long, and eventful, life. Also, the rangers gave us each an official national forest hoodie. We'd both been wearing them nonstop ever since. Using Lucy's phone, Alex posted a picture of us in them with a caption that told our story. "It's blowing up with likes," she'd said.

Alex scanned her inbox, stopping on one message and clicking it open to read. She looked up and said, "Laura wrote back."

If she had said that to me a week ago, I would've felt the hairs on the back of my neck bristle. Maybe they still did, a teensy bit. But mostly, I felt okay. "Yeah?"

Alex nodded. "She said she's super happy we're both safe, and she's really glad her cover-up saved your foot. When we get home, she wants to meet us at Michael's to hear everything."

I smiled. That was actually nice of Laura. Maybe there was hope for her yet. "Tell her I say thanks."

Alex smiled back at me. Then her fingers went back to flying over the keys.

On that last morning, while everybody else was inside getting ready to leave, the only sounds were the birdsong from the yard, the wind rustling the tamarack trees, the light clink of a set of wind chimes—and Alex and me loudly chewing our doughnuts. We had been eating constantly. Anytime I wasn't sipping on juice or didn't have a snack in front of me, one of our parents would swoop in and offer another sandwich or piece of fruit or yogurt. I was glad that these last moments at the lake were peaceful; the kind of quiet, low-key hanging out, just the two of us, that I had longed for all summer. I was ready to go home—being in my own bed would be really nice, especially after I thought I might die in the forest. You never know how much you love your pillow until you face the reality of never sleeping on it again. But I was still sad that we were leaving. Once we got back to Madison, I didn't know how much I'd see Alex. School would start soon. Things were going to be really different this year, with Laura in the picture. And now that we'd finally compared the schedules we'd gotten on registration day, I knew that we had only one class together. I closed my eyes, to preserve this moment.

"You know what we never got a chance to do?" Alex asked, wiping her hands on her hoodie. Her voice was still raspy, but she was sounding more like herself.

"What?" I blinked my eyes open. I mean, there was a lot of up-north stuff we didn't get to do, after being missing for three days and two nights, before spending an overnight at the closest hospital. And then being mostly quarantined in the living room until that morning.

"Our jump off the pier."

Buttercup Lake glittered in front of us. A loon floated on the surface but otherwise, the water was calm and unbroken, like glass. It was as perfect a lake day as I'd ever seen. "Well, I jumped in."

Alex rolled her eyes. "You know what I mean. We didn't jump in *together*."

"I thought maybe you didn't care about that," I said. Not to be contrary—I really hadn't thought stuff like that meant something to Alex anymore. Sure, the cabin was my favorite place, but it didn't have to be hers.

Alex bit down on her lip, still healing but back to a normal size. "Of course I care. So... What do you say?"

I shaded my eyes and stared out at the water, thinking about how hopeful, but also desperate, I'd felt on the drive up north, waiting for that lake-jump moment and everything it had meant to me. We'd been through so much since then—and we'd survived.

"Seriously?" I asked. "Are you feeling up to it?"

"Hey, it's a tradition, right?" Alex was already easing herself up from the chair and raising the hem of her hoodie. Her arms and legs were speckled with healing bites, shrinking welts, and fading bruises. So were mine. We were back to matching, in such a weird way.

Our lake-jump tradition was never quite like this. But as I

said, things change. People change. Friendships change. That's part of life. And the beauty of it is, new traditions can always be made. It's like the word I sneaked up to the aerie to scratch into the wooden ceiling beam, the word that fit this particular week so perfectly: *Newfound*. Because we'd both found our way home and to a friendship 2.0.

"Count of three," I said, yanking off my matching hoodie.

We dashed across the yard, kicking off our shoes. My body was so sore that running was painful, but I didn't care. Still in our clean T-shirts and shorts, we hobbled down the pier. Someone, probably Lucy, yelled from the driveway, "Hey! What are you guys doing? Don't you know we're heading out in five minutes?" We kept running. Then Lucy hollered, "Mommmm! The girls are jumping in the lake!" We just laughed and kept moving toward the water. *Better late then never.*

As we reached the end of the pier, our hands found each other and clasped tight. Then we jumped into the air, spreading our limbs like starfish. We pulled our knees up just in time for a double cannonball, hitting Buttercup Lake with a resounding splash. That, and our laughter, shook the songbirds out of the trees. We surfaced and turned back to see our families hurrying down to the pier, shaking their heads at us, but also laughing. Nolan and Mateo were already tugging off their sneakers to join us in the lake. Lucy was unbuttoning her cardigan to jump in too.

An end-of-the-week lake jump may never become a Buttercup Lake tradition. It's not exactly the best idea to start the long drive back to Madison soaking wet.

But that one time when Alex and I did, it didn't mark an ending at all—it was our fresh start.

A NOTE ON THE SETTING

The Northwoods of Wisconsin are very much a real place—filled with pine forests, pristine rivers and lakes, quaint cabins and old-fashioned supper clubs, and lots of wildlife. Anyone who has grown up in Wisconsin (myself included) has fond memories of "going up north" to reconnect with our state's natural beauty and charm. It's a wonderful place to relax or explore.

Most of the locations and landmarks mentioned in *Alone in the Woods* are real—from Paul Bunyan's Cook Shanty to the Wolf River to the Chequamegon-Nicolet National Forest, which covers more than 1.5 million acres of old-growth forest. However, readers very familiar with the area will notice that I made some slight alterations to the geography, including where the Wolf and the Nicolet briefly intersect—namely, I pretended that Highway 55, which hugs the winding river, doesn't exist. (That would have made it a little too easy for the girls to find their way to help.) Thank you for the suspension of disbelief, for the sake of story.

For those who quibble that anything below Highway 8

doesn't qualify as true Northwoods, I'll counter that "Up North" isn't really a place. In the words of the Wisconsin Department of Tourism, "it's a perspective."

I hope I captured the magic of a Wisconsin summer in these pages—and if you haven't had the good fortune yet to experience one for yourself, perhaps you'll be inspired to head up north sometime soon. I'll save a doughnut for you.

ADDITIONAL RESOURCES

To find out more about the real-life places and research that inspired this book, visit the Resources page at rebeccabehrens.com. Available for download are:

Alone in the Woods Educator's Guide

A comprehensive educator's guide for grades 4–7 with pre-reading questions, comprehension questions and activities, as well as enrichment activities and a bibliography for further research.

Alone in the Woods Discussion Guide

A two-page guide with ten thought-provoking questions about *Alone in the Woods* for readers of all ages to discuss—great for book clubs!

Alone in the Woods Family Discussion Card

A downloadable postcard with prompts to help parents and caregivers talk about the book with young readers.

ACKNOWLEDGMENTS

Oftentimes writing a novel feels like wandering a forest. I'd be lost without:

Annie Berger, who expertly guided me through this survival story with keen insight and encouragement, and the talented team at Sourcebooks—especially Sarah Kasman, Steve Geck, Dominique Raccah, Todd Stocke, Cassie Gutman, Nicole Hower, Ashley Holstrom, Ashlyn Keil, Margaret Coffee, Heather Moore, and Valerie Pierce. Special thanks to Sandra Ogle for copyediting with such care, and to Levente Szabó for capturing my story in his dynamic cover illustration.

Suzie Townsend, who always makes sure I'm on the right path; Dani Segelbaum, who is truly a lifesaver; and the whole hardworking team at New Leaf Literary.

Beth Behrens and Michelle Schusterman, readers extraordinaire.

Teachers, librarians, and booksellers—thank you for your tireless work on behalf of readers and writers.

My friends and family, and especially Blake, who's always trekking by my side. And who usually has a protein bar.

ABOUT THE AUTHOR

Rebecca Behrens is the author of the critically acclaimed middle-grade novels *When Audrey Met Alice*, *Summer of Lost and Found*, *The Last Grand Adventure*, and *The Disaster Days*. She grew up in Wisconsin, studied in Chicago, and now lives with her husband in New York City. You can visit her online and learn more about her books at rebeccabehrens.com.

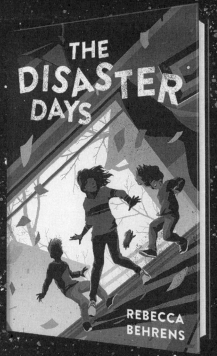